SYCORAX

NYDIA HETHERINGTON

QUERCUS

First published in Great Britain in 2025 by

QUERCUS

Quercus Editions Limited
Carmelite House
50 Victoria Embankment
London EC4Y 0DZ

An Hachette UK company

The authorised representative in the EEA is Hachette Ireland,
8 Castlecourt Centre, Dublin 15, D15 XTP3, Ireland (email: info@hbgi.ie)

A CIP catalogue record for this book is available
from the British Library

HB ISBN 978-1-52943-107-0
TPB ISBN 978-1-52943-108-7
EBOOK ISBN 978-1-52943-110-0

1

This book is a work of fiction. Names, characters,
businesses, organizations, places and events are
either the product of the author's imagination
or used fictitiously. Any resemblance to
actual persons, living or dead, events or
locales is entirely coincidental.

Typeset in Bembo by CC Book Production

Printed and bound in Great Britain by Clays Ltd, Elcograf S.p.A.

Papers used by Quercus are from well-managed forests and other responsible sources.

For anyone who lives with chronic illness and pain.

For the spoonies.

For every woman who has experienced medical misogyny, gaslighting and misdiagnosis.

For those awaiting diagnosis who feel unheard and uncared for.

For the under-medicated.

For the sufferers of side effects from medicines designed to keep them well.

For every single person who has had to shield.

For those still shielding.

For the vulnerable, the CV and the CEV.

This book is for you.

Author's Note

Sycorax the Blue-Eyed Hag

Many years ago, when I was an actor in my twenties getting to grips with Shakespeare's *The Tempest*, I became enchanted by the absent, yet ever present force in the play of Sycorax. As a character who is long dead when the action begins, has no voice or physical presence on stage or page, Sycorax, or this 'blue-eyed hag' as Prospero describes her, is silenced before she ever has a chance to speak for herself. Yet she remains a major foil for the play, its themes, and for our understanding of Prospero himself. What we do have of her are the magician's angry (and it could be argued, jealous) rants, and the laments of her son, Caliban, now become Prospero's slave. From these snippets we get to know her, or at least see a shadow of who she might have been, albeit shot through the prism of Prospero's prejudices and fears. She was, we are told, a powerful sorceress, a 'foul witch', bent of body, 'grown into a hoop', who hailed from Algiers, and for 'sorceries terrible' was banished to the island where the play is set, only escaping with her life due to 'one thing she did'. We are never told what that thing was. The other important bit of information we know about her is that when the sailors abandoned her on the island, she was pregnant.

Shakespeare wrote *The Tempest* in or around 1611. Sometimes believed to have been his final play, we now think this probably isn't quite true. For me, it's certainly his most poetically beautiful. Along with *A Midsummer Night's Dream*, the play delves more into the supernatural, the whimsical and the magical than perhaps any other of his works. With James I of England (James VI of Scotland) on the throne, a king known for his tyrannical pursuit of devilry, witchcraft and witches, the inclusion of a deceased sorceress would indeed have been a thing to whet the appetite of contemporary audiences. There are problems with the play, not least that it's the story of a colonialist, a white European duke who takes over an island and makes the only inhabitant of the place, Caliban, a North African man, his slave. Caliban's dead mother, Sycorax, is a mirror to Prospero, yet the language used to describe her is forcefully misogynistic and damning, perpetuating the duke's patriarchal rule and white privilege. Where we are told her powers were natural and earthy, and as such, base, evil and feminine, his are learned and bookish, equated with higher, good and more masculine things.

Sycorax's North African heritage has been intelligently written about by writers who have a great understanding of the subject and often lived experience. These commentators have brilliantly highlighted its major importance. With a far deeper knowledge than I could ever hope to gain, they continue to be a source of inspiration. As such, it's not something my novel focuses on. Where I feel my own experience might do justice to the novel, in the fact she was a woman in a world run by men and her state of being ('grown into a hoop') suggests someone in physical, debilitating pain, I've used it with care, passion and tenderness.

As is often the case with Shakespeare's plays, a vague historical context lurks behind the story of *The Tempest*. Like everyone, William the playwright would have been inspired by the popular stories of his time, along with retellings of news from across the globe. With this in mind, I have used history and the whispers around certain events as a springboard for my own tale. In 1535 the Holy Roman Emperor, Charles V, invaded and captured Tunis, which had been under the rule of the Ottoman Empire. Due to the success of the campaign, in 1541 he again set out towards the coast of North Africa, taking with him forces from Spain, Genoa and the Holy Roman Empire. This time the target was Algiers. The attempt was a disaster, almost costing Charles his life. His fleet of around 500 vessels and 24,000 soldiers was caught in a severe storm, resulting in an enormous loss of life and ships, many of which slipped their anchors in the violent weather and were simply wrecked on Algerian shores. This defeat was the end of the Empire's ambitions to take more North African territory. When news of the failed invasion reached England, it did so with a supernatural tale attached. It was said that a witch had predicted the storm, and it was on her advice that the city governor, even though he was aware his own forces were outnumbered and would be butchered in a fight, did not surrender to the invaders when he saw them appear on the horizon. Rather, he waited, and then watched as the enemy perished in the storm before reaching dry land.

This novel is my imagined birth and origin story of that tempest-predicting witch, the mighty sorceress, Sycorax. I admit to deliberately and thoughtfully using artistic licence when it comes to dates and historical characters, to better serve the narrative (if it was good enough for Shakespeare etc.) and therefore any mistakes are my own. My book is a feminist take on her life, and one seen through the twenty-first-century prism of chronic illness and disability, with all the connotations of pain and othering that they bring to her story. Finally, the tale is told in Sycorax's own voice, which, though absent from *The Tempest*, I've heard calling to me through the years, ringing like the warning bell in a storm. Her voice cannot be silenced. This is her story.

CALIBAN:

All the charms
Of Sycorax – toads, beetles, bats – light on you . . .

William Shakespeare, *The Tempest*, Act I, Scene II

Prologue

It is cold. The island hums. It knows I cannot sleep and tries only to soothe me. Moonlight touches my face. I lift my chin a little, bathe in the brightness, and blink. White beams reach like arms into my cave as I crouch on the smooth rock at its mouth. As always, the Moon's beauty makes me gasp. Hairs rise on the back of my neck. I like the sensation. Resting heavily upon my staff, my trusty aid, still fragrant with the sap of the tree it came from, I enjoy the fresh bite of the cool night air. It will be hot when daytime comes, sweat will cling to us. As I shiver, the song of the waking island risks lulling me back into slumber, even as its scents of hibiscus, mushroom, and mint make me thirst for the day and its heat. How I love the contradiction. I try to stretch, but my limbs are too stiff and ache. In truth, I am racked with pain, but no more nor less than usual. I shrug, and turning towards a snuffling, snoring mound behind me, cannot help but smile. There's no sadness here.

My son sleeps.

Spindle-limbed and chubby-faced, tucked into his bed of leaves and moss, of spider silk and crow feathers, he is safe. The Moon's light pools about him while the steady flicker of my everlasting candle, the eternal flame I brought to this place when he was but a fish in my belly, dances beside him. It leaps gently at each outward breath. I see his long hair, lying like a blanket, ink black and thick across his berry-brown back. It is woven through with seashells, mother-of-pearl, shining fish scales, crab claws and fingers of brittle white coral, all manner of things he's found washed up on the beach of this, his paradise playground. How he loves to adorn his body with the stuff of the island.

His island.

He reminds me of my mother.

I watch him breathe. The gentle ebb and flow of air, in and out, as the cage of his body lifts and falls. I marvel at his eyes flickering behind their lids as he dreams of tomorrow's adventures. This small stretch of land, this enchanted rock, is all the world to him. Nothing exists beyond it, other than the salty sea and the starry heavens. He belongs here and he knows about belonging. This boy needs no book to tell him which mushroom will cause palsy, which root is a sure and bitter death. Neither is his knowledge spell-gotten; a thing born of magic. It's learned from a life of running through the forests, from fishing in the brooks and clambering through the rockpools. He understands the nature of this place better even than I who made it. After all, he was born here. Even so, I fret for him.

I sigh and shiver, thinking of how my boy has no power to charm or enchant. Why should I care? I've ensured he has all he requires; he doesn't need to use magic. But my heart hurts when he pretends to be a great magician. Swooping about in his glittering child's cape woven from beetle wings, all iridescence, like a character from the stories I told him as a babe. And how it pains me when the island's spirits tease him, knowing only too well he has no magic in him. They laugh openly at his nonsense made-up spells and silly barked incantations. He cannot control the sprites. Often, they're great friends, but when the pucks are in buoyant mood, they're like bees around a honey thief, stinging and pinching him. It's his only torment, but how he suffers for it. I had to teach a certain mischievous fairy a lesson he'll never forget. It hurt me to do it, for I loved the spirit. But without my gifts or his father's allure, my son is but a poppet, an amusement for enchanted beings.

But hush. My thoughts make too much noise. See how my boy shifts, suddenly in his sleep. His hands are up now. They flit around his face as if to rid himself of some swirling, buzzing things. I must stop thinking on fear and bad possibilities before they invade his dreams further, and instead send him soothing images of clear streams with frogs, bright golden fishes, and the songs of crickets. There, he settles and grows calm again. My darling Caliban, almost a man yet still very much a child, full of curiosity and play. I wish I didn't have to leave him alone, but all the charms and spells in the world cannot prevent that now.

I've heard the call.

The voices of my ancient desert ancestors are singing me to my rest. They are louder than ever tonight, too much to allow sleep. They're becoming agitated and won't be ignored any longer. I am not afraid, for in their song is my mother's voice, summoning my soul to hers. How sweet that reunion will be, how I have longed for it. Even now as the last of the moonlight brushes the entrance to our cave, I see her, my mother-moon, her long pale fingers beckoning. But oh, my boy. To be torn from him is a misery.

At least my son will be here, the king of all he surveys.

No man can ever touch him, enforce laws upon him, or bind him in chains, hidden as he is on his mother's island. The sprites can do him no real harm, nor would they want to. He is solid, made from the stuff of this place. They are a bagatelle made of mist and air. The one I punished for bad behaviour will be released from his woody prison once my boy is truly a man. The sprite won't dare tease him again after such a sentence, even if I'm not here. Poor thing, even now I smile at the thought of that airy spirit and his cheeky ways. But how my head thrums and my mind cannot settle. For the ancient melody is all about me. Discordant notes push through the harmony. Listen, it grows.

The song is loud now.

Its pull so strong it takes my breath away.

Should I make my way to the sea, as my mother did when I was not much older than Cal? But look, my flesh becomes insubstantial. I've no time to say goodbye to the spirits. No time even to reach the shore.

I begin to fade.

No matter. For I hear my mother's voice. There! Among the choir of women.

It grows louder.

I must go.

Wait.

Let me look again at all I have done.

This island is my gift to my son and it's worth more than any jewel of the earth or gem of the sea. What good work it has been. What joy we have had.

He stirs.

Oh, quiet the thudding of my aching heart! The screaming in my mind! Quiet, you singing voices, you callers to oblivion! Let me watch in peace as he flicks his head again, annoyed by some small beetle scuttling around his thatch, and let me see his slumbering shoulders twitch as he wriggles, burrowing into the softness of his bed. Let me hear him snuffle once more, listen to the air catch in his sleeping throat. Let me linger a while.

See! His breathing is steady, his dreams are soft.

He smiles.

Look!

Must I really go?

My flesh is fading into moonlight. I hear the beat of dark

wings and see their distant shadow. Then let me whisper my name one last time for him to hear in his sleep, to remember me by, for in that name lies the story of my life. I would tarry a while, stay until he wakes, tell it all to his face, but the song is stronger than all my powers, and I'm pulled away. My voice joins in with the singing. I'm all but with them. See how I fade with the Moon.

What a life I have made in him!

He is perfect.

Dear wind and stars, look to my child, for I must go.

Let me whisper, then, quickly.

Quick! Now! The Sun rises. Golden.

Like the spirits, I am almost gone into the air.

Let me whisper my name, so he will know.

Sycorax.

ACT I

Scene 1

Although my mother's name was Atlas, like the mountains, she came from the desert. To prove her origins, when I was small and in a sulking mood, she'd brush mounds of golden dust from the soles of her feet. Then smiling, she'd shake showers of the stuff from her clothes, drop heavy but delicate petals of orange rocks from her seemingly empty pockets, and swear her veins ran not with blood or rubies, but with sand and rubble.

See! she'd cry, full of laughter and mischief, her brows lifted, her eyes glistening and bright. *I carry the desert with me, so I can never forget where I've come from. And it guides me still, reminding me to rise before the Sun, to cut my stems and roots under the cool light of the Moon, so the work is done before the fierce heat of the day hits.*

Then more glittering grains of sand would fall from her long hair as she'd flick her head, and I'd try to catch them,

9

like drops from a raincloud. Of course, I knew it was a trick, or a spell; a glamour to keep me amused. Even so, as a little girl I believed the desert lived within her and that, as strong as she was, my mother's flesh was made only of sand. Some nights I'd lie awake, scared to open my eyes lest I'd find a heap of golden dust in place of my mother. Even in my sleep I'd try to hold my breath in case, just by breathing, I'd blow her away and she'd be lost to me forever.

Shhhh, my chick, she'd whisper as she rocked me through the gloom. *I'm as solid as a fox, as warm and fleshy as the fattest goat.* And guiding my hands she'd press them onto her soft, squashy belly. I'd lay my head in that place then, and sleep soundly, my cheek nestled into the cushion of her sturdy body.

Atlas was a great one for stories. She told them with all the drama of a skilled player, like the ones she told me about those who roamed the desert, eating sticks of fire and walking on their hands. I craved to hear about her life before I existed. That she might be in a world without me seemed a strange sort of enchantment. Every day I'd beg her to tell those tales. Like how, sitting on the back of a great black bird, she'd flown over miles of sandy plains, then over verdant forests and rocky mountains, to get to the place where she would meet her love, my father. She'd known the journey would be long, perhaps treacherous, but she'd had to go. Someone's spirit was calling her with a passion too strong to be ignored. How she'd waited, spurning the caresses of men who'd appealed to her parents for a taste of their daughter (always in return for trinkets, silks and Roman fabrics, and sometimes a donkey or a camel), believing that one day, she'd hear the call. Since her coming of age she'd listened for it every day, but there was only ever silence. So Atlas had set her mind to higher things. She learned the ways of wise and cunning women. After all, with ancestry like hers, it was more than likely she'd have the Gift. To her delight, it proved to be so. All she'd had to do was nurture it. The years rolled on, until, with twenty-nine years behind her, she was a respected community healer. Even elderly widowers had started to think her too old and sagacious a prospect to be their bride. Still, each day she listened for another spirit's call. When it finally came, her heart fluttered so violently in her chest she thought it might stop and she'd fall down dead before ever meeting the one reaching for her.

Atlas left without a word to anyone. She asked a beautiful dark bird to take her to the one she could hear calling out. It cocked its head to listen. At first my mother wrung her hands with worry, for other than the gentle whoosh of wind, there wasn't a sound to be heard. The call was something only the soul could discern. Still, the bird gave a nod, shook its feathers, and grew large enough that she could climb upon its back. They flew through many days and nights. When the Sun went down, Atlas did not sleep. The bird took no rest, so neither would she. That's how she became so well acquainted with the Moon. In truth, she'd always preferred the darkness. As a child, many a time she'd been scolded for playing in the dunes at night, with only the stars for friends and moonlight for company, and then snoring through the day when there was work to be done. Now, racing across the night sky, the heavy wings of the mighty bird thrumming in steady rhythm, the familiar Moon became her guide. Atlas sang her thanks to the pale silver light. In return, moonbeams cloaked and protected her. Soon enough, the Moon too found her voice and sang back, spilling secrets, imbuing my mother with celestial knowledge.

It wasn't an easy journey. Sometimes, on especially hot days, there'd be sandstorms. Those terrible swarms of dust, so thick they could slice the hide off a bull, would rise high into the sky, so that even up between the wings of her devoted carrier, Atlas's face was in danger of being slashed to ribbons as if by knives. Each time the storms came my mother thought she might be killed, as the careless bird, used to flying over every terrain and bound to its quest, would never slow its pace. But the atrocious sands were not a match for my mother. Rather than weeping with pain and fear, she covered her head with a heavy calico hood, buried her face in the bird's cool dark feathers, hiding any bare flesh within the same enormous plumage, and held on. Until, one day, the land was green and at last, they landed beside a town by the sea.

There she met her mountain boy, her husband, her love. Although somewhat out of breath from his own long journey, he quietly waited for her to get down from the big black bird until, finally, they were face to face.

My father's people were from the mountains. He spent his boyhood roaming forests, climbing rocks and trees. Fleet of foot, sinewy and strong, he was a champion climber, even the tallest cedar, the highest pine, was scaled and conquered in minutes. The air, he told me, was so much cleaner up there, like breathing in pure sunshine, and how he loved those golden rays. He'd soak them up, his skin glistening under their fiery light. When his papa would call to him to take honey from their hives, the old man would shake his head and laugh. For his youngest son's honey shone so bright, like liquid sunbeams. It was the clearest, the sweetest honey any of the nearby villagers had ever known. Although my father had been given a perfectly good name as a babe, it was soon forgotten. To everyone who knew him, he was simply called Sunny.

Late to develop into a man, when his beard finally started to push through on his chin, Sunny felt his boyhood end. It was sudden and immediate. One day he was scrabbling in the dirt with the younger boys from his village, looking for lizards and beetles to tease and prod with sticks, and the next, his heart began to beat hard in his chest, there was a heavy throbbing between his legs and the longing started. Afraid at first, he ran to the tallest pine in the forest. Once he was up, he sat in the highest branches and waited. Two days and two nights went by, but Sunny would not come down. His brother tried to coax him with food, his friends with games, his mother with her tears, but Sunny would not budge. For he was aching with a love and desire of which he had no understanding. He asked the Sun to help him, to take his cry of passion in its golden rays and to send it to the one he sought, whoever that might be. The Sun answered. It blasted his skin until it was sore and tight, chapping his poor dry lips and pulling the love from this strange and stricken youth. Then, not finding anyone with a heart open enough to take such longing, the Sun passed it over to the Moon, who knew exactly where it needed to go.

More time went by and still Sunny would not come down. Food and water were sent up to him by way of rope and bucket. My father took the water gratefully, for he was burned and blistered, but he could not eat.

A body cannot feed when its heart is filled with yearning, he'd shouted to his worried family as he lowered the food back down to them, as he could not abide the thought of good bread going to waste for his sake.

He waited and waited, his longing pouring from him like the very essence of life, and he wondered if he might die up in that tree. Until one fine afternoon he spotted a large bird on the horizon, beating a straight path, slow and steady. At that moment his heart leapt under his ribs and rattled his bones. Sitting upon the bird was a woman, magnificent and determined, hair flying behind like silken ribbons, and a black muslin shift billowing around her body. The skin on her thighs seemed to shine as they gripped on. When the bird came closer a large shadow passed over Sunny's head. He bathed in its coolness, and his body began to throb and glow with love. Quickly, he woke from his reverie, for he knew he must not let the bird out of his sight. Down the tree he scampered, never once taking his eyes from the sky, and off he went. With his bare feet smacking the ground and his family shouting ever after, Sunny ran through the forest, over the mountains, through villages and towns until he reached the sea. And there she was, climbing down from her big bird. The woman, come for him, black feathers woven through her ebony hair. He could see at once that she had lived maybe ten years more than him, for he had nineteen and three-quarter years behind him, and she was everything his heart desired.

My mother was of the Moon.

My father was of the Sun.

Together they were night and day.

As they saw each other for the first time, they smiled until their cheeks hurt. Sunny could not help but touch the face of this woman who was instantly everything to him. His hand did not tremble as his fingers lightly brushed her lips. She laughed and he thought the joy would burst from him, making his own laughter ring even louder than hers. After a moment of mirth that left them both breathless, their eyes widened with desire. With their skin covered in sweat and their lungs gasping for air, they gulped for dear life. But try as they might, they could not hold back. They pulled and tore at each other, they licked and stroked and quenched every desire. Their coupling was a moment of completion and as they screamed with the delight of it, the sky went black. It was the day of a total eclipse, that most magical of times when the Sun and Moon stand together, when day becomes night. I was made in that moment.

So, my mother would say as she'd conclude her story and we'd brush small piles of sand out into our little garden, *we became the perfect mix of glorious darkness and spectacular light, blessed both by the silver Moon and the golden Sun in that matchless moment of eternal night.* Smiling then, she'd take my face in her hands before kissing my cheek, saying, *And look! What a prize we got, in you.*

Scene 2

Atlas and Sunny wed almost immediately. Their families being far away, it was private, done without ceremony, alone in the sea caves save for an old townswoman chewing on a bone pipe. Never one to hesitate, Atlas had run to the town on the eve of their arrival, searching for someone to befriend who might help with what had to be done. My mother found the elderly widow foraging for sap and stems just beyond the city walls. There was something familiar in the line of her jaw, the shape of her eyes. Atlas bounced on her toes as it hit her. The old beldam was from desert stock. Breathlessly, she begged the wise woman's assistance. With few words, the small, wrinkled dam nodded and followed Atlas back to the shore where she smilingly oversaw the couple's union. Sunny offered what he could by way of thanks, to make her a hive so she might keep bees and have honey at her fingertips, but the widow neither took nor asked for payment.

Be happy, she said, still sucking on her pipe. *That is recompense enough.*

The newlyweds decided to live a little away from the town. Not putting themselves at the heart of the townspeople, nor seeking them out for company or friendship, gave the couple a thrilling sense of liberty. They did not go to daily prayers or ask about council meetings. Neither had been raised for religion or politics. Especially not my mother, whose family were from an ancient desert tradition, with customs and gods and ways of doing things all their own. Nevertheless, from the start, my father worried their way of life might set the local population against them. Atlas described how, soon after their marriage, although he was yet a carefree youth, she'd felt a restlessness in her husband.

My love, he'd said to her one evening as they sat on the rocks, amazed at the waves lapping against their toes, both still newly acquainted with the sea and beguiled by it. *Look at how wondrous life is. We have everything before us. I've never felt so happy and complete as now, here with you.*

But even as Atlas sighed and smiled at his words, her head thrown back to stargaze, the salt water splashing about them as she enjoyed the sensation of his fingers in her hair, she'd felt her new husband hesitate.

Something worries you, she said, turning to face him.

Sunny looked away, and just for a moment, Atlas felt her heart skip in panic.

Have I caused you anxiety in any way? she asked. *Please tell* me if that's ever the case. We must be open with each other if we are truly to stay as content as this.

Taking hold of her hands, Sunny gulped down the fear of sharing his soul so intimately with another. He believed in the power of the magnificent woman sitting before him, in her wisdom and love. How keenly she felt his faith in her. It was almost a physical thing, a lifting and holding, a steady grip in that new, strange place, yet he hesitated again before replying.

I fear rejection, here. We are strangers. And probably as curious a man and wife anyone from the town ever saw. On top of that, we're unworldly people, uncultured, unschooled in the way of towns and commerce. It might serve us better to be at the hub of society, learn how things are done. Then people would get to know us, respect us, and perhaps not find us so unusual after all.

Atlas couldn't help smiling at her shining, golden husband. Even in the faded gloaming light, with his brows crossed and biting his lip, he was the most alluring, gentle person she'd ever come across.

Dearest Sunny, you must not worry. My brothers guided many travellers through the desert, heard their stories and became educated in the ways of all manner of peoples. And they told me, their poor sister, a mere girl confined to our commune but dying for knowledge, all they'd learned about the world beyond. I may have led a small life, but I saw much through my brothers' eyes, so that even when I wasn't present in body, I met people from bustling places and faraway lands through their tales.

My father lifted his chin and kissed his excited wife's hand as she continued.

A large port town like this is filled with folk from myriad places, and of many races and traditions. We are not so strange.

She laughed to show the foolishness of his concerns, but then stopped and raised a playful eyebrow.

And even if we are, what of it?

Now Sunny was the one to laugh. For surely his wife was right. In that place by the sea, away from the noise and gossip of the town, they could live freely without fear of molestation. He agreed and promised never to question such a wise and carefully thought through choice again.

For those first few weeks Atlas and Sunny sheltered in caves along the sea-edge, waking each morning with salt-encrusted eyes. They made their bed in the sand or on the rocks, took their fill of each other's bodies, and listened to the echoes of their own delighted laughter ringing around the caves. As thrilled as they were with the sea, its noise, vastness and might, the damp made my mother's limbs feel heavy and ache. Now Atlas began to worry. Every evening she'd ask her friend the Moon to save her from a family malady, a cruel, painful stiffening she'd watched many women in her family struggle with, even in the dry and heat of the desert. No gift or glamour had ever cured it. Her own grandmother had been left unable to walk due to the pain it ravaged on her, and she was known to be a powerfully magical woman. The last thing Atlas wanted was to encourage the demon disease to take up residence in her own body. After all, she wasn't getting any younger. And what of the future? Even if her worries about health were unfounded, could they really thrive, living as simple cave-dwellers, foraging for crustaceans and berries? Surely they must set themselves to work, produce their own sustenance, goods to exchange and sell? For although she did not want to live within the bosom of the town, they might easily use the daily market, make their way to and from the place at will. That was the meaning of freedom, after all.

As soon as the couple's ardour was quenched enough to allow him the time, my father gave his wife the answer. Coming from a long line of mountain beekeepers, it was natural for him to go about making his own hives, fashioning them from mud and straw. He knew well how to coax a queen from a wild nest, how to capture the swarm and set up his own small colony of beehives. When there was enough honey to sell to the townspeople, he made pots from unbaked clay, poured his honey into them and, taking the blanket the old widow had brought to the cave the day after their marriage as a wedding gift, he walked to the town.

After being alone with only Atlas and the elements for company, the market was a shock that first day. A cacophonous, crowded place situated just inside the city wall, my father stared open-mouthed as people jostled and shouted. Donkeys, goats and camels strained and pulled on their ropes, screaming with displeasure. There was a strong stench from the animal dung that sat in heaps on the main dusty road. My father laughed when he saw how women came out from their dwellings with brushes, to push the still steaming parcels to the edge of the track before returning to their houses and closing their doors behind them.

Although small for such a large and busy port town, the daily market was obviously a community hub. It seemed to be a place where the many who gathered there every day had known each other's families for generations and beyond. Talk of feuds, of loves and reconciliations was overheard in barked conversations across the heads of shoppers. Feeling both elated and lost in it all, Sunny set his blanket on the ground next to the other traders and offered his honey for a fair price. Clutches of townswomen flocked to him when they saw that he was happy to let them taste the glistening drops on their fingers before promising to purchase. Never had the people of the town tasted anything so sweet or seen anything so clear and bright as the honey from my father's hives. Like little pots of sunshine, they said. Everything was sold in minutes, with women bemoaning how they hadn't had a chance to buy his sweet pots. He loved to tell me how he was left dumb with astonishment on that first market day. That was when he'd felt something within his breast, a thing he'd never felt before, making him grow taller and wider. It was pride. That's what he'd say, and when a few of the local men shook his hand and slapped his shoulder, he thought he might burst with the dignity of it all. Sunny knew then that his life was good and, as he'd suspected, there was nothing to regret in community and commerce.

When Atlas started to complain of a little stiffness in

her joints, and finally spoke to her husband of her fears, the nights of sleeping in sea caves became a memory, more pleasant in the remembering than in the living. Putting a new dwelling together in much the same way as Sunny had made his hives, my mother and father built themselves a home. They chose a high and dry place, up the slopes and over the dunes. It was simple; one small room with a shutter woven from pine leaves and sea rushes that was both door and window, to keep them from the heat of the day. A pallet for sleeping and fulfilling their still ardent desires took up most of the space in the room, so they built their cooking fire outdoors, where they also kept any stores and provisions. Sunny had found a spring and dug a well when they'd first arrived, so they always had fresh water. Now he wished he'd built their new home a little closer to it. But it was easy enough to go back and forth to fetch what was needed or store extra in large pots under the shade of a tree. The important things were that their house was sturdy, big enough for the two of them, and comfortable.

As Sunny tended his bees, my mother would sit on the ground nearby, singing and weaving baskets the way she'd learned from the women back in the desert. Unfortunately, her baskets were not pretty. She'd hated lessons on house-hold matters and had daydreamed as the other girls in her commune learned all that was a woman's duty. But at least she worked quickly and prodigiously, and although her baskets were not the finest, and often strangely shaped, her work was strong and robust. My father used some as hives, trying new ways to hone old skills, and still there was an excess. So, keeping enough for themselves, the rest were taken to town to be sold. As my father was now busy making candles from beeswax and spinning comb to make his honey as pure as possible, my mother became the one to take their goods to market. Sunny said her charming face and figure would help sell their produce even though he knew no help was needed to sell his honey. In truth, he wanted to show her off, let the town see what a wife he had.

Who wouldn't want to buy from someone as magnificent as you? he said as he grabbed her around the waist and kissed her neck. And once again his breast was filled with pride at all he possessed.

Atlas didn't bother about the giggles of the townswomen when they first perused her baskets, frowning as they looked at them from each possible angle. The sniggers soon stopped when they saw what a good price they could be bought for. In any case, my mother's artistry lay elsewhere. Soon she became known, not for being the weaver of unfathomably shaped baskets, nor for being the older, strangely garbed, barefooted wife of the beekeeper, nor even as a healer, some-one with poultices and tinctures hidden in her pockets, but as the maker of Dreamstones.

Each day, after foraging leaves and herbs for her remedies, Atlas would walk the sands by the sea, selecting stones and pebbles of all sorts and sizes, filling her basket, singing as she went. She watched the sea closely, learned the way the tides worked with the Moon, discerning the best times to go collecting. When night fell, she'd take her stones outside and work under the moonlight, grinding their surfaces with sand and polishing them with beeswax. Using feathers as brushes, sometimes she'd anoint the pebbles with oil, for extra light and sparkle. Living away from the caves, her fingers were once again supple, her hands strong. Under them, and with her use of the Gift, the stones released their heart colours. Swirls of greens and blues shone through the grey rock. All the colours of sea and sky. Some burned with fierce reds and oranges, betraying a passion deep within the core of the mineral. When her pile of pebbles shone like the most precious jewels of the earth, she'd put them away and wait for the full Moon. When it came, my mother would take her basket of colourful pebbles out into the night, hold each one up to bathe in the gaze of her celestial sister. Then, she'd whisper dream-words over the surface and into the heart of each rock, locking stories and desires deep into the stones, and securing them with the magic of the full Moon's light.

Anyone who was able to buy one of my mother's Dreamstones, or were lucky enough to be gifted one, would have its protection and the promise of the dreams held within. Some townsfolk asked Atlas to make a special one, just for them, trusting her with their secrets so their dreams might be secured, bound and always ready for them. Others thought Atlas's Dreamstones nothing more than pretty adornments, something to make a room shine with colour, while there were those who made their purchase through fear. After all, if Atlas had the power to heal a colic with an infusion of leaves, why would she not charm the very pebbles on the beach? And why would she not put a hex upon their house if, with their eyes to the ground, they scuttled past her in the market without making a purchase? My mother knew how to use all these perceptions to her advantage, and played whatever part was thrust upon her. It was a game, and a fruitful one. She believed being different from others was her strength. Even so, Atlas wasn't fond of gossip.

Unlike the folk from faraway lands, who came in ships, with their fair skin, odd clothes and purses filled with coin, my mother and father's differences were too close to home; they were too ragged and poor. Sunny realised his wife had been wrong to say they'd not be seen as strange in a port town. He was soon aware of how the townsfolk looked upon him and his unusual wife. They were outsiders, in every way. As the months went by, whenever he entered the town, he tried his best to be friendly, especially to the menfolk, whom he openly courted with good humour and idle chatter. But town chatter could be vicious. He overheard whispers about his own youthfulness, about Atlas – so wild with feathers in her hair and sand between her toes, selling Dreamstones and telling stories to people who'd gather to listen as if entranced – and how she'd obviously bewitched Sunny. My father accepted the sideways looks and furtive glances with nods and smiles. Even when he strolled with his wife through the town and people openly baulked at Atlas. For she'd sing (old desert songs, full of magic and curses) as if lost in some unreachable world in her head. How could it be, they'd hiss, that she seemed not to have a care in the world when her pockets were empty, her skirts hardly more than layers of sackcloth? Surely there was devilry in her.

None of it mattered.

Sunny had only to look at his wife.

His admiration greatly outweighed any care for nasty talk.

All was fine when it was just the two of them.

But with my arrival things changed.

Sunny began to fret.

Scene 3

My mother gave birth to me in an olive grove. She was taking a batch of oddly shaped baskets to the town when she felt something break and rip apart inside her. She dropped her baskets and looked down as an ocean appeared to gush between her legs. Alone among the ancient trees, my Atlas squatted. Driving her bare feet into the dusty earth, now wet with her waters, my mother pushed and screamed but it took many hours for me to come into the world. As she worked, flocks of birds gathered about her. Crows, rooks and ravens made a circle around my labouring mother. Jackdaws lifted their heads to the parched air to caw and bleat their encouragement. Or maybe their noise was a warning to snakes, scorpions and other scaly beasts, pulled towards the smell of birthing blood, she couldn't say for sure. But once they'd found her, the birds never left, becoming my mother's constant companions.

You brought them to me, she told me one day when I was playing in our garden and all their squawking and bluster made me cover my ears, stamp my little feet and shout to shoo them away. *The birds were your gift to me and want only our friendship. Be kind to them, chick. For each has a tiny heart beating within its breast, just like you.* And she tapped my chest, in time with the thud beneath my bones.

But let us go back to the day of her labour, and of my first breath.

Finally, when the Sun was down and the Moon cast her eye over the land, I was born. I know all about my arrival. Atlas the storyteller, the bender of words and mind-pictures, wouldn't let such a tale go without many iterations. My birth was her favourite story to tell by the fireside in the deep night when, as a child, as yet unable to control my dreams, she'd wrap me in layers of muslin, her arms fast around my skinny body, and rock me as she spoke. The warmth of her voice was a sleep-song in my ear, giving me the courage to conquer those fearful night thoughts. And her face was soft, brushing against my chops, as she described her hands, moving, as they guided my head out from her own body.

What a head, she'd say, smiling. *Covered with thick black feathers, that's how it looked. I thought I was birthing a crow!*

And lifting her chin, she'd laugh at the memory.

Truly, I wondered if that was why the birds had come, to bless me for bringing one of their own into the world! Don't grimace, my love. Crows are clever beings. Of course, I knew the birds were there to protect us. And to share in my good fortune at having a daughter. For mankind may not value such a thing as highly as it might, but birds know better. All the noise and flapping they made in celebration was such a sight, along with your astonishing head. That's how I knew what your name should be. Raven! My dear Raven — in honour of the bird that brought me to your father, and it was a fair description of what I could see before me. My own raven-headed moon-child.

Once I was out and plainly a squirming babe with arms and legs rather than a crow with wings and a beak, my mother used her teeth to sever the cord. It was thick and salty and tasted of metal and meat. It took a good while to chomp through the thing. *How I chewed you free of your binds,* she'd say, laughing and shaking her head, her long dark hair falling like black water streams across her face.

When your eyes opened and you first looked at me, oh, what a gasp came from my throat. Such eyes as I never did see. Violet-blue like the sky when the Sun is low in the early desert mornings. I thought perhaps you were blind. Not even the fair-haired Europeans coming off boats in the harbour had eyes of such a colour. Then I remembered the story of the Desert Queen of the Tents who was divine, and some believe the mother of us all. She was my direct ancestor and as a child myself I was told, like my grandmother, I had something of her power showing in the shape of my nose. Her eyes were said to be violet-blue, like the finest sapphires. You see, the Gift, when powerful enough, shows in the colour of the eyes. How you blinked at me then, how your face acknowledged mine as if we'd known each other for a thousand years. I knew then you could see all right, and the jewels in your head were a great and ancient prize, touched with divinity. As beautiful as they are, I mourned a little, too. For I understood the sorrow they might bring if I didn't hide them from the gaze of others. People can be jealous and afraid of difference, my raven girl. Especially in women. They're wrong to be so. When all along they might celebrate and revel in it, as the birds did at your birth, as we have always done. As you must try to do.

When Atlas arrived home so late and still carrying her baskets, her legs and dress soaked in blood, at first my father thought some terrible thing had taken place and his voice howled, full of atrocity. Perhaps it was the townsfolk, and their nasty talk had turned to action of the worst kind. But when he saw me, sucking my fingers in the bottom of a basket, Sunny's heart soared. Never had he touched the infinite until he looked upon me, that's what my mother said, and she proclaimed that her young husband, even with a bushy beard upon his chin, only really became a man the second he saw my face.

A few days after my birth, my father agreed we might better thrive with more distance between us and the town. I was tiny and already strange with gems for eyes and hair like ravens' wings. It was decided there and then, when the time came for me to be seen by the wider world, I would do so with a sheath of muslin around my eyes, to guard me from any cruel or malicious curiosity. Sunny felt a deep need to protect me. He set to work building a new dwelling, one more suitable for his small family, a place of sanctuary. It was hard work; the walls were thicker and sturdier than the last. He chose a spot further down the coast, although not so far that we couldn't cross the distance to sell our goods, fetch food, and have friendly words with some of the more open townsfolk. For, supposed devilry or not, Atlas's smile was hearty and kind, and as sure as she could cure a rash or a cough, she was mighty good company.

Our new home was bigger than the first. A large room with a stone hearth, fire-pit and chimney at its centre, a shuttered window in the front wall, and a door at the side. There was space for hives at the back of the dwelling and a garden for planting herbs and vegetables at the front. We were close to the well, so our water would always be fresh. Importantly, the plot was hidden by dense scrub, keeping us safe from the weather and out of sight of those who might want to look if they were passing by. Being unseen became an important factor in our lives. Where once, carefree and happy, Sunny and Atlas rejoiced in their freedom, now my terrible innocence and defencelessness was all-important. No matter what, I needed to be protected. Later, when Atlas told me stories of their early days together, even though she tried to hide it, one thing was sure; with me came change. I was a catalyst.

That was my burden.

Scene 4

My earliest memories are the smells, tastes and feelings of our family life. The fragrant odour of beeswax that lingered on the walls of our dwelling and on our skin from the melting, softening and rolling of candles. Sour sweat mixed with musky earth when collecting honey with my father in the baking heat. Sulphur from the gently burning smoke-pot we'd place in the hives through a small hole in the top. The catch at the back of our throats as we rushed to capture the smoke, quickly closing the hole with twigs and mud, locking everything in, suffocating the bees inside. We'd stand back then, breaths held as we listened to the panic and chaos of the imprisoned insects, waiting for the inevitable stillness, the silence. When it fell, it would be sudden and exciting. But when Sunny smashed the hive, how sad I'd be to see the colony dead. I'd cry out against our easy violence, sob at the sight of hundreds of tiny bee

33

bodies, once so happily humming around outside our home, now lying dead in perfect circles of golden honeycomb. My salty tears soon dried though, when my father allowed me to plunge my hand in and pull out the sweet, sticky liquid sunshine. I'd watch the stuff ooze through my chubby fingers before shoving it all in my mouth, picking out brittle remains of wing and leg as I supped it down. This was my first real lesson in life: sweetness comes at a cost.

Although days were often stifling hot, night-time was always cold. Even so, Atlas craved the company of the Moon. Many times, deep in the night, we'd go for moonlit walks by the sea. Atlas and Sunny carried burning torches as we wandered through the midnight air. For the Moon's light shone pale and misty in the thick velvet black of night. When the torches moved, they sounded like the beating of great wings, and I'd look within the flames for a fiery bird. Mostly, I'd watch the dark world through sleepy eyes, toddling happily between my mother and father, my giggling protectors. Their voices, always so full of fun, rippled into the night as we tripped along, their torches licking and dancing in the chilly air, sending me into trances. I was told many times to mind the torches, to stay clear of the heat, as I was at home around the hearth fire and the wax pot. But there was something especially dangerous about a torch fire, wild and free with its hidden wings and hungry flames, moving around in the open air. Although my main memory of early childhood is being afraid of that hot, orange danger, I was also fascinated by it. I wanted to touch the fire in the same way I grabbed honey from the hives. I wanted to have it for myself, to own it.

Fire is my first memory of pain.

On one such nightly ramble, my mother and father sat for a while, some business of the day taking up too much space for walking or rolling together in the sand. After their gentle debate was through, they fell quiet and, lost to their own thoughts, looked out over the big brine. Each had planted their torch in the sea-damp ground just by where they were sitting. At first, I wedged myself between them, dug my fingers into the sand to watch the shapes shift and feel the sludge move through my hands, but I soon grew fidgety. Distracted by the cold and in need of entertainment, I slid behind my father. Time can be a puzzling thing, for in that moment (less than a moment) a million thoughts and feelings rang like bells through my infant mind. As much as I loved my mother and father, my heart was full of rebellion. I crawled toward Sunny's torch, felt the sandy ground puck and shift beneath me. Even as I saw my arm stretch out toward the flame, my hand grasp at the fluttering head of the beacon, I heard my mother gasp and shout.

I did not scream at first, nor did I snatch my fingers from the flames. I watched, entranced and breathless, as the still baby flesh of my hand caught and melted like beeswax in a warming pot with each fiery lick. It was only when I heard my mother's screams, felt her pull me away, that the pain rent a shriek from my throat.

I don't recall much of what happened after that. I was whisked into my mother's arms among cries and calls as I bellowed in agony. Soon I was lying by the hives at the back of our dwelling, panting like a dog, full of fever and kicking at anything around me. The air was suddenly thick with bees, bumping into each other like drunkards in the dark. My father held my thrashing, screaming body down, and Atlas was at my side, smothering honey still on the comb over my hand. Then something caught my eye and my thrashing stopped.

It was the Moon.

She was small and high in the blackness, winking at me as if demanding my attention, doing her bit to take my mind from the pain. I felt calmer then and closed my eyes as I listened to my mother's sing-song voice, trembling with panic but quietly asking any deity, god or goddess to help her cunning, and to save me from the terrible wound. The last thing I heard was her whisper the name Setebos, before I slipped from consciousness, into a long and starry sleep.

Although saved, I was in a delirium for weeks. When at last I was able to get up and move about, my hand was wrapped in layers of silk and muslin, so it looked like a large bauble on the end of my arm. An altar had been roughly made in the furthest corner of our home. When I saw it, I gasped, knowing of such things only from my mother's old tales, and the sometimes strange and shadowy practices she'd described being performed around them. A small bowl of goat's milk and a crust of honeycomb were placed on the altar, which was covered in seashells of every kind and anointed with oil. Sweet incense sat burning in a pot. The smoke made curls in the air, tickling my nose, making me sneeze and stinging my eyes. I looked at my mother, puzzled by this new thing. She had faint outlines of welts up her arms and over her face from the bee stings sustained the night of my *accident* – as my mother insisted on calling it, as if she truly believed I hadn't meant to disobey her and grab the flame. There'd been no time to kill or even calm the colony with burning sulphur that night. I pointed at the angry red marks, my face crumpling with guilt, but she only smiled as she sat me before the altar and said, in her most serious voice, that now I was well enough it would be my job to tend it, as it was mine and no one else's.

You must honour the divine Setebos, she told me, moving slowly and precisely, showing me in sweeping, graceful gestures exactly how to renew the offerings and give thanks for my life. *He was the one to heed my call and help lift you from death's grasp, so you're forever in his debt, now.*

My father snorted.

We turned to look at him, but he refused to hold our gaze.

Atlas sat back on her heels before saying, more quietly, *I wouldn't have begged had I not been desperate. His presence was strong, and there was no other*, and then louder, turning her face to her husband, *so this is where we are.*

My mother smiled and moved with purpose again to continue her instruction. *When we call beyond this world*, she said, *we are forever beholden. I've given my promise, now you must give yours, not through words, but through worship.*

I looked again to my father, who was still refusing to look back and shaking his head. *Whoever heard of worshipping a demon?* he whispered, just loud enough for me to hear.

A devil? I gasped, my voice croaking like a timid frog.

Angel or devil, it doesn't matter. They're the same thing, the two sides to existence. Call them what you will. Good and bad live hand in hand, face to face, and back to back. Without one its opposite cannot exist. So what is good is also bad. Atlas shrugged.

But I frowned so much, my head hurt and my eyes filled with tears. Atlas sighed and touched her forehead to mine. She smelled of wild herbs and beeswax. I wanted to please her, so tried to smile, managing only a grimace.

One day, I sniffed, *I'll be like you and know everything.* I nodded at my mother as I blinked away my tears. She couldn't help but grin, her face wide, moonlight-pale and silver, her hair as inky as the lunar night.

If we did not have light, we'd never know we lived in darkness, she continued. *Like the Moon and the Sun. Setebos is your divine grace, that's all you need to know.*

When I'd wiped my eyes and proved I'd understood by matching her actions, anointing the wood with sweet oil using my uninjured hand, she looked to my wounded paw and said, *Scars are important. They don't only show how we've suffered. They're a tribute to how we've survived. My Raven, be proud of the life you have in you. Your spirit is strong. Perhaps you're really a tiger! When I thought you but a bird.*

We giggled but her voice was serious.

Reaching into her pocket she took out a pebble and a long raven feather, placing them upon my altar. I looked at the grey rock and frowned again.

We should learn what powers you have, if any; they can protect you if you know how to use them. With your eyes, I don't doubt the Gift will be strong in you. For now, these are your tools, and you will work with them, for practice, she said. *I trust you to use them well. I didn't expect this so soon for you, but the accident has been a sign.* She looked at my hand. *It's time.*

I watched my mother brush oil across the pebble, witnessed the colours move at each stroke before she fixed the feather into my hair with the finest twine, then very slowly, as if the action itself were a holy event, my mother unwrapped each layer of fabric covering my injured hand. When all was off, she told me to look at what was there. The skin was still raw and pink in places, scabbed and scaly in others.

I knew my hand would be marked, that was only to be expected. I'd seen small injuries before, had watched in wonder as they'd healed, but I'd never seen anything quite like this. Two of my fingers were stuck. They were neither bent nor straight, but try as I might I could not move them. The rest were balled into a fist, and I couldn't stretch them out at all. I looked hard at my hand. It resembled a lump of dried beeswax. Seeing the shock as I flicked my eyes to hers, my pooling tears that began to fall in streams down my cheeks, my mother did not throw her arms around me. Instead, as my lips trembled and the look of horror turned to grief, crumpling my face, Atlas shook her head, hard. A gesture that told me crying was not the way. She held my chin up with two fingers and smiled. Then my gentle mother, bells around her ankles and feathers in her hair, kissed my broken claw, and anointed it with oil.

My unwrapping was a rebirth. The genesis of understanding how I might be in the world. Atlas was teaching me to work with the elements. To respect, honour and learn from them. That was the essence of the Gift. Trying to dominate nature would ultimately bring pain. As it was, it had tethered me to an unsavoury god. But I could still find a way to thrive, and discover my connection to natural things. For we are not greater than nature but a part of it. It was also the first time I felt my father step away from my mother and me. The fissure started lightly; a tut here, a turn of the head there. Or a short silence where once words or laughter might have been. Slowly, the breach grew. Something cracked and split each time my mother held her tongue. I felt it like a blade cleaving me in two. The rift was my fault. All I could do was watch. No balm nor bandage could heal it.

Scene 5

At Atlas's insistence, I started using my injured hand, so I might live well with it and not hide it away. I told myself nothing had really changed. Our home was yet happy. I followed my father around, helping with the bees, collecting honey and shaping wax as I'd always done, tripping at Sunny's heels as I went. If noise from the birds, who were never far from my mother's feet, diverted my attention, causing me to wander off to pet them, it was never for long. I'd soon be back at my father's side, looking up, searching his face for recognition. And there it would be. His smile. The beautiful assurance that I belonged to this man, and he to me. I was his shadow, that's what he always said. How I'd laugh at that as he'd bend so I might throw my arms around his neck and, laughing, he'd protest that there was work to do. But he loved the distraction. Many a time the honey went uncollected as he'd sit beside me to play. We'd make up tales about distant islands lost at sea, collect sticks to fashion into miniature people, creatures and beasts, who'd carry out adventures in our imagined worlds. There were stories of emperors and monsters, of pirate hunts and fairy-lore. I loved to be in his company.

My stories are all true! he'd insist, trying not to laugh. *I'm not a child and have no imagination. Every word I speak is honest. A mountain man never lies.*

But now, I had my altar.

Although we carried on for three summers as if all was well, there were fewer games, and I was often in the way.

Why are you always under my feet? Sunny started to say, as he brushed me aside. *Give me space, girl.*

I tried hard to be in the right place. But it seemed more and more that when my father turned round, there I was, hindering some work he desperately needed to do. Where once he'd scooped me up as he tended the hives, or got me to fetch pots of water, given me tasks, now he pushed me away. On the day he finally snapped I'd been in a good mood, skipping about, babbling, asking why he was doing a thing and what it was for (even though I'd asked the same question a thousand times). Later, as Sunny worked with the smoke-pot, I sat beside one of the larger hives with my cheek pressed against the wall of the nest. I'd wanted to feel the vibrations from the tiny bodies buzzing within. When I started humming a melody I believed fitted well with their own tremulous song, my father whipped around, a look of rage burning his face.

Will you ever stop with your bother and leave me alone, child? he shouted. *Haven't I enough to do without worrying what you're up to all the time? This is no place for a girl. You shouldn't be near the hives. You need to be with your mother, with women and other girls, not around a working man. Go from me!*

Stunned, I didn't move at first, but blinked into his furious face. My skin tingled, like all the bees had stung me at once. It took a few moments to realise I wasn't hurt, there was no need for tears. It wasn't sadness or upset I was feeling, it was anger. I had seven years behind me and was old enough to see the injustice of his rage.

Good! I'm a person, not your miserable shadow, I shouted, stamping my feet. *I'd rather live in my light than wither in your shade.*

My father was as still as stone. Only his eyes moved, shivering in their sockets as he stared. Though he'd never raised a hand to me nor beat me at all, I was suddenly afraid. A scream of frustration ripped from my mouth as I turned and ran down to the sea. I waited there, in the caves, throwing pebbles into the water, watching them splash until hunger outweighed my rage.

When I returned home, other than Atlas's birds scuttling and pecking about the roof, all was quiet. Neither my mother nor my father mentioned the incident. In truth, they hardly spoke. Silence lay heavy on my shoulders. I thought the weight might crush me, for I was certain I'd done something very wrong. When Sunny suddenly spoke, I jumped from my stool by the fire-pit. But his voice was steady. He said only that I was a girl and needed to be around women, so I might find my place.

That was that.

The next day I was no longer a beekeeper's helpmate or my father's shadow. I was at my mother's side learning to weave baskets and prepare Dreamstones.

Scene 6

I had a knack for the stones.

Atlas called it the *Gift*.

The Gift was an ancient knowledge, passed down through generations of women. Atlas's family had at times been richly bestowed. If the stories were to be believed, we were from a royal lineage and divine bloodline. Through the ages, it seemed, our filial talents for great acts of magic and enchantment had faded. But, Atlas excitedly assured me, along with a knowledge of the healing ways, we could usually still create Dreamstones and do other small glamours. My mother fervently believed the old tales and felt sure that even the more powerful magical gifts had never truly vanished.

They've been sleepy, she said. *Resting, waiting for one strong enough to carry them. For just as a wheel turns, everything comes around again, somehow.* She pointed to my eyes, hesitated, and smiled before continuing. *You bear the mark of the great ancient powers. Don't fret, my Raven! Even if you possess them, you're not bound to use your magic. You must do as you wish. There's no duty, no commitment.*

She sighed and looked away, as if lost in her thoughts for a moment.

I'm not sure we ever truly know what we are until our last day on earth, she said, her voice breathy and quiet now, her own eyes staring and distant.

Frowning, I tilted my head to one side, questioningly.

If the gifts of our foremothers lie strong enough in our heart, she explained, *their spirits will come for us at that final moment. And as our earthly body melts into the air, leaving nothing but a trace of desert sand, we will join them as one. That is our great privilege. There's no death for those with the Gift, not in the earthly sense. Only a different way of being. So you see, the ancestors are always here, in the ether. When the time comes, if we've truly been granted the power of enchantment, they will call us back to them.*

What if we have no gift? I asked, my eyes wide and wet and searching.

Then we are buried beside the ones we love, and the earth shall make good of us. There's no need to worry about that now, child. Perhaps it's just a story, and one I shouldn't bother you with. Women are flesh, after all. In any case, there will be a mighty strength to whatever you set your mind to do, with or without magical things, I'm certain of that.

And handing me a basket of dull, grey stones, she watched as I set to work. I pulled heart colours from the pebbles with incredible ease. As soon as I'd pick them up, they'd start to shine. Selecting one stone, I stroked its solid surface with my feather. For my mother this part of the work was exhausting. She'd be as if in a trance, focusing on the very essence of the pebble before her, beads of sweat bejewelling her forehead. I had no need of such concentration. I sat back, giggling as the different hues swirled and moved through the stone, until at last I guided them to their rightful place within the rock. It took no effort. The spirit of the mineral seemed to commune naturally with my own and with a few last touches of my feather, the pebble was transformed. Atlas wrapped her arms around me, cocooning me in the calico and loose muslin of her tunic as she rocked and laughed and kissed my head.

As I thought. You have a powerful gift, she said. *What a future you'll have!* And laughing, she stroked my hair.

My small pebbles were the brightest in the baskets. Still, Atlas would not permit my whispering to them under the full Moon. I was too young for the task, she said. I didn't mind. There was a sparkle in her beautiful eyes as she looked at me. That was all I needed. In truth, I cared little for the stones. Other than delighting in their brightness and colour, I thought them merely trinkets. But when Atlas imparted her cunning ways, teaching me the healing properties of oils, plants, mushrooms and insects, I was eager, attentive and quick to learn.

We mustn't abuse nature for our own purpose, she'd insist as we walked the tracks around our home, examining all that grew and lived thereabouts.

Being from the desert there' were plants and trees near our dwelling she hadn't yet fathomed. But we soon understood how to work with them. Sometimes it was in the smell of the stems, or the quality of the sap, how sticky or how wet, how sweet or how bitter. We learned together which leaves to pound to a paste with her pestle and pot, which to boil in water and drink as a broth. Her instincts were strong. With a simple touch to a flower head she'd know if it should be avoided. For mistakes, she warned, could be deadly. Neither did my mother take more from the world than she needed.

We mustn't be hungry for excess. Greed and want will cause us pain in the end. And remember, it's only right to replace and replenish what we use, she'd say.

Atlas taught me to show thanks and reverence by giving back to the earth something of what we took. When our work was done, we'd sprinkle libations over the ground or bury a pinch of what we'd created under the sandy soil. Her instruction was keen and careful, and I cleaved myself to every word of it, like an apprentice to their master.

Everyone has wickedness in them, even us. We're as prone to fear, pride and greed as anyone else. Healing takes as much goodness from us as it does these leaves and stems. We must be vigilant, do our best to keep the bad at bay, especially when working with the things of the world. But don't be afraid of what you can do, my Raven. Your potions and pastes are already strong and fine, imbued with your energy. They will help many people.

How I'd grin at that, my smile so big across my face it made my cheeks hurt. I liked the idea of healing and helping people, wanted it more than anything. When we went to market with the Dreamstones and oddly shaped baskets, I happily listened to the clink of our small bottles of tinctures and potions, heavy in my mother's sagging pockets. But the bottles were not proudly displayed on our blanket next to my father's honeycomb and candles. Atlas kept them with her, hidden in her skirts. She gave them quietly to any who might be in need, asking nothing in return.

I knew our remedies were secrets because women who learned the workings of the world were not trusted in the town, not openly. Even if we could save lives from fevers and infections, knowledge was the domain of men. And they fiercely guarded it from the weakness of the feeble female brain, through suspicion and fear.

Time passed, and although my world was small, I did not want for much. Nor was I scared or lonely, not even when strangers came to our door to call Atlas away. She'd be gone for hours, sometimes only returning the next day, or the next. When Atlas was gone it was strangely quiet in our dwelling without the noise of her birds. My father would smirk and say it was a blessing to be rid of their blasted din for a while. But I heard the irritation in his voice. Although we became used to my mother's absences, they could send Sunny into bouts of sombre mutterings about old women or the dangers of being *too cunning*. He seemed to know where my mother went off to, but such was the risk to his mood I never dared ask. I learned to busy myself, to avoid his grunts and frowns until his bleakness passed. Then we could enjoy our time alone together. We might tell our old, enchanted island stories and play with sticks, like we used to. Sometimes I'd even hope for a messenger to come for Atlas. For when his humour was good, my father was still the most amusing person to be around and I relished being the centre of his attention. It often occurred to me that if I really had the Gift, as my mother believed, then I might simply make a wish and conjure someone up to call her away. Many times, I thought to try. But I was afraid of magic. What if I sent her away forever? Such an idea was too painful. The Gift was no prize, only a burden that would make me monstrous. Like the strange creatures in our games. I wanted none of it.

Sometimes, when we sat on our blanket at the market, someone might call to Atlas across the lane, and she'd take off. I'd be left, sitting among our baskets and beeswax, wondering at her urgency. Other than being desperately curious about where she was rushing off to, I liked being my own mistress. And on such occasions, she always came back before day's end. Only once do I remember being afraid. I had nine years behind me, so was yet quite small. We were at the market and Atlas had gone with the old widow, only this time she did not return. Night began to fall and, worried I'd be left in the lane, alone in the dark, I packed up and dragged our blanket of unsold goods home. By the time I reached our door I was breathless, fretful and sobbing. Sunny took me on his lap and, with my hot cheek against his chest, swayed until the weeping stopped, then gave me a hunk of honeycomb, all for myself. When at last Atlas returned the next morning, he would not speak to her nor even catch her eye. How sad my mother looked, to be cast from his loving gaze.

Scene 7

With no playfellows of my own age and kind, animals and insects fulfilled the role. I loved them all, from the lowliest worm to the mighty sea monsters in my father's tall tales. That such great beasts could exist, swimming around under the waves, seemed impossible. Even so, I wanted to believe they did, to find one and befriend it, like I had the lizards and snakes in our garden. Each time I walked along the shore I'd keep my eyes open for a sign: a swish of a tail or the spray from a nostril. Until one day, on the beach collecting pebbles with Atlas, I saw one for myself. Never again did I question the possibility that the earth and sea were filled with magical things. I only mourned what little care people gave them.

It was dead when we found it. A giant of a thing, and although it was motionless, with all signs of life gone, it filled me with terror and excitement. My mother lost no time. She lay hands on the leviathan like I'd seen her do countless times with trees and plants, as if somehow trying to get the measure of the beast. With a fearful look in her eyes, she told me to run to the market quickly, find the old widow, get her to fetch as many townsfolk as could come and tell them to bring knives. For having only ever heard stories herself and having never seen a whale before, she too thought our drowned creature a monster, something evil from the deepest regions, that might awaken at any minute.

When you pray to demons, expect to be visited by devils, she'd whispered to herself as I turned to leave. I knew I wasn't supposed to have heard, but feeling somehow responsible, I ran quicker than I'd thought possible.

When the people arrived, a fever ran through them.

I watched as they hacked the beast to bits. Exhilarated, laughing and chatting, they were nervous but full of elation as they worked. Blood, stench and bile flowed from the corpse, soaking everyone, causing gulls to scream and circle above our heads. When it was done, after setting the blub-bery fat aside in baskets and pots, the large lumps of flesh were burned. For although the townsfolk, who'd lived by the sea all their lives, knew the thing to be but a whale, its arrival was no less monstrous to them as it was to Atlas. Better to give the meat to the unclean fire than let the carcass rot. Such decay could bring all manner of malevolence, not to mention grubs and worms spreading disease and sick-ness or worse. They were certain *the Great Fish* was sent to remind them that the salty depths were full of horrors. For as exciting as it was, the elder men and councillors agreed, the appearance of this mighty dead thing was a sign of devilry, an omen. Who knew what might follow if they didn't thoroughly deal with it.

As the fire took hold, it was difficult to breathe without holding sea-dampened cloths to our faces. Even hidden behind the band of muslin, my eyes pricked and streamed. Black billowing smoke from the whale's pyre went as far as the eye could see. Still, there was a festive feel to the congregation on the beach. Everyone lingered around the flames, the braver souls getting as close as they dared. The sense of joy in the crowd was palpable as men and women whirled about, covered as they were in a mess of innards and blood. This finding, it seemed, this chopping and burning had been a thing of communion for the townsfolk. No matter how imbued the situation might be with possible evil, how unclean the burning, this coming together was something to celebrate.

Atlas held me back, and as always, except for the old widow, who stood with us and chattered in low tones using words I didn't understand, we stood apart from the others. With my mother's arms about me, we watched the fervour calm and the women of the town gather in clusters on the beach. We listened to their laughter as the men, Sunny among them, went about the serious business of gathering and cleaning blades and knives in the now red-foamed sea. It was strange to see my father slapping backs with other men. He was one of the crowd, a worker and a neighbour, like all the others. I felt a deep fracture, a physical tearing apart of him from us. At one point he stopped his work and looked towards his wife and child. He'd been smiling with the men, but as he caught my mother's eye, the smile faded before he quickly looked away to continue the work again. I felt my mother's grip tighten on my shoulders.

Don't worry, she said. *He'll clean up before he comes home.*

And she pulled me away to walk silently back through the dunes.

After everyone had left, long after nightfall, Atlas took me back to the beach. The hunks of whale meat still burned on the pyre as, taking a stick, we pulled a single lump from the flames. The weight of the still crackling meat bent the branch, making it bob as we walked to the shoreline before we cast it into the waves. The townsfolk had taken from a creature of the sea, so Atlas needed to give something back.

It's the balance of things, she told me. *If one side outweighs another, we open the doors of hell. Mark me, child, it's a place that truly exists. Not in a mythical land under the ground, but in our minds and beating under our hearts.*

The stink of burning whale flesh would linger for weeks – in the air, on our clothes and in our food. The fat, although possibly brought to our shore by ways of demon endeavour, was more than plentiful and handed out, equally, to all households. After all, it was a useful fuel – for fire and light – and might even be rendered into soap. A clutch of men, including my father (who was likely to lose trade for

55

his candles if such a gift be allowed), had seen fit to make the decision while still working on the corpse. We were not forgotten. The old widow came to our dwelling to offer us a share of the precious whale fat. Although he held his tongue in front of the old dam, I saw Sunny frown and shake his head when Atlas refused to take any. It wasn't through fear of hellish curses she'd declined the gift. She simply said the whale had not died for our benefit, so to use its remains was against nature and that truly was the way of the devil. The old woman smiled at my mother and, sucking on an old bone pipe, said that was exactly what she thought she'd say, and went on her way.

Scene 8

Ever since I was a babe, my eyes had been covered. For no matter where I was or what occupied my time, their curious colour was always to be hidden. Whenever out or away from our dwelling, muslin bands torn from an old shift and dyed in seaweed and salt to a murky hue were tied about them. As I grew, so did Sunny and Atlas's anxiety about the gems in my head. Not a day would pass without it being impressed upon me that I should never be without my muslin. Wearing it became as natural as putting on clothes. To me, the world was a hazy place, seen mostly through the curtain of my parents' worry. When in town, if asked why my eyes were covered, Atlas would say I was sensitive to daylight and glance at my injured hand, knowing most folk thought one ailment was as good as any other. Sure enough, it satisfied them that I was a poor creature. Probably witless. Definitely in need of pity. Some would gawp, as if at a caged monkey, especially children and those who came off the boats in the harbour. The townswomen usually looked the other way, humming their condolences at Atlas for having an unfortunate daughter, glad of the fact their own child was not so stricken.

Even seeing it through shadows, going to the daily market with Atlas was to be in amongst an explosion of colour and noise. It was fascinating. My head would snap about. I wanted to take everything in, hear every conversation. We'd sit on our blanket in the bustling lane, selling our wares alongside the other traders, and I'd watch from behind my muslin, amazed at Atlas's movements as she smiled and chattered. She was so fluid and graceful. Next to her I was invisible.

It was impossible not to notice how people looked at her.

My mother was thrillingly strange to the townsfolk, and she knew it. She took pride in her difference. Even back in the desert the men and women of her community would smile and shake their heads as she passed, and the children would run up to tug at her skirts, excited by her appearance. For her clothes were never quite right, her hair unkempt, and her manner more open than most. I'm certain that sometimes she courted the glances that came her way. She was certainly unafraid to flaunt her sandy feet, unslippered and strong, to shake her ankles adorned with seashells and silver bells, and to flick the feathers in her hair. I'd giggle as she'd make a show of playing with the crows and jackdaws pecking at her feet, the starlings swooping to her side. And she would always have a smile on her lips, and a laugh in her belly. With the addition of my unusual appearance, we were sure to be never far from market gossip.

It didn't bother her in the least.

On top of everything, Atlas had a mighty fine figure. Wide hipped and full breasted, she enjoyed the feel of fabric against her skin and thought nothing of showing it. The movement of her own flesh thrilled her in a way the other women in the town obviously found confounding, perhaps even shameful. Maybe they secretly envied her. Of course, some people had filthy mouths and minds to match, and the market wasn't a place to hold back opinions. For them, that a woman might be comfortable in her body was an aberration, something to be mocked and ridiculed. Speaking with their backs turned, though in full voice and plenty loud enough for us to hear, they'd say it was only to be expected from a desert wench, most likely in league with demons and evil forces. They'd heard the stories of ancient desert witches, their dirty ways, curses and spells. My mother would tut and laugh loudly, roll her eyes and, replying to the backs of their heads, bellow that folks should try not to show their stupidity and ignorance so openly. It wasn't like they'd never met people from the desert before. Just like the Europeans, many now lived right there, in the harbour town. In truth, Atlas knew the townswomen had seen nothing like her before and that some, in order not to fear her, filled their hearts with hate. No matter what she heard, my mother didn't flinch. She was never without a

smile, a kind word, and a gentle touch for all who passed
her way. Atlas was a healer. And for that, along with her
goodness and despite the sometimes filthy talk, she wasn't
wholly disliked.

Although never displayed on our blanket with the other
goods, my mother's remedies were our most important
commodity. They were asked for in whispers, to which I
was attentive, keen to learn of ailments and cures. Being
easily unseen, it wasn't difficult for me to gain all manner
of information by listening to market chatter. I heard many
stories about Atlas, mostly fabulous and silly. But also about
how, although married and not yet old enough to be thought
wise, my mother had sometimes helped with birthing other
women's babes. I was sure this must have been before I
was born, for she never spoke of it. To some, it seemed,
she'd been seen as a charm in the birthing chamber, like a
monkey's paw hung above the bed pallet for luck. Others
had thought her work was more talent than superstition and
had appreciated her methods. One day, as Atlas nattered
away to a group of girls, a tired-looking woman with a belly
as big as a whale approached me.

Your dam need keep away from labouring women, she snarled,
quietly.

Her lips were curled back, and she covered her nose as she
spoke, as if I smelled of something rotten. I gave myself a
sniff, just in case, but found nothing rank.

It's unfitting, she growled. *A mother of childbearing age should
not be in a birthing chamber.* She rubbed her hands over her

large, round stomach and coughed. *No good can come of it. Deviance shall be punished.*

The woman stared at my hand then, until I covered it with the skirt of my shift, and she finally hobbled away. I dared not ask Atlas about the encounter. But that snarling woman's words set my mind alight. My mother was like no other woman, and although a strange pride filled my heart as I watched her, I shuddered, wondering where she went when called away and what punishments might be due.

Menfolk were different around my mother than other women, too. They could be saucy and bold; say things they'd be ashamed of thinking near their own wives and sisters. Atlas was no simpering flower. She knew how to be bawdy back, how to lift enough skirt to show her calf. She'd bat away their dirty talk like flies from one of our honey pots with her loud and hearty laughter. Caught in the shadow of my spectacular mother, even years before I was of age, those men sometimes tried to catch my attention, too. But by Atlas's side, they had no hold on me. Although quiet of nature, I wasn't a timid girl, and it took little effort to shrug them off with a flounce of my head, a shake of my feather. Then they'd laugh at the child with her bound eyes and broken hand, imitating such a one as her mighty mother. Then there were some, fine upstanding men, who'd whisper of shady secrets, of sorcery and witchcraft. Years passed but the talk was always there. My mother heard it, but only laughed at their jabbering.

If they accuse me to my face, she'd say, *I will ask those foolish men if they'd like me to prove I'm not a witch by running naked into the sea, so they can watch me slowly disrobe — which is what they really want, the lustful pigs — and observe how quickly I drown — getting a good eyeful at the same time, of course. They can decide for themselves, then. For they surely know a true witch — whatever creature they imagine that is — cannot be drowned. I will happily describe to them how they could watch me, paint a picture in their minds of how I would look, flailing and gasping for breath, the water clinging to my drenched skin, my breasts bobbing in the waves. And afterwards they'd forever be ashamed of how hard they grew, imagining weed floating through my parted lips as the sea entered my poor body until at last, gasping, I died. They'd soon stop their talk of witchcraft and devilry.*

Scene 9

Atlas was indeed magnificent, but her allure was more than physical. It was in her boldness, her power to charm, and her affinity with nature.

The day the lion came down from the mountain and wandered, lost and angry, into the town, my mother and I were at the market in our usual place. I had almost thirteen years behind me and was feeling sick, uncomfortable and anxious, having just started my bleeding. Everywhere I looked people seemed to stare, and I was sure, somehow, the blood was showing, and all the townsfolk knew my shame. My mother was sitting beside me on our blanket, closer than usual. Every now and then she put her hand on my back and petted me like a goat. Or snaked an arm around my shoulders and squeezed. It didn't help. In fact, it made me more out of sorts than ever. But no matter how many times I shrugged her off, she continued her efforts to comfort me.

Dreamstones and baskets were spread about us, the honeycomb having sold early, as was often the case. It was another hot dry day. The breeze from the sea was thick and warm and full of the smells of the harbour. It gave little relief. Several jackdaws and pied crows pecked around my mother as she fed them seed and touched their small heads with her gentle fingers. She cringed every now and then, rubbing her hands and flexing her increasingly stiff digits.

As you are growing up, I am growing old. She laughed as she winced.

The market was busy, and I'd quickly become weary of it, bored of brushing dirt from my face, scratching at the chafing muslin around my eyes and coughing back the kicked-up dust from the feet of passers-by. I was yawning and tired among the bustle of men shouting, cocks and hens flapping and cawing, animals shitting as they went, and women haggling over the price of food and goods. My belly and back felt heavy and ached from the bleeding. A feeling like knives shooting down my legs added to my unhappiness. No matter how many times Atlas stroked my hair and told me it was a thing to celebrate, a crossing from childhood to womanhood, all I wanted was for it to stop. The thought of bleeding like that at every turn of the Moon for the rest of my life filled me with horror. And Sunny had started to look at me differently since it started. He'd insisted I was to be kept by Atlas's side whenever we were in town from now on, although Atlas had baulked at this, asking if he thought shackles might be a good idea, too. Finally, my father refused to play our games of island adventures any more.

You're not a little girl now, he'd said, *you need to be dignified, well behaved for finding a husband.*

I was miserable.

All my mother could do was smile and say, *Everything changes. Even this. The bloods will stop when you're old. You'll miss them, then.*

I doubt that very much, I said sulkily. *I'd rather be old than have this. Or be a child forever. Anything but . . . ugh. Why must it be women who are made to suffer this? Is it because we bleed that we must hide behind our fathers? Or forever be shushed and quieted, like the townswomen? All so we might be chosen by a husband to keep his house? Then be kept in his home like an animal, with little dignity or freedom? I am not a goat!*

Atlas snorted, threw her head back and laughed.

You've a hot head, my Raven. You're capable of much more than you know. There are things we can accept and things we can't. You'll see.

Scowling, I sighed.

I longed to be by the sea caves, to secretly untie the tight binding over my eyes, let the light in, drink in the sights. How I loved the jade water, sparkling as if touched by shards of gold and silver, shining under the Sun's rays. All I wanted was to lift my child's shift and wade through the cool waves. But I was sitting on the ground. My backside was numb, my legs and arse itchy under layers of new thick underthings, my eyes were covered, and my feet thick with dirt.

Then, just like that, everything changed.

I looked up.

There was a drop in the noise around us, a shushing of voices. A nervousness appeared to be spreading throughout the market. Townspeople were suddenly still, like spiders hanging on threads, waiting. The air seemed to crack like a struck stone, and just for a second, everyone looked to be holding their breath. Then it came.

We heard it before we saw it.

No, it wasn't the beast we heard first, it was the screaming.

We watched from our blanket as clutches of people ran from the market and down towards the harbour. I flinched and readied myself to flee whatever trouble was obviously coming, but my mother gestured to remain seated. That's when we heard the deep, echoing roar of a mountain lion. Later Atlas said it was the sound of fear because the animal was lost and scared and wandering in an unknown terrain. To me it was savage, from another world and so loud it seemed to shake my bones from their sockets. I grabbed my mother's arm. All around us now, people were scrambling to get away from this terrifying, unseen menace. Even the birds took flight.

We sat tight.

My mother was stone-still, head turned in the direction of the thunderous roar, nose held high, sniffing the air. I tried to speak, to protest, but she shushed me. Again, the sound came. Louder than before. Closer. A group of men was shouting and gesturing wildly at us to move away.

Quickly, quickly, they shouted. But my mother would not budge.

Then we saw it.

The lion walked slowly through the dust toward the market. There was such a hush, the very waves in the harbour seemed to still themselves. The animal's great golden head, beautiful yet monstrous, shook from side to side before it opened its maw and roared again.

Its mane was magnificent, sleek and full, and unlike us, covered as we were in sweat and dirt, perfectly clean.

A male, Atlas whispered.

His paws were as big as meat platters, yet so graceful. They looked soft, gentle even, as he padded effortlessly, slowly forward.

My heart was banging in my breast. There'd been stories of men killed in the mountains by such animals, the flesh shredded and ripped from their bones which were found splintered, dried and bleached under the torturous Sun. Tales of babes stolen from villages to be made a meal of by these terrifying beasts. I knew only too well that the softness of the lion's tread hid the ferocity of its claws, sharper and more brutal than any soldier's cutlass.

I shifted; my mother stilled me.

Watching the animal's fine flank, all muscle and grace, I was so scared I thought I might disgrace myself. Yet my awe outweighed my fear. Though terror gripped me like a fist, I was glad we hadn't run away like the others. I wanted to be close to the creature, to feel its heat. The thrill was almost too much to bear, and I felt tears rise in my covered eyes. Then to my horror, my mother got up from her knees, brushed the dust from her skirts and started to walk with outstretched arms, slowly, towards the beast.

A scream rose to my breast, but I could not let it out, nor could I move at all. Until at last, my mother was standing before the awesome creature, a footstep away from its mouth.

Stricken, sweating and shaking where I sat, I watched her with a mix of terror and admiration. There was a fluttering, throbbing and turning sensation in my belly, like laughter bubbling up. As if in all this, the thing fighting to get out of me was joy.

The lion came to a halt.

He regarded my mother with his pale yellow eyes before his large, thick tongue licked his chops with an audible slap. He moved his head slowly from side to side, heavy breath pulsing through his wet nose. I noticed then how his mane was darker in places, and how that simple nuance made him all the more regal.

He was beautiful.

Atlas slid her foot forward in the dirt so as not to disturb the dry earth, moving ever closer. Holding out her hands, she stretched to stroke him, but the lion stepped away. Then she started singing, softly, in the language of her desert family. When close enough, she finally touched the lion's muzzle, and bent to the beast. He held his mighty head up and she slipped her arms around his neck, singing in soft, loving tones and nuzzling into his mane. The behemoth responded in kind, like a kitten on its mistress's lap.

After a moment, Atlas stood.

She cast about, twisting slowly around to face away from the market.

The lion looked at her as if with affection, or respect, and turned its great bulk.

They walked together, then.

My mother and the lion.

Away from the market.

Away from me.

The tips of Atlas's fingers rested on the lion's head as they glided off. The gentle swing of her hips and movement of her skirt matched the sway of the animal padding beside her in perfect synchronicity. I could still hear her singing, and remembered how she'd told me that if it's given in truth and kindness, a song can be used to charm.

They walked on.

Blinking under the tight fabric over my eyes, I could see the body of the lion pressed against Atlas's thighs, could almost feel its weight and power as she must have. She did not look back at me. Her focus was entirely on the lion, and his on her. Other than the distant sound of waves and the wind in the trees and my mother's charming song, all was quiet. They kept walking until they disappeared, and at last were out of sight.

When I turned back to the market a crowd of townsfolk stood, as still as houses, looking out to where my mother had been guiding the lion away from them. The men were lined up in front blocking the womenfolk, who peeped and strained to see from behind the wall of their husbands and sons. Something akin to admiration filled the men's faces, but not quite. It was something else, something I couldn't place at first. Until I suddenly understood what my mother had always said. It wasn't esteem I could see, it was desire.

Their faces, even the way they stood, betrayed a yearning they knew they shouldn't contemplate, for a woman they could never possess. This strange desert woman with her young husband and broken child, who was secretly present at the birth of their babes, who could control the temperaments of wild beasts, who had knowledge beyond their reckoning about the properties of trees and insects, was beyond their reach. I saw something else there too, something I wasn't expecting.

I saw their fear.

ACT II

Scene 1

Years fell away, my legs grew long, my shoulders shapely. My breasts bloomed upon my chest in a way that both alarmed and pleased me. My hipbones jutted out below the gentle rise of my belly, sharp under my thin, young girl's shift. Sometimes I'd knock them, painfully, on the edge of the table, leaving bruises and making me curse my clumsiness as I went about my work, boiling brews of leaves and herbs for remedies, making Dreamstones, and rolling warm beeswax into sticks. I wanted more than anything to be like Atlas and marvelled at my transformation. But there was a mourning, too. As if my childhood self had been ripped, unbidden, from my person.

Moments of solitude became ever important. I'd crave them. More often I'd wander alone to the seashore to clamber over rocks and sit in the caves. I especially loved to scrabble through the sand dunes, where I'd stop to lie down for a while, feeling the Sun scorch my skin. On very hot days I might shed my clothes, walk naked through the sea breeze as I'd done in childhood. It was somehow different now, though. How I loved the feel of it on my skin, nature's breath, touching me, giving life to my unseen parts, my flesh fizzing at its touch. I had no idea how well I was. All I knew was I felt alive, and young, and the world was full of possibilities.

Like my mother and father, I'd grown nervous of my eyes being uncovered. Unlike Sunny, this was not for fear of putting off the attentions of a possible husband, the idea of which made me feel sick. But the fabric had become part of me. As much as I disliked wearing it, without it I was raw and vulnerable, like a shelled crab. Even when the rest of me was bare to the elements I'd often keep my eyes covered, the muslin (stained so none might see what was hidden beneath) wrapped and tied tightly around them. When I dared take it off, I'd imagine terrifying scenes. Screeching gulls swooping down to peck out my eyes and make off with them, greedy for their precious colour. Or I'd picture a sea monster rising from the waves to steal me away. It would cast me into the brine, leave my flesh to rot in the salt water, so it too could gaze upon the gems in my poor dead head. I knew the sea was not a benign thing. It held secrets, often leaving gifts of unrecognisable fleshy decay scattered along the shore. It was an unfathomable barrier never to be crossed. Eternal. Powerful. Made for atrocity and destruction. And how I loved to be close to it.

With fifteen years behind me, other than the midnight whispering I still wasn't permitted to perform (*You must know your power before giving it to others*, Atlas would say), I'd taken over from my mother at making the Dreamstones. Though I cared little for the work, they were in demand. Bought by sailors spilling from the many ships in the harbour as gifts for their sweethearts and mothers, as much as by the girls of the town. I liked it when those young maidens tried to buy one in secret, flicking their heads hither and thither to see who might be watching. I'd imagine them hurrying home to stash the pebble under their bedding, hoping to ensure a night of dreams where their deepest longings could be played out and sated in full. I'd point to a pebble full of reds and pinks, saying they were the colours of the heart, of blood and the passion of true love. I wanted them to know I'd never judge someone on their needs or desires.

In truth, I knew nothing of the heart.

Things had shifted after the incident with the mountain lion. My mother was a less popular character at the market. Gone were the happy conversations, the thrown-back heads and open mouths full of laughter. Although women approached our blanket as usual to buy honey for their husbands, and baskets for chores, only a few still asked for the little pots of ointments and cures Atlas had secreted in her skirts. Or for advice on which leaves to use to make a broth to aid digestion and which direction to stir the pot. Now, if they asked at all, it was with nervous, trembling fingers, and furtive glances, and nobody came to call her away any more. I watched her grieve the loss of complicity with other women that her healing had brought.

You'd think they'd be grateful, I said as we watched the townswomen file past us at the market, turning their heads away, never stopping to pass the time.

As her absences from home dwindled, so did her strength. My mother became slow and stiff of limb, easily exhausted and always in want of sleep. I attended to her as best I could, made up remedies for restoration. If they worked, it was only ever for a short while. When one day someone did finally come looking for her, I couldn't help but notice the light flicker and flare in her eyes.

It had been a slow day with little trade. We were despondent, sitting on our blanket, sweating under a furious Sun with nothing to do but pet and feed Atlas's endless parade of birds. A girl of around my age came running toward us waving her arms. She was breathless, gaspingly saying she'd been sent to fetch the desert woman. Things had become too difficult, the girl rasped. Wringing her hands and speaking through tears, she spoke of endless torrents of blood, loudly insisting again, so everyone could hear, that she'd had no choice but to find the desert wench.

Every tongue seemed to stop, every eye and ear turned in Atlas's direction, as without hesitation my mother hobbled after the sobbing girl. Of course, I was forbidden to go. Sunny would never have allowed it and my mother only ever wanted harmony. Alone on the blanket, the snarls and disdain of our fellow traders turned on me. Seeing no need to let myself be so abused, I packed up our things and left. Sunny's annoyance at my returning home early and alone would be easier to bear than their baseless hate.

After that, things got worse.

When people walked by us in the market, their chatter would stop dead. More than once I heard whispered voices spit the word *witchcraft*. On several occasions men prevented their wives from buying a Dreamstone from us, even after the woman protested it was to be a wedding gift and not for herself. My mother looked bowed, as if her body were falling into itself. When I told Sunny she needed rest and care and to be away from the sharp tongues of the town, he agreed. Atlas was getting too old for the work anyway, he said. He'd take his honey to market himself. The talk and behaviour of the townswomen didn't seem a bother to him. He was even in good humour about it. After all, they were just women. They'd stop their nonsense soon enough, especially with a man around. In any case, after years at the hives, he'd enjoy the clatter and noise of the town, the talk and company of fellow townsmen.

As Atlas grew thinner and slower, she spoke more often of the family affliction suffered by her kinswomen. She thought she might escape it, she said, but now she knew it had taken her. Her fingers were stiff, swollen and inflamed, her grip so weak she'd drop things and bark insults at herself for being feeble and inept. As a child she'd watched her aunts and cousins do the same, until finally they were bent in two and could not walk on their swollen feet. She'd already stopped making baskets, saying it was a waste of time as they were too oddly shaped to sell, anyway. I knew that wasn't the true reason. Her gait was less fluid, and I watched sadly as she hobbled about, her face twisted into a grimace of pain. Often, she was too tired to do anything more than raise herself from the bed pallet.

Each morning at my altar, I'd sprinkle oil over a sandstone and ask Setebos to ease my mother's suffering. Softly I'd whisper the words as I watched the oil roll over the altar: *Setebos, of Moon and stars, of wind and sea, make her better. Take away the pain.*

Some days, Sunny permitted me to go alone to sell my Dreamstones at the market. I'd leave Atlas sitting by her cooking pot, slowly stirring leaves to make poultices and infusions that would never be used and humming to the birds at her feet. I rarely went with my father to help sell his honey, comb and candles. When I did, he'd watch me with an eagle's stare, so afraid my muslin might slip from my eyes. I'd bind the fabric so tight my eyes would almost be closed, and I could hardly see at all. I told myself his feelings came from a place of love, and a sense of his duty to protect me, so I was willing. When he began to drape scarves over my injured hand, bark at me to tuck my arm behind my back whenever anyone came near, my spirit broke. Atlas had taught me not to hide the injury, to be proud of my history and of who I was. Now the heat of confusion and shame rose in my cheeks. I felt like a prisoner, bound by my father's care and fear, just another of my mother's faulty products, like her baskets, useful but wrong, misshapen.

Soon, I refused to go back to the market.

Sunny was only too happy to comply.

Scene 2

To keep me from mischief – as my father called my making of Dreamstones – I was trusted to work with the hives again. Such was my joy at being with the bees, I'd sing to the little creatures as I'd dance and twirl my way around the colonies. How I enjoyed those days, the feel of my loose hair entwined with feathers and seashells (like my mother's), long and slapping across my face, my thin shift swirling about me as I worked. And with Atlas sitting close by, smiling as she watched her carefree, beekeeper daughter. It seemed we were at peace with our place in the world.

One breezy morning I noticed that the bees were more troublesome than usual. I was certain all would be well and tried my best to assure Sunny, making light of the insects' angry hum. But anxious they'd swarm, my father thought it best to forgo his day at the market to stay close to the hives. Such a change to his plans left him foul of temper, and try as I might to smile, to be attentive and sweet, he stomped around, scowling at every turn. Nothing I did could please him.

Is this how they are under your care? he growled as he shouted orders at me.

I longed to throw everything down, tell him to look after his own bees as he obviously didn't trust me, and to run to the dunes. But I would not disobey my father and it would have only made him worse. When Atlas appeared, humming as she came out from our dwelling, a lone jackdaw perched upon her head, I couldn't hold back my giggles. My father turned from the hives, his face full of thunderclouds, and rather than join in with her song and sweep her into his arms as he might once have done, he mocked her. My mother stopped singing. The bird, entangled in her hair now, flapped and fretted as she waved her hands about her head, wincing as it finally pulled away. All the breath seemed to fall from her body, and I thought she might tumble over. But she pulled herself upright and looked him in the eye. At last, she was beautifully angry. By her feet was a pile of old baskets; in one swift move my mother grabbed the baskets and threw them at her husband. My father ducked down before they could hit him, and they flew over his head. Atlas covered her mouth with her hand to hide the smile she couldn't stop from spreading across her lips. It was a ridiculous situation. I found I was smiling, too, and awaiting the laughter that would surely follow. But our smiles quickly dropped away as the accusations started to fly.

Sunny looked at me and I wished for all the world I was a jackdaw so I might take to the skies and never come back.

They might accept her, he said, pointing at me. *If we were among them, at the heart of town and society. I might be on the lower council with other men my age, become a merchant, and then she might marry, even as she is.*

Atlas glared at him, then spoke in a low, quiet voice.

We are accepted, husband. Only not for what others believe we should be. We have all we need, here. Nothing has changed, other than you.

Sunny did not soften.

He riled, bawling that when I was a child and they were both vibrant with the stirrings of youth, a carefree outsider's life was fine. But now, with my mother's black hair streaked with grey, lines upon her face and the way she hobbled about like an old hag, he worried for our future. I flicked around to look at Sunny and roared at him like an animal, no longer able to silence my anger.

My muslin loosened.

It fell from my eyes and fluttered about my shoulders.

He glared at me and for one swift moment I thought he might march over and strike me. Instead, he turned back to his wife.

They say you're in league with demons. You and her. And I cannot honestly deny it or defend you. So I'm quiet, and condemned for it.

Who says these things?

Do you mark me? They damn me in the same breath!

Those stupid men, stroking their beards and sucking on pipes. They are fools who know nothing of the world, nothing of us.

They say our daughter is a mangled crow. They call her Sycorax. Do you know what that means?

It's a cruel name. It has no meaning.

You're wrong, woman. It's Roman, a fancy way to say Pig-Crow. She's branded a filthy, evil thing. Do you see now? That name will hold the story of her life.

My mother took a breath to speak but Sunny hadn't finished. He pointed to me again, his arm outstretched, shaking with accusation.

She is my daughter. You may do what you wish, as you always have, but what's said about a girl reflects onto the father. You're unruly and free, but she belongs to me.

Atlas raised herself.

Our child is not a thing to be owned! she shouted.

She's not a child! The girl is of age, but no one will have her. The idea of making a marriage is a fantasy.

Sunny paused briefly, lifting his arms in the air as if in desperation, then throwing them back by his sides with a loud slap.

Young men laugh at her, he continued. *That is, if they don't turn away in fear and disgust. But we might change that if we lived better, more normal, moral lives among the townsmen.*

My mother's chest was heaving, her hands trembling, but she took a breath and calmed herself as she'd always done when shaken.

Setebos will guide her, she said, her voice gentle and steady.

Setebos! Sunny exploded. *Can't you see what you've done, woman?*

His words came out with such force I saw the spittle fly from his lips.

You gave her a demon for a god. I've turned a blind eye for too long. What else do you teach her? Devilry through those stones, enchantments, and who knows what magic with your potions.

Magic is only a matter of belief, husband.

My father laughed then, but there was no joy in the outburst, only contempt. He took a step toward his wife, stopping quickly to avoid grabbing her shoulders.

Never have I asked what you really are, he said as his finger stabbed the air, pointing accusations at my mother, *or how you bewitched me, young as I was, to leave my family and come to this place. Is it true what they say, did I marry a desert witch?*

My mother's eyes were suddenly aflame. Without another word to Sunny, she turned and fled. I went to follow her, but she screamed at me to stay where I was. So I watched Atlas hurry away as crows, ravens and rooks gathered about her in a cacophony of caws. They circled above and around her, making a mist of their dark feathers, masking and protecting her, hiding my mother from me as she headed towards the dunes.

I worried then, that she was going to find her big black bird, conjure it from the sea so she could climb between its wings and fly back to the desert. The thought of Atlas leaving made me dizzy. Bile rose to my gullet as panic settled in my gut. My throat contracted like a snake swallowing prey, and I retched as the argument about my future whirled around my head. Atlas might never come back, all because of me.

I didn't see my father for the rest of the day.

He stayed inside as I waited alone on the path outside our dwelling for my mother's return. Although I felt sick with fear and sadness, and was desperately thirsty, I was also too afraid to leave my post lest I missed her approach. Atlas appeared just as the Sun was going down. I ran to her. She was soaked and heavy with seawater, violently shivering and trembling. As she reached me, she dropped to her knees. Her eyes were hooded with exhaustion, her face wrung and taut. My muslin was still hanging around my shoulders like a shawl; in my distress, I'd forgotten to put it back in place. Atlas grasped my face with both her hands and brought me to kneel before her. Reduced and small, sodden and bedraggled like a drowned bird, the side of her face was badly grazed. There was blood over her hands where she'd scraped them against rocks or the sea-cave walls. She held me with her eyes, dulled now, as she spoke.

Don't let anyone call you a witch. It has no meaning but to spread hate. If magic is in you, I know you'll use it well. They want to lessen us, to frighten us into submission. You must be stronger than me. We are healers. I'm a woman, not a witch.

Her bloodied face was dirty and streaked with tears she no longer had the strength to hold back. Her eyes closed, as, in a diminishing voice, she repeated the words, *I did not drown. I did not drown.* Until, at last, she dropped to the ground like a piece of sacking, and thinking she was dead, I screamed.

86

Scene 3

My mother lived, but the life was gone from her.

Sunny strode about our dwelling and would not be still, guilt and worry not allowing him a moment's rest. He wrung his hands and shook his head, mumbled half-thought sentences under his breath. How could it be that his strong, happy and clever wife was unable even to stir herself, yet she had no fever? Again and again, he'd go to her, stroke her face and in pained tones repeat, *She does not shiver nor sweat*, that it might prompt me to assure him it was indeed a sign she'd soon be well. But I could not.

The truth was, I couldn't say what ailed Atlas. I tried everything to rouse her. One evening I brought a clutch of birds in from the roof where they'd settled, pecking and scuttling, impatiently waiting for their friend. I thought seeing them might excite her from her stupor. But they flapped and squawked and made a mess of the place, shitting on every surface, causing my father to moan and pull at his hair and me to run around, shouting for them to get out. Atlas did not blink an eye.

The next morning, I woke to the sound of Sunny weeping, adrift among the chaos of shed feathers and bird faeces. He turned to me, his eyes red and heavy with sorrow, a look of hopelessness carved into his face as if into wood. He seemed older and smaller, standing there in the morning shadows. Not knowing what else to do, I rose from the pallet and started to clean the mess. Sunny was soon at my side. We spent the morning scrubbing and making good. It was a purification of sorts. We were cleansing ourselves as much as our dwelling, washing our familial bonds clean. I felt the intensity of it then, his need to protect me, his love for Atlas, his battles within himself. It was all there, under his strong hands as he washed and swept and wiped, it throbbed with each thud of his heart as he worked.

When the Sun was high and hot and all was done, we rested. Not wanting to neglect the promise I'd made to my mother; I went to my altar to kneel and give thanks. Sunny put his hands upon my shoulders and softly squeezed. There was a moment of panic as I thought I'd been careless. Maybe I should have forgone my libations, for the sake of unity and sympathy, knowing his feelings as I did. But my father kissed the top of my head.

Do what you must, he whispered, before going to sit by his wife where she lay, unmoved and waxen, to stroke her hair and gently hum the songs she'd once sung for us.

Since Atlas had taken ill, I'd mixed my remedies with the best ingredients I could find, but none gave her relief or succour. My inability to help seemed to become a physical thing. When my own pain came, it did so quickly.

At first, I thought it natural, my body's reaction to the deep dismay within my breast, for I was tired. But the change seemed to occur while I slept, so I began to wonder if I hadn't been visited by a demon. One morning I woke, and the simplest movement was agony. It worsened as the days fell away. I'd wake up heavy with fatigue, aching and sore, and hobble about on swollen, pain-ridden feet. The fingers on my uninjured hand became stiff and clumsy, my limbs slow and awkward.

Some days I thought a bag of rocks lay across my shoulders, and I feared I'd be crushed by the weight. My back ached and began to curve slightly. In the mornings my joints screamed. The flesh around them looked angry, fiercely red, all hot and tender. I bound my ankles, knees and wrists as tight as I could in rags bathed in cold seawater, like I'd seen my mother do when her own body failed that way. I drank her bitter tea of orange spice. The cures helped a little with the swelling, which was a blessing. But again and again, it returned, and I'd wake, agonising pain shooting through my feet and fingers, my shoulders and back bent with cramps. I said nothing to Sunny, played false that all was well. I couldn't bear to burden him more. Still, I remembered all my mother had told me about the family affliction.

I longed for the days when trouble seemed but a cruel dream. When my body felt free and light, like some airy spirit. Now my body was a dungeon. There seemed no escape from it, no cracks in the walls for light to break through. My mind banged against its confines, until bloodied and raw. I couldn't recognise myself, thought the pain perhaps a divine sanction, and that I might be to blame for my mother's condition. For I was the one with dangerous eyes. I remembered what the woman with the belly the size of a whale had said. That deviance does not go unpunished.

It went on.

Day after day Atlas lay on her pallet, gazing up and rarely moving other than for the most basic of ablutions. Sometimes, she'd allow her body to simply function without bothering to make provisions, nor even clean herself. Her flesh was a shell, and like the ones we'd find by the shore, it seemed emptied. Sunny was almost always by her side. He'd stroke her face and hair, hum and whisper, gather and hold her in his arms, and sway her like a babe. All to no avail. He fed her, mixed water with honey-drops, saffron-dust and aromatic herbs for her to drink, but could only watch as the liquid ran down her chin, not a glob swallowed.

Our dwelling acquired a putrid smell.

I swilled, scrubbed, and tried to make good to rid our home of foul air and evil miasmas. If all else failed, I burned precious incense, herbs, and powders to at least cover the stink. Afraid Sunny and I might fall into the same stupor and wondering if my own physical suffering might be due to poisoned air, I fixed all my attention on the need to clean. It kept me busy. But my already pained body screamed for rest and relief.

At the end of each day, when all was done, Sunny would step outside to check on the hives. I'd sit at my altar then, beg Setebos to free my mother from her torpor. I left libations, flattered with oil and pretty words, and prayed for my mother's freedom, not knowing what that might be.

Sunny also tried everything he could think of to entice Atlas to move. Once he went to market, bringing back a bolt of beautiful cloth. As he unravelled it and lay it about her, I gasped. Never had I seen such opulence. The cloth looked to be the most precious stuff the world could offer, and I wondered how he could ever afford such a gift. Atlas moved her head when she saw the bright fabric. Her hand twitched and Sunny put her fingers onto a piece of the cloth. It was woven with ten thousand threads, deep sapphire blue (*the colour of your daughter's eyes*, Sunny said) and silver. We held our breaths as my mother's face softened, and the trace of a smile played upon her lips.

Excited, Sunny jumped up. There was a sudden lightness in his step, a song in his speech as he began to jabber about his trip to town, describing in great gestures all the colour and bustle of the daily market. But when he went to the hearth, drew broth from the pot and took it to Atlas in her favourite wooden bowl, she silently turned away. Her face was as stone again, except for a single tear that rolled down her once soft and plump, now thin and taut, face. My father sat heavily on the bed pallet next to his wife, the beautiful cloth strewn about like a dead thing, and sobbed.

He looked defeated. An impotent man in the face of her decline.

Scene 4

Sunny would not countenance leaving Atlas again. There were no more trips into the town. Nothing more was done. Behind our dwelling the hives were full but didn't get tended, and my pile of sad grey pebbles lay in a heap by the door, untouched and useless. We stayed inside, listening to the cries of birds as they gathered in flocks around our dwelling. Our little garden was filled with ravens, jackdaws and rooks marching about like guards. Further down the track, in the bushes and trees, we heard the calls of finches and shrikes, woodcocks and swifts, all waiting for Atlas.

Without a store of provisions, every day the risk of starvation became more apparent. Our bellies moaned their emptiness. Still Sunny refused to be away from Atlas. If we were to survive, I had to act. Bundling the few pots of honey we had into the blanket, I tied my muslin around my eyes and stepped out.

I stopped to watch the rooks and jackdaws on the flat roof of our dwelling, pulling at mud and twigs, lifting their heads to complain to the sky. For some reason this was a comfort, as if in the spaces between their feathers lay the essence of my mother. Her laughter sang through their cries, her joy was the sheen on their backs. As long as they're here, no harm will come to her, I thought.

My progress was slow.

At each agonising step I listened to my breath as it rushed in and gasped out of me. It was something to concentrate on, away from the pain. The wind was picking up. The ends of my muslin flapped and fluttered at the back of my head. I could sense something pulling at me. I'd always felt connected to the elements, as if my body were attached to air and sea by way of flesh and sinew. As a child, I'd tell Atlas when rain was on the way. I'd smell it, feel its approach, even as the Sun shone. Now, the air tasted bitter. As I neared the town, it became leaden and viscous. I rolled my tongue over my teeth. They were gritty.

It was the birth of a dust storm.

I closed my eyes, felt the agitation on my skin, and wondered if I should mention it at the market. Dust storms could be deadly for those trapped in them. I wasn't yet able to fathom when the sands would come, only that they would. The townsfolk would probably think me raving. It was best to do my business, come away and get back to my mother as soon as I could. They'd realise soon enough. My belly was growling. I did not wish to delay my return.

When I arrived at the town and sat on my blanket in the market, people stopped to look, though none came near. My bones felt awkward, too big for their skin, and I was shaky and light-headed. I stared at my knees and stuck my injured hand behind my back.

At last, the old widow who often spoke with my mother came over and crouched by me. She said the townsfolk had been worried. Our absence from the market had not gone unnoticed and she hoped we hadn't taken heed of any bad talk.

People will always talk, she said, *then they get tired. I know, I've had my share of it. But things blow over soon enough, like any storm. Then there are other things to jabber about*, and she assured me Atlas's helping hands and cures had been missed.

The old woman rocked on her heels. She touched me lightly on the shoulder and asked about the health of my mother and father. Her voice was deep, like a man's, and she smelled of goat's milk and salty cheese. My belly growled again at the thought of savouring such food. The widow took some flatbreads from her pouch. *Eat, child.* Although my face burned with shame, I couldn't resist and wolfed it all down, thanking her between ravenous bites.

I've had nothing but honey and thin broth for days, I croaked, trying to smile at the woman's deeply creased face. She shook her head and tutted.

Where is your mother? she asked, with obvious concern.

I couldn't stop the sob from bursting through my throat. I swallowed it down with the last of the flatbread and wiped my mouth with my shift. I'd had little experience of being alone in the company of the townswomen and hadn't expected such gentleness. Looking again at my knees I told the old woman that Atlas had gone too far out, fallen and caught a chill when looking for crabs. I was sure the lie showed on my face and in my voice. I don't know why I said it. It wasn't in my nature to lie, but I feared the truth.

All at once the woman stood. She called out and suddenly I was at the centre of a whirl of womenfolk. Each one spoke kindly. Some touched my shoulder, asked me to send good wishes to my mother. Before I knew it, olives, cheeses, flatbreads, cherries and figs were brought to me. Coins were left, the honey sold. Then as quickly as they came, the whirling women were gone.

I gathered the food up in my blanket and rushed home as best I could on my swollen feet and aching legs. The joy of my haul, the encounter with the townswomen, all made the pain somehow more tolerable. And I remembered Atlas once saying, *Kindness is a powerful balm.* Those words rang around my head. They were my song now, my prayer to the world. I opened my mouth and let them out. Perhaps the townswomen's gifts would be the cure my mother needed. How simple things could be. My feet, as stiff and sore as they were, seemed to fly as my mind swirled and danced. Perhaps Sunny had been right. I might yet be accepted by the people of the town. After all, I thought, I am not so different to them. Maybe I would have my own hives, my own family. We'd lived so much apart from the townsfolk; I'd never imagined we could be beloved of them. I sang again, my voice loud and ringing, all the way home.

When I got there, my thin shift soaked with sweat, I was breathless. I stopped to gather myself. All was quiet and calm in the darkening light. So different from the town and the noise in my head. Panting like a thirsty dog, trying to get my breath so I could pass the well wishes on to Sunny and Atlas, I looked at our small home. Only then did I notice the birds were gone from the roof. The air was heavy, and all about me was silence.

Nothing moved.

Like a child afraid of waking a sleeping giant, I stepped lightly through the doorway. The dwelling was empty.

The pallet vacant.

I called out for my father. My voice screeched through the void, too loud for the space. Dropping my pouch by the fire-pit, I came out and walked around to the back, staggering now, my body having remembered its pain.

The hives buzzed.

My father wasn't there.

Something shimmered in the air.

A crow screamed in the distance, and I thought my heart might stop.

Turning, I ran.

Shouting for my mother, screaming her name, I stumbled, running, tripping and falling, to the dunes. The earlier stillness was gone, and the wind had picked up. Sand was blowing around. It was in my mouth, scraping hard against my skin. The air was getting thick with the stuff now. Golden dust spiralled and swirled around my legs. It blasted my face.

The dust storm had started.

I called out until my throat was raw, and started to hurry again, down to the shore, to the caves. The sea was an angry beast, gnashing its teeth against rocks and shoreline. I pulled the muslin from my eyes to get a better view, let the fabric fly away on the tumult, but the wind was blowing the sand with such force, I couldn't keep my eyes open. Walking against it, pushing into it, the noise of the wind was tremendous. The storm was howling and crashing and screaming around me. There was a strange thrill in my guts as its energy filled me, and I wanted to embrace it. But I was so alone, and afraid.

Then there came another sound, a distant voice.

Sunny!

He was calling her name, wailing for his Atlas.

I moved through the storm, my thin shift pressing against me, sand hitting me with the force of an assassin, cutting me, raining down like slivers of glass or metal. I was shielding my eyes with my hands but could see nothing before me. Then, there, at my feet, through the chaos, something caught my attention. It was glinting, like a star fallen from the sky and landed on the beach. I got down on my knees and saw my mother's anklet of seashells and bells. A sickness grabbed me, my head swam, my belly lifted. I tried to breathe but the air stuck in my gullet, mixed with bile and sand.

The blackout took me before I understood what was happening.

Scene 5

When I woke on the beach my face was cut and my arms grazed by the sand, but the storm had passed. I could hear the sea, still lashing at the shore, seemingly angry with the world around it, and I was shivering. My uninjured hand was balled into a fist. I opened my fingers and there was my mother's anklet. Struggling, I got to my feet and looked across the sea to the horizon and over the expanse of sand to the rocks.

Nothing. Then I saw something. A heap, rolling in the waves on the shoreline. Squinting, my eyes still scratched and sore, I couldn't help but rush toward the thing.

I knew what it was before I got there.

Sunny was face down in the lapping waves, all life gone from him. The water's swell gave gentle motion to his arms and legs in a strange death dance, so much more graceful than his usual heavy movements. I didn't turn his body over. The thought of seeing his dead face was too appalling. Falling to my knees beside his ebbing body, I wailed and let the sea push and suck around me, soaking my already storm-wet legs and dress. The salt water bit at the wounds in my skin. I thought of bee stings, of Sunny, happy at his hives.

Grief roared out of me like the cry of a mountain lion.

I threw myself onto my father's corpse, feeling the solidness of the man, holding it, never wanting to let go. I stayed there a while, wrapped over Sunny's body, protecting it, like a carapace. When I finally moved, I rested my injured hand between his shoulders, as if to give comfort, and looked to the dark horizon. The tail of the storm was fighting with itself as it slowly disappeared. I tied Atlas's bells around my ankle, somehow believing she'd left them for me. There was no need to hurry, she wasn't to be found, and it was too late for Sunny. I waited there with his body for as long as I could stand the cold of the brine. Singing songs he'd taught me as a child, I wailed incantations of love to help his soul find some peace because I didn't know what else to do.

It took all my strength and more to pull my father from the sea. Hooking his body into the crooks of my arms, I grabbed it with my one truly functioning hand. When I got to the rocks, I rested my back against the hard stone and caught my breath. I was shaking furiously. Tears burned my face where the sand had torn the flesh. I wondered if I should go back into the town to beg for assistance, but that didn't seem the right thing to do. It had always been only us, at least when it really mattered. Atlas, Sunny and me. My mother had wanted it that way. I thought, then, of the townsfolk, of all their myriad differences. Some were so old I thought they must have lived forever, some so young their youth glowed about them like a new shimmering light. Each face was a landscape, a history of frowns and smiles heavy with stories. I thought of the well-fed folks, plump in clothes clinging and tight. And of those who shuffled about half starved and stricken, with nothing but rags hanging from their bonelike limbs. I couldn't bear the thought of all these different people coming to gape at my father's body as they shook their heads with pity. Atlas once said people liked to thrill at the misfortunes of others, whether they meant to or not.

Finally, I turned my father over, managing to avoid looking at his face, and moved him again. He was as heavy as the rocks themselves as I dragged him into the cave. But it was quiet, and peaceful, and away from the rush of the sea. He would be safe there.

I went home, still shivering violently with cold and grief. My mother was gone, too. I felt it, the void, the loss. But how glad I was not to have found her corpse. For I wanted to believe there was a deep glamour in her. One wondrous enough to ensure she'd not leave a fleshy shell behind. So that she might endure, in the air and the fire and the sea as her body faded to mist and she was joined, eternally, with her ancestors. Because enchantment never truly disappears. It leaves a trace, that's what she'd said. Her talk of the Gift and of magic had been a source of discomfort to me, of fear. And how I'd tried to turn from it, to ignore what my eyes and soul knew to be true! Now I wanted it. So that somehow, she'd still be with me. Even so, I'd look for her where birds gathered, in case they took me to her earthly remains. Because, if I was wrong and she was naught but rot and bones, she'd want to end her worldly time in the proper way, so her spirit might rise to meet her husband's.

Inside, I made a fire, and set the pot upon it for broth. After I'd rubbed myself down with a cloth, I put on the new shift Atlas had made for me before things went bad. Like her baskets, the seams were all at odds and the fabric hung at an angle, making it useless to wear in any sort of company. For a moment, I smiled, but the grief flooded quickly back. I ate what I could, then went to the pallet and climbed under the covers. The bed smelled potently of my mother. I breathed her in. Holding her aroma inside my chest for as long as I could, because it was all that was left.

I listened then, for rooks and jackdaws.

If I could hear their calls, there might yet be hope. For hope is a sort of magic, and surely, never truly lost. The return of the birds would be a sign that my feelings had been wrong, and that Atlas was near, and I should get things ready for her return. After all, she couldn't really be dead, the thought seemed ridiculous, impossible. My mind searched for her. When I finally closed my eyes to sleep, I found her there. She was walking from the market toward the mountain path, hips swaying, skirts swinging, bare feet kicking up dust like a smoky breath. The mountain lion was at her side. His great beast's head shook once, then turned up to her. I could feel his hot, wet breath seep through the layers of her dress, warming her thigh as if it were my own. His yellow eyes were sparkling, full of love and admiration. And I sent out a sleeper's prayer, that I might never wake, so I could stay in that dream forever.

Scene 6

Morning came and I awoke.

Lying on my pallet, blinking into a new day, a new world, I listened for the familiar scuttle of claws on the roof, for the tchak, cackle and caw, and pecking of beaks. None came. Hope had failed me. Atlas had not returned. Still, it wasn't quiet. Grief and loneliness were cacophonous companions. I heard the hives humming outside, Sunny's voice resounding in every buzz of every bee. But my mother's absence was a terrifying scream. I thought its force would shatter my bones.

Without her, there was no peace.

I'm not sure how many days came and went. Mostly, I stayed inside. The dwelling was always dingy, for I lit no candle. The thought of Sunny's corpse lying in the cave, maybe being feasted upon by watery creatures, horrified me, leaving me too afraid to step outside, except for when the Moon was small and high, the night so impenetrable I could not see. Then I would slip out, as silent as a snail, and crawl to the sea-edge. Feeling my hair down my back, salt and sand encrusted, I'd lift my face to the Moon.

I'm here, I'd howl, and wait.

But my mother's spirit did not come.

Only the cold white moonlight answered, hollow and empty, until I'd shuffle home, a pain like knives stabbing through my feet and legs.

Grieving seemed only to deepen my bodily afflictions.

My toes refused to bend, even the fingers on my un-injured hand were as useless twigs. On bad days, my back curved so much I was unable to stand straight. I thought I was decaying. What was left of the young woman I'd been only weeks before? Now I didn't know the person sitting in my skin, or understand how she might live.

I had provisions from my trip to the market, so I fed myself, I slept, I defecated. Sometimes my body trembled and could not be stilled. Along with pain and stiff limbs, dread and loneliness were my intimate acquaintances. I was hollow. My spirit ached for those who loved me. Sadness was an engulfing fire that came in blooming, burning gusts, making me wail with agony until silence spilled into me again and everything was nothing.

I thought it would destroy me.

I wished it would, so that at the very least, I might rest.

If I slept, I dreamed I was nothing but ashes. Sometimes I'd wake ranting and slavering. All propriety was gone. I lived and felt like an animal, or maybe an amalgamation of beasts and insects, hardly moving from my pallet, scuttling to the corner to piss when the need came. I did not kneel at my altar. Instead, I covered it with the fabric my father had brought home for Atlas. The feel of the weave under my unsupple fingers took the breath from me as I remembered the spark in my mother's eye, the hope as she first beheld it. How could the cloth still be here, existing in the world, bright and wonderful, when she was nowhere?

The thought that another person might ever look upon me again made me shudder. Neither did I want to see myself, nor touch any part of me, even to tend to the wounds and burns on my face and limbs from the dust storm. My eyes were scratched from the sand and watered constantly, sending down a stream of warm tears that made the tight, dry skin on my cheeks break and weep. I wondered about the different parts of my strange, broken body. My spine crawling up my back like a great centipede. My crow legs ending in thick claws – so swollen were my feet – my flesh, chapped and scaled like a lizard, blasted by sand and wind. And my hand, my monster's paw.

Ah, but that was the only part of me I tended.

Those scars were my history, my truth.

Thoughts of my own flesh consumed the hours. I didn't know how much time had passed since leaving Sunny's corpse in the cave. After what felt like a lifetime alone in perpetual night, through the dimness, came a light. I was sleeping on my bed pallet when, from a crack in the doorway, a spear of moonlight, brighter than any natural thing, impossibly lustrous and strange, shot through the dwelling and woke me with a start.

The light spread like quicksilver, invading the corners with a harsh, bitter brightness. I cried out and pushed myself into the farthest edge of the pallet, legs kicking, frantically looking for purchase in the straw below me. Finding nowhere to hide, I stopped, listened to my own breathing and peeked over my cover. The light did not abate. I squinted into it, half expecting an angel or a demon to be standing before me. Was it Setebos, come to scold me for my insolence at his altar? Or another thing from the world of spirits, sent to cast me into the abyss for leaving my father's body to fester in the cave while I hid away to live in nothing but nervous degradation? For filth and fear, I knew, were an abomination. I waited, breath held, sweat seeping through my cover. But no devils appeared. The gods, too, had forsaken me.

All there was, was light.

My heartbeat slowed to a thud. I lowered my cover and looked around. I'd never seen the place illuminated by such brightness before. Seeing the dirt and chaos, I was ashamed. This was our home. The Moon had come to visit and all I could offer was a pit fit for rats and fleas. Atlas would be disappointed, having such a creature for a daughter. The brightness dimmed a little and although I was terrified, the effect was calming.

There were colours then; silvers, pale blues tinged with golden edges, yellows and mauves, swaying slightly, like the swirls on my Dreamstones, gently floating around the room. I wondered what enchantment was tricking me, tried to remember the divine words for protection from unworldly things, but nothing would come.

The colours shifted.

There was an outline, a shadow.

I saw the shape of a beak, of beating wings, and beneath them the claws of a mighty bird. Raven-like, the shadow flew, moving the light around in great swoops. As the colours paled, like drops of ink in water, I could see another image. It was my mother's face. I cried out, reached for her, but there was nothing to touch, only light.

Get up, she said, *you are young and strong.*

I sank below my cover again, and whimpered like a wounded animal.

But how could I fear my Atlas?

Put your hand to your breast, she demanded.

I moved slowly, entranced by my mother's light, yet afraid. So afraid.

Do you feel it. Beating?

I nodded, wide-eyed, panting, my heavy breath wetting the hot, dry air around me.

When you feel the thud inside, that's me, that's your grandam, and all the women who came before. You are not alone. We are with you, one day you will come to us and we'll be as one. But not yet, my Raven. You've a life and you must live it.

My Atlas of light had a voice like the bells around her ankles. I reached down to where I'd tied them to myself.

Had I hoped to shackle my soul to hers through the power of that one object? Did she leave it for me, a way to commune with her, a necromancy of sorts? I'd thought so when I found it, I'd hoped.

And here she was.

Get up, she cried.

Her voice was loud and insistent, making me jump and yelp.

Go out into the world. Show who you are.

I didn't care if she was calling to me from a place of benevolence or a place of evil, she was here. Finally, I'd conjured her, and I wasn't alone. Letting my grip loosen on the bedcover, I nodded.

The light dimmed.

The voice hummed and softened.

First, you must do the rites for your father, said my mother of moonlight, but her voice and colours were already fading.

Panicking, I reached out.

Lunging violently forwards I landed heavily on the ground. My already sore knees seared with agony, and I screamed. But I didn't care about the pain; it was only pain after all. Afraid to lose her I grabbed, again and again, at the air. But it was a bagatelle, a faint and weakening light, a dream.

Do not leave my husband's ghost to wander in misery, said the voice of the dream. *He loved us and he loves us still. Feel it when you touch the bowl he ate from, the hives he worked, the walls of our home. Feel it and do what is right and good. Free his soul, for it suffers so.*

The light that was my mother was a wisp now.

It lingered briefly over a pile of discarded cherry stones.

I cried out, begged Atlas to stay, sobbed, and screamed her name.

It was too late.

As quickly as it had come, the light disappeared, and all was shadows.

She was gone.

As I lay on the floor, the darkness swaddled me. I listened to the thump of my heart, losing myself to its steady marking of time and life, until at last, I slept. When I woke, the smell of jasmine floated in from my mother's garden, so sharp and sweet it made me laugh. Sound came to me, too. So clear it might have been scrubbed and made new. Starlings and finches whistled in the pines outside, the bees buzzed happily in their full hives, as the sea called to me.

It was warm.

Golden beams of morning sunlight lay in strips across the room.

Thirsty, I opened my mouth to find some moisture in the air. The taste of salt danced lightly on my tongue. Its sharpness was a medicine, a wonder. I sat up and blinked into the fine and beautiful world. Then I went out to see the bees and, as my father had taught me, I put my face close to their full nests and spoke to them. My words came out small and rasping as I told them how I'd moved Sunny's drowned corpse to a cave and left him there, and how Atlas was lost but she'd sent me her moonlit messenger. The bees hummed their reply, freeing me, at last, from some of the burden of it all.

Returning to my pallet, I rubbed myself down with the washing cloth, and dressed in my old shift, shaking out the sand as I threw it on. Then I covered my eyes with a fresh muslin and walked away from the dwelling and out into the day.

Scene 7

By the time I reached the town I was breathless. My limbs felt as heavy as rocks, my heart heavier still. I limped dizzily around the market feeling the weight of many faceless eyes upon me, hearing the tutting of tongues. I looked down. My shift was filthy, stained from sea and cave dirt. It was hot and I was sweating, so that the thin fabric clung to me in places it shouldn't. Trying to ignore my own distress at how I looked, and pulling at my clothes, I eventually found the old widow. When she saw me, she stood from the rug where she was selling sweetmeats with another woman and frowned as I staggered toward her.

Please, I said. *My father is dead.*

As before, there was shouting and whirling as the old woman gathered women and menfolk together. Eventually a small throng was awaiting instruction. I told the widow where I'd left Sunny, my voice quiet and broken, and she waved the men off to the sea caves. Then she took my un-injured hand, held it tightly in her own, and we walked slowly, heading a line of women, who collected flowers and leafy branches as we went, until we reached the shore.

The women asked no questions. They lined up before me, and one by one, each made a mourning gift of the collected flora, handing their offerings to me with bent heads and words of consolation. Their compassion filled my empty spaces. I thanked them and let them fill my arms with their gifts.

When the men arrived with my father's body, carrying him on their shoulders, already washed and cleaned and wrapped in his winding sheet, the gentle chatter of the women stopped. The only sound was the rushing wind and the waves shouting at the shore. I thought the sea was angry – perhaps it had thought to claim Sunny for its own – but here we were, about to give him to the earth.

The women followed behind the men and set about trilling, keening and wailing. I'd sometimes heard the ghostly cries of mourning women floating on the wind. It seemed an unearthly sound, yet as beautiful as it was strange. I stood and watched as strangers carried my father to the burial place beyond the harbour. I'd never been that far into the town. The thought of Sunny being put under the ground for eternity, in a place I didn't know, filled me with horror. I pulled at the old woman's sleeve.

Must I go? I asked, my voice small and juddering.

The widow shook her head. Then simply asked, *Atlas?*

All I could do was drop my own head in reply. She gave a mournful sigh.

Go home, child, she said. *We will see to it. But wait.*

The old woman walked a few steps to the shoreline, picked up a pebble, and returning quickly, put it into my uninjured hand. Nodding at the stone she told me to make it a good one, for it should be my own Dreamstone.

A sob wrenched from my chest.

The woman put her arms around me, held me until I quieted. When she left, following behind the funeral procession, I watched her walk away. The breeze blew, lifting her soft overskirt in a cloud of twisted fabric. Finally, she was nothing but a smudge of colour. As she disappeared from view, I unfastened my eye covering, so I might see clearly what was left of my life. There was the sea, the sand, the clouds, and me. I waited until the rose-coloured sky turned black, then, with my arms still filled with mourning gifts, I turned towards home.

There were no stars, and the Moon had covered her light.

Scene 8

The day after they buried my father, I tended to myself.

Brushing sweet oil through my forsaken hair, I freed it from the sandy remnants of the storm. Where knots had formed, I cut them out. I did it with my mother's curve-bladed knife, the one she used to gather plants for her remedies, which I now kept tied around my hips in its goatskin pouch.

The weight of Atlas's knife in my uninjured hand felt good and strong. But my fingers were stiff, my grip weak, making me drop the blade after each cut and slice. At first, I cursed the thing and myself. I screamed my already grating throat raw, clawed at my flesh until blood spotted my skin. But I didn't give up, and at last, digging the handle into my palm, I mastered the knife.

The blade was so sharp it sang as it cut.

The joy of each resounding swipe replaced my sobbing with laughter.

When, finally, I looked to my wounds from the storm, they were already healing. There would be no scarring. Still, I made a poultice from various seeds and the large, nap-covered leaves Atlas had called 'soft beard', bruising and mashing them until they formed a paste. Using only these things that grew in my mother's garden, I bound the mix with spider silk and bade the silver threads to impart their strength with a song. The work was hard. My voice grated and rasped as a sheen of sweat covered me, but it was good, satisfying labour.

Stopping to rest for a moment, I heard the distant squabbling of cormorants across the dunes. The sound came closer, carried on a gust of wind, and died away again. What a funny din they made. I'd watched those birds since childhood, marvelled at their angular forms diving into the sea, or resting on rocks. Outside my dwelling things were no different now to then. Life was too full of marvels to be at odds with it. I wiped my tired face and went back to my task.

Over those first days and weeks alone I grew more curious about the work that was now mine alone to do. I'd begged Sunny to find ways to gather honey without destroying the colonies or killing the bees. He'd said one day we'd see, but in the end, he was always too busy. I did it now, cutting two holes rather than one into the hives, singing to the buzzing occupants as I guided my mother's knife. As I stood back to look at my work, my face hurt from smiling. How fragrant the air around me was, filled with the tang of sea salt and the sweetness of beeswax, and how I loved it. Not for the first time that day, I heard my own laughter ring through the air. When I began to be gentler with myself, the world seemed to bend to my needs.

Hunger was a problem, again. I'd finished the last of my food from the market and was once more living on thin broth and honeycomb. Though my bones felt hollow from lack of sustenance, I dreaded the thought of going back to town, of being looked upon. Strangely, there was something almost pleasing about feeling so empty, like my body might float away on the breeze. I decided to let myself grow thin. After all, it didn't much matter now I'd relinquished any idea of marriage. I could get just enough nourishment from the plants in my garden and the bees in my hives to at least stay alive. But the very next morning I opened my door and at my feet was a misshapen basket filled with flatbreads, cheese, sweetmeats, olives, figs and a jug of goat's milk. I guessed it to be the old widow again, and looked about, but there was no one. The thought of her old bones dragging the load from the town so I wouldn't starve melted my heart, and yet it stung. Had I become so selfish? Atlas would be horrified.

After feasting until my belly was round and tight, I sat in my garden, idly sweeping the feather my mother had fixed in my hair across the surface of my grey pebbles. The colours came as always, swirling and moving. Then, there was another quality to them, something I'd not seen before.

I watched as the Dreamstones invited in the deepest, shaded tones along with the light.

Yes, I said to the stones. *For brightness to truly shine, there must be shadow. Let it in.*

How they shone in response, as I laughed through a halo of eddying colours. When the batch was done, I put them in a clean basket, lined with a soft, white cloth. They looked like jewels, a treasure fit for emperors or gods. Wanting so much to show them to someone, I carried them to the back of the house for the bees to see. But the hives were quiet, the insects resting. There was no one to look on them but me and the moonlight. Staring up to the pale crescent above, I thanked her for the companionship. With nothing left to do, I went inside to sit on my pallet and wait for dreamless sleep.

The next day, I remembered the pebble the old widow had handed me as my father's body was taken to its grave. It seemed suddenly curious that Atlas had never encouraged me to make a Dreamstone for myself, only for others. Now, I desperately wanted my own. At first, I felt unsure so selfish a glamour would work. In the end, it was the best I'd ever made. Even when I set it down, the tones continued to move, to twist and change. Like me, my Dreamstone wanted to feel all the colours. Unable to resist, I picked it up once more. In my hand it began changing again, so quickly now that light flashed about the place. It was dizzying. I laughed and spun about trying to catch the colours on my skin. But unable to settle, the pigments began to merge. Soon the pebble turned grey, then black. Then no matter how many times I went back to it, the stone held no hue or shine, only an absence that seemed to shake my spirit. I thought about what I'd seen in my father's eyes when Atlas and I took our Dreamstones to market. It wasn't admonishment and suspicion, it was fear. Putting my black stone on my altar, I watched it for three days. Waiting, hoping, with Setebos's help that the colours might reappear. But they were gone. I buried the pebble in my garden, grieved its loss and, feeling lonelier than ever, waited for the sadness to fade. Waiting was the worst part of being alone. Yet all I seemed to do was wait.

I'd wait for the night to pass and the day to come. I'd wait for hunger, for the pot to boil, for my body to piss and excrete. Then I'd wait for night to fall once more. And in the morning the waiting began again. Of course, as I waited, I busied myself. At home, I cleaned things; made a fire and put it out again; boiled infusions of herbs for remedies and potions and poured them into pots of unbaked clay. With every passing moment I sighed to the depths of my soul, for it was relentless.

Several days after my Dreamstone turned black, I noticed the pebbles I'd already prepared with my feather begin to glint with a strange urgency, as if calling to me from their basket. At first, I thought it merely my starved imagination, until I remembered the full Moon would rise that very night, and I had yet to whisper into the shining stones. The glamour was only half made, it was bidding me to finish my work. Believing Atlas would want me to continue, I forgot my buried sadness and waited for day's end. Oh, it seemed it would never come! When at last it did, I dashed into the garden, keening and dancing on swollen feet like an unleashed thing. And how I fell upon my basket of colours before ever thinking what to say. I whispered my desperate messages over the stones then, locked my passions into their hearts, so that along with all that was good, and with no thought to their eventual dreamers, I gave the Dreamstones my pain. But how unburdened I felt, how listened to, as tears of relief ran down my face. When at last I sat back to look, though, something was different. The stones still shone and had not blackened. Yet as bright as they were, there was a faint but definite darkness to them, more than a mere shadow now, like a billowing sky just before a storm. I blinked at the pebbles, wondering at their complexity. So what if the dreams they gave weren't filled with the joyous perfection of Atlas's? They were beautiful. And perhaps my stones had deeper messages. The right dreamers might even see me in that sleeping world, and rush to me when they awoke, hearts bursting with affection. But for that to happen, I'd have to go to town.

The mere thought of the market brought a wave of panic and sickness. As desperate as I was for company, I'd kept away from the town. Rejection from the townsfolk terrified me. There was nothing I really needed from the market. I wasn't dying of starvation. Each time I was at the end of my provisions I'd open my door and a new basket of food would be there, as if conjured by my hunger and left by fairies or spirits. If it was the old woman, I'd never heard the tread of a foot as she left them. She'd never once knocked to enquire of my health. *Where have you come from?* I'd ask the figs as I took delicious bites of their flesh. *Why should I ever go back to the town?* I'd whisper to my morning candle. If I did take myself to the market, I told myself, it wouldn't be to beg sympathy and friendship. It would be as a woman with agency, as my mother had done before me, to sell dreams and to offer my services as a cunning woman. The townsfolk knew my heritage; it shouldn't be a shock. Grief and loneliness had made me live in shadows, but I'd bury them, put them in the earth with my black Dreamstone, and look to my gifts to bring back the light. Yes, I would go to the town.

I would be a healer.

Scene 9

I'd set my pots of honey and various remedies on the table by the cooking pot, thought of everything I'd need for going to the market. I practised how I'd greet passers-by and counted out my most colourful Dreamstones (magnificently full of light and dark; how proud of them I was!), knowing exactly where I'd put them when I was finally sitting on my blanket in the dust for all the town to see. Again and again, I played the scenes through in my head, imagining how folk would rush to embrace me. They'd breathlessly ask how I was managing, alone in my dwelling. I'd smile and show what I'd become. Not someone rotting from loneliness, but a gifted woman of compassion, ready to share my remedies and use my charms for good. How stupid I'd been to feel so afraid.

In truth, each time I readied myself to take the path into town, my courage failed, my belly flipped, and I could not go. Biting my lip until the salty sting of blood sent me to sit with the hives or take to my bed, I'd remind myself that there, alone in my dwelling, I was safe. That place, where my precious things lived, where the cooking pot was my friend, the bed pallet a dear companion, and my altar a sure reason for greeting each new day, was all I needed. But the Dreamstones were ready in their basket, bright and full of the dreams I alone had poured into their stony hearts. In showing them, my pride would make me brave.

It was time to go.

I left before the Sun was fully up. I'd oiled my hair, secured my special feather with thin twine and added others of different lengths, kinds and colours, along with new pieces of shiny nacre from broken seashells. It wasn't easy. My fingers were stiff and sore, but I persisted. The adornments were beautiful. I wanted to feel their beauty radiate through me as I walked slowly towards the town, my basket of goods slung onto my back and tied with Sunny's old blanket.

To keep me steady I had a sturdy branch, fallen from a dear old pine in the dunes, the one my mother had called the Wishing Tree. I leaned upon its solid strength as I pulled myself along. I'd seen ragged old folks in town resting on gnarly staffs as they'd beg for scraps, so I knew how I'd look, bent, limping, and leaning on a stick. I tried not to think of myself like that, shabby and broken. Walking any real distance without help had become impossible, so I accepted the assistance the branch gave and was grateful. Anyway, it was a beautiful thing, long, and of the best wood. I liked the feel of my staff. Somehow, it felt like a friend.

Although my feet were tender, my toes stiff and I winced with the pain of each step, I revelled in the feel of the dry road under my bare soles. For at last I was on my way, walking proudly into my future. My mother's bells jingled around my ankle, providing music as I went, and her knife at my hip made me feel strong and fearless. I'd spent time sharpening, whetting and oiling it. Any bandit or beast would not get the better of me with such a blade for a companion, no matter how tortured my body.

The sound of the waves beyond the dunes gave a steady, helpful rhythm to my walk. Gulls screeched their hungry song and I laughed into the breeze at their noise. All was as my mother had told me; nature was my helpmate, my companion and friend. Until a chattering of jackdaws made me look up, and a little breathless, I stopped.

Are you here, my Atlas? I whispered to the circling birds, too high in the sky to be anything more than a dark swirling smudge.

An unseen crow screamed from the branch of a cypress tree, giving my nervous heart a jolt, before it swooped down next to me. It hopped from foot to foot and bowed its feathery head in a comical dance. *Hello*, I said, and it cawed again, as if in reply. The light caught its shining eyes, black as my buried Dreamstone, yet brighter than the stars. I stared at the bird a moment, but couldn't see Atlas there, either. It was just a crow. I gave the bird a half-smile. The crow shook out its ruffled wings and marched about. It had the look of a richly clad merchant from one of the big ships in the harbour, nose in the air, *All arrogance and idiocy*, Atlas would say when they paraded by. As I started back down the track, the crow followed, hopping and shouting behind, making me giggle and snort as I went.

It was early and there was little chance of meeting anyone on the way, so feeling braver than usual, for most of the journey I held my muslin at my side. Feeling it ripple in the warm breeze, I filled my uncovered eyes with the landscape, with the birds, beetles and the morning lizards scuttling through the scorched grass as I passed them. When at last I saw the tall buildings on the horizon, the high sails of boats in the harbour, and got the whiff of rotting fish in my nose (the town always smelled of decay to me), the crow, who'd stayed close all along the way, lifted its beak and let out a loud caw. I quickly fastened the binds around my eyes, blinking heavily as they watered. Not for the first time, I cursed my blue-eyed desert ancestor, along with the townsfolk for their silly superstitions. But I thanked the crow for its timely warning. The bird lifted its beak again as I stretched to stroke the soft feathers on its neck. Then, tilting its head, I saw that glint anew, deep in the magnificent darkness of its beady eye. And something moved me so I almost gasped. No, my mother wasn't there, hiding in its happy black orb. But I was sure I'd been touched with an important glow, and that it was something I'd never known before. A profound light of warmth and friendship.

Scene 10

I was first at the market so laid my blanket where Atlas had always put it, at the very edge of the soon-to-be-busy commercial lane. A few sailors were already wandering the streets. They came to me as if drawn by a spell, falling upon my coloured stones, not even asking their purpose or price, so ready to spend the jangle in their pockets. My honey, too, delighted them, and as the other traders began to arrive and set out their blankets, I'd already sold half my pots and many handfuls of small Dreamstones. The crow seemed delighted by our early trade, strutting around the blanket, watching me with its ever-blinking, clever eyes. I put my fingers out to stroke its fine feathered head, and the crow rubbed against them, like a kitten at play.

A woman, around my mother's age, whom I recognised from our many days sitting on the ground next to her in the bustling market, was next to set her blanket down. She'd often chatted to Atlas, so it was surprising now to see how much space she'd left between us. Traders fought for places to sell their wares. It seemed an extravagant waste of space not to have our blankets touching as they usually would. Trying not to pay attention to the gesture, I nodded as she set out her bowls of plump cherries, smiled at her pots of red-hot pepper-spice, all neatly in a row, but she did not respond in kind. She stole glimpses of me, merely frowning and wiping her hands nervously on her skirts as she turned her back.

Soon, the market was full, packed with traders on their blankets, edge to edge. Their knees touched as they sat cross-legged, shouting and laughing with each other. But no one came close to me and the crow. The gap between us was obvious, leaving me outside the hubbub as the commerce started in earnest. I continued to smile and nod, but garnered no response. Womenfolk mostly frowned. They stood in small groups a little way from where I sat. Staring, they chattered and sometimes pointed to me, shaking their heads, making horrified gestures with their hands whenever the crow lifted its head to shout at them. I supposed they felt it safe to be so openly brazen, all together like that. Atlas would never have stood for it, but I sat there, smiling as if I hadn't noticed their cruelty.

As the day drew on, the Sun's heat burned my neck. I was too hot and had started to feel sick. Not only was I uncomfortable with my eyes bound so tightly, but my legs and back were mightily sore from sitting. As I sweated into the fabric of my thin shift, I felt like a lump of rock, unable to move in case it caused heads to turn, eyes to stare, and voices to whisper in my direction. Even in the loneliest moments on my own in my sad and empty dwelling, I had never felt so alone. I felt tears wet my muslin. Some escaped, rolled down my face and onto my lips, where I licked them away, aching at the taste of salt on my tongue. All through the morning and into the afternoon I cast about the market for the old widow. For most of the day she was nowhere to be seen, and I gave up hope of talking to her. But when the Sun was low in the sky and the dirt of the day encrusted my blanket, she finally appeared, hobbling slowly up the lane.

I wanted to jump up, to shout and wave my arms above my head. The relief of laying eyes on the nearest thing to a friend in the town made my heart thrum and I became breathless. Of course, I didn't jump up; I couldn't. Instead, I willed her to see me. When at last she did, she stopped in her tracks and shaded her old eyes with her hand from the blasting Sun. How I wanted her to come to me, to crouch beside me on my blanket, speak of normal, inconsequential things, and maybe to smile. But I was afraid to look directly at her in case my desperation showed, or lest she wasn't there at all, and what I'd seen was a spirit of the imagination, a shadow made from anguished thoughts. I turned my face a little. Dust swirled around her skirts. It was true, she was there.

Come to me, I whispered, so softly not even I could hear the words.

Come to me, I said again.

Being a little away from where I was, and with my own eyes covered, I couldn't make out the look on her face.

Come to me, come to me, I repeated, wishing her to my side.

Her feet shuffled in their baggy leather slippers; it looked like she might turn away, go back the way she came. Panicking, I narrowed my eyes behind my muslin.

Come to me old mother, I whispered again, more urgently, gripping my staff tight. The wood was warm under my hand. I know not why, but I hummed a low note then. The sound was gentle as it vibrated around my mouth, tickling my tongue. And as it lingered, my staff seemed to tremble under my fingers. At last, I saw the old woman take a step and begin to make her way over. As she approached, I looked at my staff, still now, as inert as any wood. And I couldn't help but remember Atlas's story about the Queen of the Tents.

She was ancient and divine, the mother of us all, she'd said. *Her eyes were the colour of sapphires, like yours but brighter, bigger, bluer. And her magic was the first and the strongest. They say she spoke in melodies, with notes both short and long. It was known that if she'd wanted, she could move the Moon and the stars just by humming a song, turn night into day with a simple tune and a wave of her blessed staff. This mother, this sorceress, this first woman of enchantment was our direct ancestor.*

And in my mind, I saw Atlas, laughing, spinning, pretending to be the great mother of magic as she sang in full voice to the birds at her feet.

Listen, she sang, *the power of creation is in our ancient songs.*

The old widow nodded as she neared the edge of my blanket. I shook myself free of memories and attempted a smile, but my mouth refused to comply. She had lines carved deeper into her face than I remembered, yet sat easily on her haunches before me. Lifting my chin with a short, stubby finger, the old dam snorted. Her fingernails were lined with dirt. Another grunt and she picked up a pot of honey, putting a coin on my blanket in return.

You kept away too long. It's been weeks since we buried your father. No thanks was given to those who mourned in your place. People talk. You know how they are.

The woman's voice was deep and quiet; her heavy accent was like my mother's but flatter, and to my ears, it was a dull song.

No, I said, my own voice small and gruff. *I know nothing of people.*

The woman looked at the crow standing at my side on the blanket, flicking its head one way then the other as if trying to get to grips with the situation. Turning her attention back to me, she stared for a long time before speaking. I couldn't say if it was pity or suspicion I saw on her face, with its creases and crosses. I fidgeted, uncomfortable under her gaze, and brushed the rough fabric of my shift across my legs, which stuck out before me like those of a child's poppet, too painful and stiff to bend beneath me.

Has your mother returned? the woman suddenly asked, looking at the twist of bells and seashells around my exposed ankle. I shook my head.

I'm alone now, I answered. *But my honey is good, and I've learned all her remedies, and others. My instincts are strong.*

I hesitated then, scared I was saying too much, surprised by the force of the words spilling from my mouth.

I have the Gift, I said in a steadier, less childlike voice.

The old woman nodded once more and gave a slight sigh. *Can you describe what that means, what it feels like for you?*

There's another, invisible world around us. I know it's there because I'm connected to it. I hesitated, trying to find a way to explain the inexplicable. *I feel the unseen things*, I continued, soft-voiced and timid. *There's no hardship in it. It's as natural as breathing.*

Sycorax, she said. *Do you understand that people like to tell stories?*

I blinked at the woman, flinching at the name, unsure how to answer. Was it a riddle?

She sighed again. *It thrills them or confirms their fears*, she continued, *for they carry fear like a babe in their arms. They suckle it.*

As she turned her head away, the old woman spat on the ground. I watched the frothy spittle soak into the dust, leaving a trace where it hit.

We're all afraid, I said, unsure of her meaning. *I know that to be true.*

She frowned.

Don't mention your remedies unless asked, the old woman grunted. *Not yet, at least. We have time. Your gifts will only be welcome once you're loved and trusted.*

Confused, I took a breath to question what she meant. But she raised her hand, drew closer and asked what I'd known about my mother's work in the town. Surprised, I shook my head and said I knew of the remedies she brought to market, hidden in her skirts. I'd helped collect the ingredients, sometimes even stirred the cooking pot as the goodness was extracted, and I'd seen her dole them out, passing them secretly from hand to hand when asked for by townswomen in whispers. And I knew that sometimes she went away. But I'd never known where to or why. Only that someone from the town would send for her, and my father wouldn't speak of it. Then I told her about the woman at the market, heavy with child and accusations. And that at the time I was so astounded by her passions, I hadn't thought to untangle the knot of her hissed words as anything but the woman's own fear of childbirth.

The old woman settled herself beside me, opened her pot of honey, stuffed in a dirty finger and sucked on it. Smiling at the sweetness, she told me that her and Atlas were companion women. Now I was the one to frown. They were the ones called for, she explained, snapping her tongue as the honey stuck to her gums, if a townswoman went into their travails. They'd stay in the birthing room, guard against interruption, take control when the labouring woman couldn't, and guide and help the babies out. They stemmed the blood, she said, calmed the fears, swaddled the babes, and sometimes they buried them.

For some folk, women who do such work are dangerous. We're close to death, see? We alone witness the first moment of life. And we understand the hidden parts of men's wives, sisters and mothers. These are all considered mysterious things. Such foolishness! There's nought strange in any of it. Still, it's quiet work, if you get my meaning. Not secret exactly, but not to be talked of in company. Especially if menfolk are about. They'll call us witches, accuse us of bad things, for they'll not abide a woman with knowledge and ability.

She thought it normal Atlas hadn't told me of their work together. The birthing chamber was an intimate and dangerous place. My mother would have protected me from possible allegations. The old woman smiled then, and said Atlas had been a tender companion. So, despite her odd ways – things that might normally render people suspicious or afraid of her – for many townswomen, my mother was much loved. And missed.

My jaw went loose, my mouth lolled open as I searched for the right words, but I knew not what to say. I'd known my mother had helped with births, but she'd made me believe it was only a few. That she could have been so involved with matters of town life seemed impossible. She'd always been against us being close to townsfolk. Seeing my confusion, the old woman tried again to explain.

There are some, menfolk mainly but women too, who say there's devilry in you, she snorted. *They think afflictions are punishments for evil thoughts. Deeds maybe. Atlas would protect you at all costs. Keep you away from any possible harm. See?*

I shook my head, utterly confused. The old woman

touched my shoulder, sighed again, and nodded at my injured hand.

Women, or their children, are not twisted for nought.

Finally, I understood. I wanted to scream at such an appalling accusation. I'd had an accident, I insisted, and on top of that was in terrible pain from an ancient family illness, and if all that wasn't terrible enough, I was now an orphan. Surely, I should be helped, cared for, not slandered. Trying to calm my agitation, the woman shuffled closer and took my injured hand in hers.

It's nonsense, of course, child. They're superstitious in this town. Be like your mother, ignore them, but look to yourself. The towns-folk are full of curiosity and blather. It will pass, but for now they talk about you, wondering if you killed your father with enchantment and put a spell on your mother so she'd go back to the desert, leaving you to take everything.

Take what? I cried, gasping for air as if her words were a blow to the gut. *I have nothing. I'm utterly alone.*

The crow lifted its beak and cawed.

Now, child. Don't fret. They'll become accustomed to you, with time. It was the same with your mother when she first arrived. But she showed her gifts were born of goodness. You can do the same. You'd best marry, quick. You're not without allure. Some men like it. And she squeezed my scarred hand and laughed, showing her almost toothless gums. *Remember not to stay away so long. You need to be seen. If you want me, ask for Yemma. They all know me.*

The woman spat again, patted me gently on my leg, and left.

I didn't move until the market emptied, and there was only myself, the crow, and a few ships' boys left on the dusty lane. Then, at last, I took up my things and without unfastening my muslin, nor listening to the sounds of the world, I made my way home. The crow jumped along before me, waiting for me to catch it up as I limped slowly after.

That night, the crow stayed.

Lying on my pallet, still and quiet in the dark, my breathing shallow, my hands and feet screaming with pain, I listened to it move around on the roof, picking at straw with its beak and tap-tapping its claws as it went. My mood lifted with each shuffle and clack. I thought maybe it wasn't a bird at all but an angel, sent to save me from a lonely life. As my head began to swim with sleep, swaying at the steady scratching of crow claws above, I thought I heard another sound: the distant roar of a mountain lion. Its cry seemed to call out to me, rolling through the night like a ship on the sea.

Sycorax, I thought it sang. *Sycorax*.

I was certain then, that for now and ever more, that would be my name. I'd not let it be a statement of filth and suspicion. I would free it from the dirt, take it from the mouths of scoundrels. And most of all, I'd carry it, like the mountain lion as he walked beside my mother, with pride.

ACT III

Scene 1

Paying heed to all Yemma had said, I returned to the market the following morning. I'd not stay away again. The crow nodded its agreement as it trotted beside me on the road into town. When we sat on our blanket in the usual place, I adopted a breezy sensibility, nodding and smiling as I chatted to the crow. The bird cawed its loud replies and the good people of the town looked the other way as they shuffled by, sending dust dancing around our heads.

No one stopped.

Not even for a pot of honey.

We stayed until sunset and left with the other traders, ignoring their disregard. The next day, we went back, and every day we could thereafter. Until finally, we were as natural a sight to the townsfolk as the dry earth beneath their feet.

As the weeks went by, just as Yemma had predicted, my

goods started to sell. Honeycomb, candles, and even Dream-stones were looked upon with greedy eyes. Pots of honey were in demand again. Young girls might stop to shyly enquire about the stones, flicking their heads as they spoke quickly and quietly, hoping not to be seen as they asked for dreams. How wide their eyes were, shining with nervous excitement and a thing I now recognised as hope. I spoke to them kindly and always with a smile.

No one asked about my remedies, no townsfolk at least. Not yet.

From my quiet place at the market, I watched the townsmen and women. Their children grew from buds to saplings, and new ones appeared, tiny and squealing, swaddled to the breasts of smiling girls and tired-looking women. I wondered if Yemma had pulled them into the world and longed to be a part of her secret life, as Atlas had been. Instead, I was barely visible, an outline of a person, like a smudge of ash from a cold fire. For as strange as I was with my crow and my staff and my feather-adorned hair, I wasn't Atlas. Timid, always peeping from behind my muslin, I was hidden. In truth, I wasn't entirely unhappy. But with seventeen years behind me, I wanted to be more than the shadow of a girl.

I'm a healer, like my mother, I'd say to Yemma when she came to sit with me and the crow, as she did on market days. *I should make it known so I can help the townspeople. Like you do. It's my duty.*

The old woman would snort at that – *Duty!* she'd once

said. *Let the devils take it, child. And you along with it, if you're in earnest.* But then she'd pat my leg, hum and nod. Even so, her frown told me her true thoughts: it would be better if my place in the town was as a simple market trader on a blanket. If I wanted a decent life, unmolested by *the fear and stupidity of folk*, as she called it, it was best to keep my gifts to myself. So that even as my pockets bulged with bottles of thin liquids and thick poultices, I watched as townsfolk scratched at rashes and shook with fevers and could be of no help.

At least I had the ships' boys.

They came to me for all manner of cures. My eyes were opened to a world beyond my imaginings by those scurvy lads. I was grateful, and never stood in judgement of them or their harbour whores – poor wretches. That there should be such suffering through want, and such an abundance of riches, side by side in the harbour and in the town, seemed an unholy injustice. I swore to the sky, to the trees and to the sea, that if ever I could be of assistance, whether to a beggar or a king, I would.

Scene 2

Each morning after sitting at my altar I'd go to the shore to collect pebbles and seaweed. Then back in my garden I'd gather plants and tubers, caterpillars, beetles and bugs to study. On days I didn't go to the market, the afternoons were for tending my bees, or candle making. My life was as the ebb and flow of the sea. That's what I'd tell myself if sadness took hold and shadows descended.

There's no ebb without the flow, no light without the dark.

Sometimes I'd sing the words into the world. It was a mantra of sorts, something to save me from the saddest places of my mind. Working on remedies helped with that, as did telling stories to the crow, who rarely left my side. I began to understand idleness was my enemy, a friend only to melancholy. In truth, when the pain in my limbs didn't prevent it, I had more than enough work to fill the hours until nightfall. And if walking and standing were difficult, I had my trusty staff to lean upon. Such a beautiful, powerful object. Even to look on it made me smile, and with strange qualities all its own my staff was more than an aid or a helpmate; it was my door to freedom.

The day I'd found it, my pain had been overwhelming and I'd been barely able to stand. Even so, I'd felt a pull from the invisible world. It came quickly and then how I yearned for the splash of sea spray and spume on my face. Such was my craving for a taste of salty air, it seemed a sort of madness. Unable to resist, I dragged my sorry self out. Hauling myself along, I all but crawled towards the sea, crying out with each movement. Nearing the Wishing Tree, exhaustion hit like a blow to head, and I reeled. But how happy I was to see the woody fingers of the old pine beckon to me. The Wishing Tree had always been an arresting sight, a majestic being that grew alone in the dunes. It was a twisted thing, centuries old with bark all blackened by age and fungus.

But it was unlike any other.

There was a strange beauty to the five contorted limbs rising from its trunk, for all the world resembling thick, gnarled fingers. It was more than a pine tree, it was a behemoth of a hand, forever waving to the world. As a child I'd imagined it inhabited by spirits. Airy, ancient things who'd sculpted their tree-home into the shape of an eternal greeting, so their human neighbours would know they meant no harm. Pine trees were known to represent the triumph of life over threat and forbidding things. Atlas had assured me that the tree was magical and might grant wishes if we asked. That's how we'd named it. Sometimes we left small gifts in its branches, lengths of stringy seaweed, or garlands of seashells held together with twine.

That day, thinking only to lean against the trunk, to rest beneath its shade a while, I slid to the ground, feeling the rough wood support my aching back. A warm breeze sang through the branches, and for a moment I was lost to its calming melody. But then I flinched. Somewhere in its whistling song, I thought I heard Atlas's voice.

Make your wish, my Raven, it whispered.

Desperate, I grasped the trunk, heaved myself up and reached out. Suddenly a long, low branch broke free and swung backwards. Afraid I might lose my head, I ducked. Agony seared through me. I screamed and, crouching, rocked myself back and forth. But again, I was arrested by a noise from above. Looking up I saw it wasn't my mother sitting among the pine leaves, but the broken bough, hanging and tapping at the trunk. The knocking was so insistent I could no more ignore it than grow wings and fly. Pulling myself up again, I reached for the branch, tentatively, as I might an animal in need of comfort. There was a loud crack as it fell into my hands.

It was a gift.

Too tired to go on to the shore then, I thanked the great pine for the bestowal, and leaned upon the stick like a staff. It took my weight. My steps were steady then. As painful as it was, I moved with confidence and surety, felt rooted, stronger.

This is freedom, I said to the breeze.

Some days later, when the stiffness in my hands would allow, I stripped the branch, better for use. The bark peeled back easily, like paper, showing the richly coloured, smooth wood shining beneath. Warm sap seemed to flow through it, as if the lifeblood of the Wishing Tree continued to feed and keep the fallen branch vital. There was the smell too, deeply fragrant, and vibrant, more living than dead.

As the weeks passed the staff became as much a part of me as my agonised limbs. Each time I touched it the wood seemed to awaken and come alive. More than that. We had a living connection. An energy ran through the staff and into me, like we were indeed made of the same stuff, part of a sole foundation. Each day I thought to bless it, to anoint the wood and give thanks, only I didn't know when or how to do such a thing. In the end, it happened on a particularly hot day.

Scene 3

The heat was sickening, I'd not slept well. Bothered by the idea of being out in the noise and dirt with a constant swirl of flies, I didn't go to the market that morning. After languishing sleepily on my pallet for hours, teasing the crow, my now constant companion, I noticed my staff leaning by the door. Caught in a sunbeam it seemed to vibrate red and orange hues and looked for all the world a thing divine, beyond nature. As I watched, the colours grew stronger. They flicked and danced as if calling for my attention.

It was time.

I waited for nightfall, for the heat to wane. When it came, the waxing Moon was large and pink. With the crow sitting happily on my shoulder, we made our way to the dunes and rested a while under the cooling rosy light. I'd taken a torch from the small fire-pit I always kept alive outside my dwelling, and brought a basket filled with things I thought I'd need for a blessing.

The air tasted sweet as, over a burning candle, I melted a nub of dried sap from the Wishing Tree, collected long ago by Atlas and stored away with remnants of bark and dried leaves. We listened, the crow and me, to the spit and sizzle of it in the pot. The bird cocked its head, and its keen eyes reflected the small leaping flame. When I thought the time was right, I added sage and other aromatic stems, anything that seemed good for a blessing, chopping them with my mother's curved knife. Then dipping my feather into the potion, I began brushing the staff, anointing it.

The mixture soaked into the hungry wood, deepening its colour. But there was only enough to leave a small stain, nothing more than a spot, a bright blemish on the surface where I wanted saturation. Taking a bottle of sweet, unctuous oil from the basket, I poured it all over my staff, enjoying the slick spill of the stuff over my hands. At last, as I hummed to the sound of waves crashing to the shore behind the dunes, and as the crow raised its beak to caw out its own melody, I asked for the grace of Setebos.

Under the oil, the wood began to glint and shine.

It was magnificent.

My heart hammered at my ribs; my belly turned.

My skin tingled, as if pricked by pins as I watched the staff change, becoming as resplendent as any bejewelled thing. The transformation was not due to any blessing I might want to bestow, it was charm-made, supernatural and magic. Finally

I understood the source of my craving the day I'd found the branch. It hadn't been a strong but simple yearning for the salt-filled breeze, but the calling of a deeply potent, powerful spell. And I ached for it again. For if enchantment existed, it would surely sit in the branches of a great natural being like the Wishing Tree. That's why my mother had taken me there so often. It was never just a game. She'd believed in the potential for natural magic born of earthly things, and she'd been showing me where to find it.

I'd take it, now.

All of it.

First, I shouted into the night, to assure myself no one was lurking behind bush or tree. There was no scuttering, no human movement or response. Emboldened, I lifted my shift over my head and stood in the dark. Even after the heat of the day, it was cold now, and I shivered. But I enjoyed feeling the bumps rise across my skin, the hairs on my arms bristle at the touch of the breeze, my muscles stiffen in the cold. My pulse was fast, a deep thrum in my throat and temples as I caught my breath.

How alive I was.

It was somehow more powerful to be without the barriers of clothing, to let my body feel the world around it. Besides, I'd always loved the feeling of cool air on my bare skin. But night-time and moonlight made everything seem more daring, exciting and secret, and suddenly I felt a bolt of shame. Surely, I told myself, it was normal for young women to give themselves away as a show of commitment.

Wasn't that the common view? That girls should make sacrifices of their bodies, often having them sold to the highest-bidding man by their fathers. I'd heard the talk; I knew the worth of a daughter's skin. My anger rose at the thought, but still my cheeks warmed with disgrace at my own naked abandon. I picked up my discarded shift, held the rough fabric close to my chest, praying over again that I was truly alone and would not be seen. Then remembering I was no one's daughter now, I let go a cry and dropped my shift again. My skin was my own.

Naked, I closed my eyes, and listened to the sounds of the night.

A high-pitched moan seemed to creep toward me from the beach.

I shook with cold as the wind began to blow in earnest. The moan became a wail, rushing across the surface of the sea and hissing through scrub and branches to catch me in its grip, I gasped. The crow, feathers ruffled, cawed beside me, and my courage quickly rose again like waves in a storm. Still the wind would not abate. Howling and fierce, it almost knocked me from my feet. But I had my staff to save me. Catching my breath and laughing into the gale, I threw my arms open. The Wishing Tree branch, still clutched in my uninjured hand, continued to keep me steady as it sent out shards of light in every direction. My face burned, raging like the midday Sun, and the wind blew ever harder, whipping my hair around my head like a madness, wailing its haunting song.

You're not in the storm, you are the storm, it cried, spectral and ghastly.

If I was not born for magical things, I asked myself, why would the world answer so?

There was an ache across my skin, my body jumped and twitched like a moonstruck beast before the feeling burrowed down inside and I was still again. It wasn't painful, it was something else, a want that gave both sorrow and joy in equal measure. Somehow strengthened by it, I whispered a plea.

Give me glamours unknown.

Then, crouching to tie a knot in a blade of grass, I made my declaration, a promise of allegiance, not only to Setebos, but to every natural force. For at that moment, I was more elemental than human and knew that true divinity lived not in demons or gods but in nature, in myself, in belief.

Again, I stood. There I was in the wind, not staggering, not shuffling or crawling, but rooted, like the Wishing Tree made flesh.

If it is, then let it be, I shouted, lifting my staff above my head so it could catch the rose light of the Moon, capture and hold its singular power and strength.

If it is, then let it be.

Again, the wind grew, screaming around trees, throwing dust into my uncovered eyes with a violence that made me cry out, until finally I fell to the ground.

Then, sitting with my staff across my legs, exhausted, I swayed as the weather lulled and calmed. After a moment

I took my feather from my hair, brushed the branch again, and the pine showed its heart to me. The grain of the wood flowed gently, ever moving in thin lines around the surface, forming new patterns, each one more glorious. Sap bubbled to the surface, leaving small globs, like shining stars, all along the staff. At first, I was worried it would turn black like my Dreamstone. But when the staff changed again, it was not into a voided, dead thing, it was into something as soft as muscle and sinew, that rippled beneath my hand. Appalled, I threw it down, grabbed my curved knife and swiped the blade across the terrible, undulating thing, which instantly resembled my beautiful staff again. But blood was running down the wood from where I'd made the cut. I felt a sting, looked at my arm and a scream ripped from me. A deep slit had opened in my own skin, identical to the mark on the branch, but although it was gaping and open, it was dry.

Only my staff was bleeding.

I touched the warm liquid, viscous and thick, as it rolled down the wood and smeared it along my sliced skin, pleading the flesh to knit together. In an instant, the wound was gone. Only a smudge of dried blood remained, encrusted and tight. My staff, too, was unblemished by the blade.

It was only then I noticed there was no wind now.

All was calm.

Even the waves had stopped whispering at the shore.

Still, I shivered as I dropped my shift over my head, put the basket under my arm, and leaned against my now solid staff. The crow spread its wings, jumped up and perched atop it, making me smile at its sense of elegance and drama. Then, unsure of what I'd done, of what was real, or phantom-made, I staggered home.

Scene 4

The next morning, I woke to the Sun blasting through my window. When I tried to move, I couldn't. Where once I was made of flesh and bones, now agony seemed the very fabric of my being. It was impossible to leave my pallet.

What have I done? I asked the empty room.

It darkened a little in reply.

Tentatively lifting my head, pain shot down my spine and knocked the breath from me. I'd pushed my ailing body too far going out in the night like that, done too much even when I knew the risk of retribution. And now my demon disease, with its tongues of fire and teeth as sharp as the wildest dog's, was hungry for its reward and claiming the right to feed. I growled my frustration, barked and whimpered into the stillness of the morning. But anger and upset only made things worse. I took in a lungful of air, slowed my breathing and lay still. My mother had once said everything must have a name. So, I named the illness Aamon. For truly, it was the devil prince, and I was its prey.

Blinking, I looked at my staff, shining and magnificent in the corner. Seeing it in daylight made everything real and I saw the truth of what I'd done. Perhaps I was being punished for attempting enchantment. Had I fallen into witchcraft, given myself to evil forces through hubris and ignorance?

No!

I'd not think like the townsfolk.

I'd think like my mother.

Opening my eyes wide, I listened for the memory of her voice. But it came only as a wretched thing, a suffering ghost, forever pleading:

I'm a woman, not a witch.

And there was her face, looking up to me, grazed and bloodied, twisted and afraid. Such a vision would not gain admittance. For I'd not access her torment, let it settle and reside in my own breast.

Atlas, I whispered, feeling she was close. *You were wrong. We are witches. If our minds are hungry to know the world, and we refuse to acquiesce and follow, then we are witches. By nature of our pain and illness, we are witches. By the colour of my eyes, I am a witch. By the shape of my hand, the feathers in my hair, the bells around my ankle and the crow at my side, I am a witch. By every digression, we are witches. If you hear me, be happy, Atlas, for your daughter is finding what you couldn't. To name a thing is to condemn it. The town calls me Sycorax, and so I am she. I call my pain a demon, and so it is. Yet it comes from my own body. You said we have gifts. Others cry witchcraft and would see us murdered for them. The Gift is mine to be used, and I will use it.*

Perhaps my illness was simply a matter of equity. Atlas had suffered too, another gifted woman grappling with pain. Hadn't she told me the malady struck many of our grandams? The bloodline of the Gift. And she taught me to never take without giving back, so that order might be kept, balance restored. The thought almost gave me comfort, that my pain might be spawned of fairness. But no, there was nothing good or fair in suffering. And I wasn't being punished, for such a notion grew only from cruelty and lies. Even if my body felt like an unknown being at times of intense pain, like a separate thing, belonging not to me but to some demonic force, in the end I knew the truth. Fortune may not have been kind, but it was no disaster. I was unwell and needed rest, that was all.

My mother told me the women of the desert understood the value of resting. As a child she'd watch them. They wore coloured silks around their heads, fringed with braids and filigree metalwork. Their skirts hung with coins that shone like sunlight and sang like the wind, same as Atlas's wedding garb. Sometimes my mother would shake her marriage outfit from its basket to show me, explaining how in the heat of the day, the women would slump together in their billowing tunics, chains and talismans dripping from them like starlit water as they snoozed and snored.

Snorting like chained beasts in the shade of the tents, she'd laughed.

Those women, my kindred, lived through the rhythm of their bodies and I would do the same, trading bad days for good.

Being away from the town would mean more talk. If the townsfolk noticed me at all it was when I wasn't there. They saw my absences, not their cause. Nor did they ask. But there was nothing else to be done.

I rested on my pallet for several days.

Soon, I was well enough to move, to sit at my altar, and finally to make the journey to town again. I'd make things right as I'd done before, charm the townsfolk, not with spells, but with Dreamstones, honeycomb and candles.

Ebbs and tides, I told myself. *Ebbs and tides*.

Scene 5

While I'd been away, somehow word spread about my cures. So, as I sat with the crow on my first day back at the market, a handful of townswomen came to me for remedies. When, delighted, I breathlessly asked Yemma why and how I'd suddenly become a healer for these people, she shrugged.

They must've missed you, she said, smiling.

Suspecting she'd had a hand in the townswomen's sudden interest in the contents of my pockets, I threw my arms around her, bone pipe and all. She protested and whined at me to *leave me to my peace, child*, but she did not push me away.

After a few days of questions regarding potions for rheumy eyes, warts and all manner of skin complaints, I was suddenly consulted on questions of maternity. My heart slammed with excitement. The woman was young, just a girl really. When she told me her troubles, asked how things should be, although I didn't say so, I knew nothing. In the end, I packed up my blanket and took her to Yemma. As they sat in the shadow of a tall cedar, the old woman took the girl's hands in hers. Their heads were together, but standing close, I watched and listened as they talked. After the girl left, full of thanks and relief, I had so many questions for Yemma, my own chatter left me dizzy.

I wanted to know everything, from copulation to birth. Of course, I knew some of the former, having spent much of my life sharing a bed pallet with Atlas and Sunny, neither of whom were shy in the matter. And my mother explained things in her own way when my bleeding started. But how it all worked and what came after was a mystery.

Yemma sat me beside her.

Jumping like a flea, waiting for all to be revealed so at last I might start learning the ways of wise women, I growled at the old woman as she took a breath, sucked at her gums and paused before finally speaking.

It will come with time, she said.

I stared at her, my every muscle a length of taut twine, ready to snap. But her eyes sparkled as she confessed to being satisfied with my eagerness. So, although disappointed, I went home with excitement rumbling in my belly.

More often then, when townswomen came to buy my wares, they spoke in whispers of matters of the womb — which seemed unfathomably to be blamed for every pain and fever. It made me laugh out loud when a widow of middling age told me the apothecary had assured her the ache in her knee was due to the inaction of her womb. He'd explained that due to its awful desperation, the woman's poor, dried-up organ had gone wandering down her leg, looking for moisture to quench its thirst, and – *thwack!* – it had got stuck in the bend, and now her knee was sore. His only recommendation was she must find a new husband, and quickly, before her wretched womb set off again and did any more damage. I asked if he'd made a proposal himself and the woman roared with laughter, snorting as her face went purple and tears ran down her plump cheeks.

The apothecary was a stupid man; of that, I was certain. In return, although he'd never spoken to me, his brow furrowed, his nose turned up, and his lip curled if I passed him by. How he'd scuttle about the town, always in the shadow of the councillors, or courting favour with merchants. He was more interested in gold than the wellness of the townswomen. It showed in his long, brightly coloured tunics, lavish headdresses, and the polished silver on his neat fingers. Many were impressed by his wealth, of course, or afraid of it. They bowed to him and listened when he spoke, for a man who'd gained such riches must surely be a source of great knowledge. I gave the widow woman yellow spice and black peppercorns for a tea to help calm any inflammation in her knee, and drops of bitter oil to be taken with honey to mask the taste. I told her to bind the knee tightly with a warm poultice, then with rags soaked in cold seawater, and to rest it as much as possible as the ache was due to overwork and wear. My cure worked. The woman was so delighted she brought her kinswomen to me with all manner of ailments. I was not embraced by all in the town, but the change put a lightness in my once heavy heart. How happy I was to be trusted, even by a few.

The Moon rose and set.

Marking time, it anchored me to the earth as I carved a life for myself. When it waxed, I used its energy, made remedies, honey and Dreamstones. As it waned, I paused my making, let grief lead me in reflection and rest. For as we turn, rotating through the days, all things must have balance.

And through it all, Yemma was the axis around which I'd pivot.

Scene 6

Right from the start, Yemma showed a keen interest in me. On those first days back at the market sitting with the crow, I'd catch sight of the old woman standing in the hubbub, watching me. All day she'd be there, leaning against a wall, arms folded across her chest, simply looking. After a while she'd approach and stop for a few moments' conversation, enquiring after the state of my hives, or just to ask how I was getting along. The conversations grew in length and subjects, until she started to sit on my blanket with me, spend her days telling me tales of this or that family, so I'd know who might be passing, and eventually, what remedies they might need. In that way, I always had something to offer an ailing body or a tortured soul.

I loved Yemma almost instantly.

She was a wise and wickedly funny soul. With that pipe of bone forever hanging from her lips, a strip of faded calico wound around her head, and a laugh like cackling corvids that could shake the leaves from the trees, she was hard to miss among the crowds. She was a bawdy old bird, too. Even the young men, beardless as they were, couldn't escape her eye. But it was the older ones she liked best, with their fleshy chins covered in grey bristles and their bellies hanging loose around their middles.

Something to get hold of, she'd say, shoving my shoulder, shrieking like an old deckhand as she'd cough and hawk up foamy globs into the dust.

Even with her rough ways, Yemma was trusted in the town. She'd outlived two husbands and five children and had been a guiding hand in resolving many a dispute over the years. Even townsmen lowered their gaze in respect when they saw her, though she mocked them, fiercely, once their backs were turned. Snorting at their arrogance and swagger, no matter how wretched, riddled with disease and crawling with lice they were.

Look at the way they carry themselves, like kings, she'd squawk, sticking her nose in the air and grabbing her crotch like a sailor, to give the imagined beasties a scratch.

There was one townsman Yemma never laughed at nor spoke of in a slovenly way. He was tall and broad and something high in the town council. The man lived in a fine house on the hill, beyond the reaches of harbour smells and market noise. Up there, the dwellings, with their many windowed rooms, were built of cool white stone so they shone over the town like pale lanterns. The man looked the age Sunny might have been. But his skin was supple and chestnut smooth, not lined and dry from being out all day, and his clothes, although never overly showy, were cut from good fabrics and well-made. Like the Governor, he was a foreigner from a prosperous country, and it was said he spoke many languages. Yemma told me the man was called Afalkay the Beautiful. At least, that's what the townspeople called him. Whenever he was near, she'd raise an eyebrow, whistle through her gums and say, *Beautiful by name, beautiful by nature*. Then after a pause and with a wink, *Or so they say*, and she'd leave it at that.

For this man, with his head covered by a loose twist of finest muslin to guard him from the Sun's harshest rays, and with a perfectly groomed greying beard, was not only a feast for every eye, but known as a goodly person.

And he was most dear to the women of the town.

Afalkay the Beautiful was, in fact, an old friend of the town's revered and much feared Governor. He'd arrived by galley some years before, unmarried, to take a high position on the council. No doubt to be an ally for his old confidant. At first, he was greeted with suspicion. Being close to the Governor, a formidable one-time pirate known for brutality and ambition as much as for leadership and protection, it was thought Afalkay the Beautiful must be cut from the same cloth. But he quickly became friendly with townsmen of both high and low birth, taking an interest in their lives, whether they be merchants, farmers, or poor ship hands.

Townswomen particularly found him an agreeable addition to society. Unlike other men of influence, he listened to their complaints and heeded their counsel. Known as a watcher, silently taking stock of comings and goings, he'd give aid before circumstance forced any man to ask or beg for assistance.

When it came to finding a wife, he'd not hesitated in his choice. Afalkay the Beautiful married the eldest daughter of the poorest fisherman, a widower barely able to feed his hungry brood. The marriage not only changed the fortunes of the family but gave the young woman a standing in the town she never could have dreamed of.

He'd only seen the wretched girl once, Yemma said, *before making his proposal. No matter how plain she was. But her belly's been full every passing year, and she's never without a smile across her chops. You'd think her a cat with cream. So all's well there. It's a wonder he chose her, mind. Him being savvy and full of wit. For looks aside, she's an ignorant kind of a girl.*

I frowned and asked Yemma what kind of a girl I was.

You're not of a kind, she said, smiling. *You're free like your mother, like the Moon.*

But I knew the Moon was prisoner to the Sun, and the Sun could never break away from the earth. They were no freer than a rat in a cage, no freer than anyone is from their own bones.

When, later, I started to visit the harbour, I was surprised to see Afalkay the Beautiful so often there, though it was a rancid place. Sometimes even before I saw him, I'd feel

his eyes upon me. Of course, it was not a location for good
women to be. But when I'd look up to see him, he'd not
frown at me like the sailors and merchant men, he'd smile.
How I'd snap my gaze away, my heart beating fast and wild,
my thoughts swarming like bees until I lost myself in the
crowds. I hoped he knew I'd not gone to that despicable
place through free will alone. It was the Gift that took me
there.

As a seer of storms.

Through our idle chatter, the sailors and ships' boys who
bought from me at the market soon learned that I could
predict the ways of the winds. At first, when they'd ask for
predictions, it was sport. I enjoyed our conversations. When
my words proved true, they let it be known I was a watcher
of storms. Some called me the Storm Witch. This was why I
covered my eyes, they said. For without my muslin, I'd see
the invisible stuff of the world, all the spirits and poor dead
souls cleaved to the earth, desperate for rest. To take it off
would send me raving. I saw no reason to contradict them.

When the chatter reached the townsfolk, there was talk.

Whisperers claimed I was in league with the devil. Or that
the crow was a demon, and I its witless servant, a mouth-
piece for diabolical doings. If I'm honest, it amused me, and
anyway, I could do nothing to prevent silly rumours. I felt
sure those who knew me wouldn't believe such tall tales.
Most townsmen, if they thought of me at all, would probably think me a desperate maid whose troublesome, unused
womb had gone wandering around my body, wreaking

havoc, leading me to jabber at sailors. Neither was it impossible the mischievous organ had somehow given me powers to change the climate, or at very least, foresee changes. Such was the strength of a woman's virginity, her essential need for any man's seed. Whatever they thought, the veracity of my predictions was not questioned. I was proud to be known for my gifts. And I wasn't invisible any more.

How keenly I felt it, to be seen.

Scene 7

I started to concentrate, to work hard to hone my senses. Rather than ignoring them as I'd so often done, now I'd take note of the smallest signs and warnings. Each pricking thumb, each tingle of skin and hair, could be interpreted. I became more sensitive to changes of odour and texture in the air, registered whether moisture was coming from above or below, from the south or from the east, and heeded the movements of clouds. Every gentle shift in colour and light was a thing to be read and understood.

I studied them all.

I learned.

Then there were the birds.

Did you never question why your mother was forever surrounded by wrens and jackdaws? Yemma asked one dull market day.

I'd been excitedly telling her of the patterns I'd seen in the comings and goings of geese. If the flocks flew high and out to sea, the day would be fine, warm and calm. Low flying birds of any kind always meant foul weather and a single crow on the wing was a sure signal for rain.

The prophecy of birds, Yemma hummed. *Do you know what an augur is, child?*

I shook my head and looked to the crow as it lifted a proud beak.

The bird knows, the widow exclaimed, laughing.

What does this old crow know that I don't? I asked, smiling at my feathered friend.

If you can read the behaviour of birds, you're an augur, like your mother, she continued. *For Atlas, the prophecies were less sure. She'd understand feelings through the movements of swifts and corvids, gauge tensions within the town, or between people.* Yemma paused as she fixed her skirts around her knees. *It was her gift, an ancient art. By watching the birds, she could say if a babe would be born a boy or a girl or know if a birth might end badly.*

I looked at Yemma, my head tilted like the crow, slightly amazed but desperate to understand.

I was but examining patterns to predict the weather. Yet you speak of prophecies? I asked.

The old woman sucked on her empty pipe as she stared into the far distance. Her habit of falling silent when I became excited and asked questions was an infuriating quirk. One the old woman seemed to delight in. I huffed at her.

Birds loved Atlas, she said, at last. *There was a bond of trust. Like you and this crow. It didn't choose you as a companion for nought. It feels the connection.*

The crow lifted its head again, opened its beak and let out three loud bleats.

See? laughed Yemma. *Your mother said you'd be powerful.* She pointed a stubby finger at me. *Keep watching the birds, child. Find their messages if you can. They might bring you what you need.*

And what do I need? I asked, still a little grumpy.

But the old woman had said her piece. Now she was eyeing the large behind of an old townsman, struggling with his donkey. He struck the beast and Yemma cackled, howling with delight as it bucked and hee-hawed in loud rebellion.

After that, I looked for auguries of every kind.

I grew to love standing in the dunes, my staff held before me, the crow by my side, watching starlings wheel and fly to the horizon.

As talk of the Storm Witch spread, instead of rag-tags and dirty boys, men in finer clothes with shining buttons, and hats upon their heads would appear at my blanket. They expected a hag, they'd say, a crone with boils about her wrinkled face, a festering, ancient thing. But they didn't curb their disgust for the youth they found instead. With my eyes covered, the grand men thought me blind. They'd make faces and crude gestures. Yemma said not to worry, it's not that they found me ugly, quite the opposite in fact. *They're intrigued by you*, she'd say, and claimed their lustful fascination terrified them.

Young flesh is a spell to them, she'd say. *Use it when you can. For mark me, it won't last forever.*

NYDIA HETHERINGTON

But Yemma could keep her talk of lusts. I wanted only civility and respect, and for those who sought my counsel to value it. After all, my words might save their ignorant skins from a drowning, or worse. Nevertheless, I laughed along with those mocking men. Better that than let them know their cruelty hurt. Until, one day, with Yemma and the crow beside me, I told an obviously disgusted sailor of medium rank not to grimace as if he had shit under his shoes as he spoke to me.

I see you, well enough, I went on, smiling as I gently stroked the crow's head. *I keep my eyes covered as an act of kindness, so their bewitchment does not harm you by driving you to destruction with want for me. For truly, if I unbound my eyes, you'd tug so hard on your sad little cocky, it would come off in your hand.*

He soon scuttled away like a frightened lizard, leaving Yemma laughing like an old bawd, but I saw his fear, and it was a mighty thing.

Well now, said Yemma between great snorts as she tried to get her breath. *You should be careful what you say, girl. Sailors are more superstitious than even the menfolk here in town.* Then she laughed so much again, she fell backwards into the dust. *But his face was a prize to see!* she hooted.

Soon, the sailors' sneers or any talk of devilry by the townsfolk paled. There was a growing disquiet, a nervousness of a different kind. It spread like a disease from the harbour and into the town. Only this time, their fear was just.

The threat of war and invasion was never far away in a

port town, everyone knew the dangers. But the Governor wasn't only a bandit, he was a naval hero, and a known terror. If anyone could keep them safe, it would be Barbarossa. His presence was enough to ensure people slept well in their beds.

Until now.

Scene 8

Once known as the Pirate King, tales of Barbarossa's cruelty, of how he'd sacked a thousand ships and brought rich booty to our shores, were part of the town's mythology. Knowing he was governing the town from atop the hill, watching over the people like some ferocious red-haired deity, was a mighty thing. If he went away to visit powerful friends, townsfolk walked the lanes with their heads down, cowed by worry, and dread ran through the town until his return. It was always there now, a profound fear, reaching into the lives of the people, piercing flesh and breaking spirits. People were like cats in the dark, listening, sensing, getting ready to flee, to hide or to fight. A neighbouring town had been invaded. The descriptions of slaughter, of women violated in the most brutal manner, then cut to pieces in front of their men and babes, or simply left alive to relive the barbarism, was so terrifying, even Barbarossa's presence could not calm the despair.

Those who'd survived the attack in the neighbouring town now lived as slaves under the Roman Empire. Some of our townsfolk had family in the invaded city but could only guess their fates. So mothers and sisters were mourned. For there was little hope.

Women are used as instruments of war, Yemma said. *Our bodies are another land to be invaded, destroyed and conquered. And when all's done, we're easily killed. There'll not be many left alive.*

Fear bred fear, along with a deep mistrust of strangers or anything out of the ordinary. The proof of the townsfolk's foreboding was in the desperate eyes of hungry soldiers with dull cutlasses at their sides (perhaps they'd once gleamed), hands trembling, heads flitting to look who might be coming up behind. In the privateers with bellowing voices and proud scars, ready to slit a throat for a bag of coins without allegiance or care, their lives inevitably ending in some horror or other. There was no glorious victory for any of them. The only victors, it seemed, were those who made money from the misery of war. They strutted proudly around the town, buttons as shiny as their unused weapons. I'd see them in their fine robes and jewels, the men of wealth, like the apothecary. He always kept his nose in the air, swaggering through town and harbour stink alike, showing himself. Even as he mingled with the dirtiest creatures alive, his posture was that of a prize cock.

The Storm Witch gradually became a more valuable source of information. There wasn't much to flatter in the situation. With distress so high, soldiers and sailors were ordered to stay by their ships, so I was summoned to the harbour. Refusal was impossible. But I was promised gifts of payment beyond my imaginings, and underlings were dispensed with. It was an honour, I was told, that I was to be seen by captains and their merchant men, to personally give them my predictions of tides and tempests.

Yemma had told me of the malodours and mischief around the harbour. The first time I stood in the shadows of carracks and galleys, those mighty vessels licked by the fiercest waves, I admit to a quickening of my pulse. But any fascination vanished like sea mist, for Yemma's warnings were a poor reflection of reality.

Nothing could have prepared me for the stench of the harbour. A mix of sea rot and human degradation. The steaming innards of the washed-up whale of my girlhood would have been but a floral tribute compared to those gut-wrenching odours. Folk flitted to and fro, quick as lightning. Some pushed great chests filled with all manner of goods as fleas and lice jumped from fetid shirts and jerkins. Many a time some unseen hand grabbed between my legs as bodies jostled against each other. I learned to keep my chin down. Murderers were known to lurk in the shadows. There were tricksters, thieves and the poorest people on earth. I passed women alone with their babes, singing lullabies, swaying on the damp ground, and children playing in the dirt. They'd had no choice but to live in the filth with the prospect of violence at every turn. I got to know their faces, took honey-comb or anything else I had to hand. Sometimes they refused the gifts, but I left them anyway. The townsfolk knew how things were around the harbour. Most turned their faces away, busied themselves with their own troubles. More so than ever with fear of invasion. The only other person I ever saw approach those poor wretches was Afalkay the Beautiful. Sometimes he'd stop to speak to children who were nothing more than bones and rags, and through all the awfulness, they'd look up to him and smile.

A single visit to the harbour was enough to make me understand the meaning of true fear. No matter how many times I was shoved, I refused to step onto any creaking vessel nor go near a captain's cabin. Never would I stand upon a ship with those poor shabby boys, and slaves still in their irons, all dying of thirst and disease. Those great wooden monsters smelled of something sour and against nature. As if we, in our tiny fleshy bodies, might tame the ocean with carpentry! I was glad to know I'd never have to board or sail on one. They pushed me and shouted, but the ragged sailors were pleased at my pig-headedness, for the deviant nature of our bodies meant a woman on a ship was bad portent. And my refusal forced their captains and the fine merchants to come to me. It was shameful enough to be consulting a woman on serious matters. How it made the filthy lads laugh to see their betters out in the stink, in communion with such a slattern as me, barefooted and bent, leaning on my twig with the crow flapping on my shoulder. I despised the spite on the vinegar breaths of those richly attired men, the curl of their ungrateful lips as I spoke. And afterwards, they'd throw riches to the ground and watch, arms folded, as I'd struggle to bend to gather up my rewards.

Sometimes I'd feel him there.

I'd look about and there he'd be, Afalkay the Beautiful, watching with the rest. But never laughing, only smiling. His eyes would linger upon me in what felt like an unholy way. Heat would rush at me, then suddenly I'd shiver, try to stay steady, hold my staff tight. On my more brazen days, I'd match his gaze. Until at the bark of some great man, I'd flinch and turn away.

At least I was paid well for my trouble. My small home was soon stacked with fine fabrics from places I could only dream of. I had pots of silver coins, oils and spices of every kind. The useful things I took to market to exchange for food; most of the silks and sundry trinkets I gave to Yemma. The old woman sold the fabrics, their colours being too bold, their weaves too fine, to be of use to her. But she kept the oils, for Yemma loved the feel of them on her skin. To see her eyes light up as I'd present her with a pot of unctuous liquid, was worth every hellish second in the harbour.

It was fine indeed to be a bringer of joy. In return, she gave me the thing I needed most, a treasure above all objects: her friendship.

Scene 9

The first time Afalkay the Beautiful spoke to me, he appeared before me like an apparition, a divine vision kneeling on my blanket.

I hadn't planned to trade at the market that day. I'd known very well the weather would take a bad turn. Awaking at sunrise, my every nerve had fizzed with it.

The birds confirmed my feelings.

Walking along the shore that morning, flocks of gulls filled the skies, wheeling and screaming, blocking the day's new light. I'd seen great numbers of them settling on rocks and gathering around the sea caves, seeking shelter. Their noise was appalling, a ghastly and cacophonous warning. A storm was brewing, it said, and the winds would not be kind. No matter that the waves shushed gently at the shore and the breeze was yet a benign thing, the rain but a spatter. None would imagine such a morning prelude to cruel weather.

But the signs made me nervous. I became restless, snapping at the crow for every small irritation. To lose myself in the world of the market, the lives of other people would have been a fine distraction from my aching limbs and lonely thoughts. In truth, something had compelled me to go. It was a hunger to be sated, the visceral feeling that destiny would be broken or lost if I stayed away.

Once there, the crow balled itself up beside me on the blanket, wet-feathered and grumpy, beak stuck under its wing. As the rain was thin in the air and a yellow Sun peeped through the clouds, I'd had to beg Yemma to retreat to the warmth of her small home. She would have crouched beside me all day if I hadn't insisted. But when I spoke of the birds, at last she crept away, sighing loudly as she went. The old woman lived in a hut on a lane curving towards the harbour. One of many meagre wooden dwellings the town had to offer, clustered together like frightened children. It was draughty and damp. But with a fire lit under her cooking pot, cosier than sitting out in the oncoming bad weather.

I did my best to warn everyone I saw about the possibility of a deluge. Not for the first time, many thought me mad, said it was just a light shower and would soon pass, heavy rain being so unusual that time of year. As the weather worsened, they shouted about the strangeness of it, pointed at me with blame-filled fingers as, tentless, their goods spoiled in the onslaught.

My protection from the rain was a richly patterned sheet, heavy, woven with a thousand red and silver threads. It was finely made, a reward from a ship's captain, kept for its thickness and strength. I'd taken it with me that morning knowing exactly what I'd need it for, and with thoughts of my heritage – a true reflection of the Queen of the Tents herself – imagined how I'd look sitting beneath it. Now it was erected, the fabric sloping toward the ground behind me and secured in place with branches of cedar, it did indeed look wondrous. But I was a beacon, standing out from the others with their rags and baskets thrown above them, slowly getting soaked as they determinedly sat it out.

Dry under my shelter, I kept my chin down and tried not to catch anyone's eye. When the fine-looking town councillor stuck his smiling head under my awning without notice, I screamed with the shock of it. My face flushed then, as I saw the beauty of the man crouched at my side, so close I could smell him. His skin seemed to shimmer. A wave of heat gushed through me. Suddenly I was sweating under the tangled rug I'd wrapped around my shoulders for warmth. He lifted his hand to show he meant no harm and was sorry to have startled me. Instinctively, I slid my injured hand behind my back.

I've heard much about you, Afalkay the Beautiful said, raising his voice against the sound of rain hitting my makeshift fabric shelter.

I had no idea how to reply to this man whose breath and damp skin smelled of almonds and sweetest jasmine. This figure who'd watched me at the harbour, causing my heart such disquiet.

And I you, I found myself saying before I knew I'd drawn breath.

Despite the clammy chill, my face grew ever hotter. I couldn't for the life of me look at him for fear my head might boil and steam like a pot of broth, so gave my attention to a splash of mud on my blanket. There was an impossible lull, a deep cavernous silence filled only by the interminable sound of rain on rain on rain. As the man looked at me, his perfumed breath blew in little gusts against my cheek. Time seemed to slow. It felt like a chasm was opening before me. How I wished to the heavens for such a hole to appear, deep and frightful, so I might fall into it and never return, even if it meant eternally languishing in hell itself. Anything to flee his scrutiny.

The man continued to stare, silent and smiling, until it was impossible not to look back, and I flicked a peep at his face. His midnight eyes, like endless circles of starless nights, appeared to be studying me. His chin tilted a little, like a fisherman examining some strange sea creature caught accidentally in their net, questioning, *Can it be eaten? Will it poison me?*

How close he was, yet a fathomless sea surged between us.

With almost eighteen good years behind me I was of age. But under Afalkay the Beautiful's gaze I felt my youth in all its folly. No matter that I'd run an independent life and provided well for myself for three full years. At that moment I was a poor market girl in a child's shift. The good councillor was of the same generation as my father, but from a world unlike any he'd have known. Not one of dust, blankets, wax and bees. Nor one of charms and glamours. But of fragrant chambers, of long debates around cool, stone tables, of cleaned linens and choices. His continued scrutiny sent my head spinning as my skin turned cold again. Still moist from sweating, I was as slimy and unappealing as a freshly landed barb. Was I so monstrous? I wondered as the dreadful silence dragged into eternity. Until at last the crow, bothered by rain splashes and no doubt feeling the weight of my discomfort, shook its head and let out an almighty caw.

Afalkay the Beautiful laughed so hard I thought he might fall backwards and land, in all his finery, with his legs in the air like an upturned beetle. Instead, he shuffled toward me, ducking further under my shelter. The silver and red fabric caught a momentary ray of sunlight and reflected against his skin. It moved in gentle waves, and then it was all I could do to stop myself from staring at his truly beautiful face.

I'm glad of it, he said, pulling me from my dreams and making my belly churn as I blinked under my muslin. *Then you'll know I wouldn't come to bother you for nothing*, he went on.

Still having no idea how to respond and having forgotten what he was glad of, I kept quiet. I couldn't keep my eyes on his without my face burning, so I turned away and looked in glimpses again. A drop of rain dripped from his impossibly silken beard, oiled to perfection. He was smiling but there was a seriousness about him. The curve of his mouth was flawless, like it had been painted on. I imagined touching it. Until, jumping like a startled frog, I watched his long-fingered hand flick droplets of rain from the green muslin swirling soggily about his head. Perfect half-moons rose on each of his pearly fingernails. I'd never seen such physical grace in a man before. I was indeed a frog, or a great farting toad, my mouth gaping as I gulped at the air. He carried on chatting, as if crouching before me like this, so close, in the now pummelling rain, was an everyday, normal thing.

My wife is fond of your honey, I heard him say, nodding at a pot by my knee. *My babes, too.*

The idea of his wife and children tugged something at the bottom of my stomach, and as I swallowed to push the feeling away, I began to cough and choke.

Are you unwell? he asked, concern creasing his brow. *It's no surprise in such weather. Perhaps these are not days for a delicate person to be sitting out.*

I assure you I'm not delicate, I snapped back, appalled at the accusation and determined to show just how un-delicate I was. *I'm only a little unused to the closeness of a fine townsman like yourself. I'm glad your wife has enjoyed my honey. Please do take her some, no payment needed.*

He shook his head.

I'm not here to rob you of your living, mistress, but to ask for your help.

He was surely in certain danger of cramp in his legs, the way he crouched there, but he didn't move away. He only smiled with his painted-on mouth and rolled his shoulders until they crick-cracked.

But these are not good conditions, he continued. *There's to be a meeting at the town council building up on the hill. Do you know it?*

I was looking straight at him now, squinting under the wet binds covering my eyes. I'd never ventured too far into the town. I knew the council building of course, and the other fine houses that loomed over the town, only because I could see them from my market blanket. Still, I nodded as if I'd been a guest there a thousand times.

I've been tasked with asking you to attend, he said, and raised a playful eyebrow. *The invitation comes from the Governor himself.*

My jaw went slack as my mouth fell open again.

I was dumbstruck.

The townsmen, especially those of high standing or men of the council, never spoke to me nor gave any hint of acknowledging my existence. It wasn't even their wives who came to me for honey and Dreamstones, but their servants. To think the Governor, the mighty and feared Barbarossa himself, might ask for me was too incredible to believe. He could not know me. I was certain there had been a mistake.

You're confused. Please don't be concerned, he said, his perfect smile never faltering. *You've been at the harbour. It hasn't gone unnoticed. We wish only to ask your advice. If you're willing, I will take you to the meeting now. We've time to pack your things away.*

By the time I'd gathered my belongings, stuffed them into my blanket and fixed it to my staff, the rain had abated. My fingers and toes were stiff and sore. Wrapping a swollen hand around my staff, I winced, then limped as I took a step. Bowing, Afalkay the Beautiful offered his own hand to carry my load. The eyes of the other market traders were turned upon us, I could almost hear the pull of each muscle as they strained to watch my every move. I was of low birth. More importantly, I was a woman and as such the one to do any fetching and carrying. I could not accept help from the councillor. Those were the rules and I felt them keenly, as if scratched into my flesh with a pin. He acknowledged the mistake, apologising with a lowering of his chin. Then, as if in a dream, aware of the eyes of my fellow traders, weather-disgruntled and watching, I followed the good councillor through the market and down the lanes.

Scene 10

Our journey through the town was plodding and silent.

I had no words to give the man walking beside me, and he apparently felt the same. I could smell his sweet aroma wafting on the breeze, and it was beyond me not to inhale, deeply. There was a damp heat coming from his clothes and I wondered what possible stink I might be giving off. I wasn't unclean as such, but my shift was old, the fabric stained under the arms and around the wet hem where it had trailed in every dirty puddle and the many pools of piss and shit the town had to offer. So many times Yemma had told me to wear women's skirts and not the childish clothes of a girl half my age. I'd brushed her off, told her draperies were of no concern to me. How differently I felt now, suddenly longing to be dressed like any other young townswoman.

Walking so closely, I could get a better sense of the man. The good councillor was tall, broad with muscular arms showing beneath his tunic, and long, thin, but strong hands. Some curls had escaped his turban and lay across his neck. The soft, brown hair was tangled with strands of white, proving that despite his youthful smile and supple skin, his boyhood had long been left behind.

Occasionally he turned to ensure I was keeping up. The crow, hopping beside me, too lazy to fly, flapped and screamed dissent at the long trek. Afalkay the Beautiful didn't hide his amusement, especially when the bird jumped up to rest on my shoulder. I ignored the smirk and the snort, relieved to have my friend close. Agitated, the crow lifted my rain-dirty hair with its beak. Tilting my head away, I clicked my tongue and hissed. I was in no mood for games. It pulled, and as a clump of my thatch was tugged from its roots, I shrieked. There was another mighty squawk of irritation from the crow, and a small but audible chuckle from the sweet-smelling councillor. The thought was absurd, but Afalkay the Beautiful seemed content in our company.

The lanes weren't busy after the rain. As we started up the hill I was immediately lost. Thick stone steps, ancient, shiny and treacherous-looking, marked the only way up. No amount of explaining could make someone without pain understand how hard it would be for me to ascend. I said nothing and slowly began the climb, stepping sideways, pulling on my staff to drag myself up. Accepting I'd need to stop many times, I ignored how strange it must have been for a strong, healthy man to dawdle and wait.

Ebb and flow, I silently said to myself. *Ebb and flow.*

The elevation, and fear of losing my footing, made me light-headed. Looking over the town, I felt like a bird, so high above the places I knew. Blinking at the now almost empty market below, I recognised the dirty dwellings and the harbour, all so small, all so poor.

Further up, we reached a web of tidy lanes, meandering but perfectly ordered, lined with stone dwellings. They were clean and bright. It was the smell that struck me most of all. There, up on the hill, the air was tinged only with the odours of cypress and olive. There was no thick stink of bilge or effluence, no rot of sea stuff. I opened my mouth wide and took in as much as I could. A light rain started up again. It quickly grew heavier, and I let the raindrops melt on my tongue. My head spun again, but not with sickness, only a tingle of fresh, clean air. I watched Afalkay the Beautiful as he walked before me. His elegance, the softness of his tread and the movement of his hips with each step. By the time we reached the council building, I'd almost convinced myself he embodied the spirit of my mother's mountain lion and even looked for a long tail, swishing under his coat.

As quickly as it came, the rain stopped again.

The black clouds were seamed with golden light.

My mind had been so occupied, I'd paid little attention to the weather.

How unusual it was.

Sodden, and tired, weighed down by the elements and the strangeness of the day, I wished only for the comfort of my home. Although dry now, the air remained pregnant and heavy with water. That's when I felt it. A force pulling at me as I stood before the mighty steps of that building. It was a terrible sensation, more powerful than I'd known before. I was burning and freezing all at once, and the pulling, all the time, something pulling at me, as if devils' hands had burst through the earth and stone to tug at my ankles. My skin too felt a mighty shift. I thought myself a snake, ready to shed its scales, as all over I puckered and crackled. My bones seemed to soften, and for a moment I was afraid I'd melt away. I looked to the sky again. It betrayed nothing. The clouds had cleared, the Sun had regained its place and around it was nothing but blue. Yet it seemed so empty.

I listened.

All was calm and silent.

I realised then what was missing. Other than the crow, there wasn't a bird in sight. Bad weather was on its way.

And worse.

Scene 11

Up close, the council building seemed as rich as an emperor's palace. The stone hall with its high white and gold walls was bigger than I'd imagined possible. Inside, furious torches encased in bronze jutted out at intervals as tongues of spitting flames lapped the walls. Shadows danced around the place, faceless phantoms, bending and shuddering like demons until, coming together, they dissolved into shivering pools of darkness. I hesitated at the entrance, cowed and unsure if I should be there at all. Afalkay the Beautiful gestured to advance. My bare feet slapped against the cold stone floor and my staff tapped like a hammer. I'd never felt so small and dirty. There were many high townsmen and councillors filling the space before us. A hum of low voices, like the sound of agitated bees, abruptly stopped as I entered. It seemed a thousand heads turned to look at me, and a thousand breaths were held. In truth, there were probably less than twenty men gathered, but they had the power of multitudes.

I shivered.

Afalkay the Beautiful put his hand gently to my elbow.

As we moved forward, I thought I was entering the lair of a magnificent yet terrible beast. I was a sacrificial maiden, like in the stories of dragons and monsters my father once told. The good councillor directed me to sit on a low wooden stool in a shadowy corner, behind the crowd of finely dressed men. The crow was at my feet, head darting this way and that, firelight reflecting gold spots in its black-bead eyes. When I sat, the men turned their backs to me. They moved as one, a many-limbed creature, as they gave their attention to an ornate table filled with tomes and charts. The hum of voices returned. I was invisible again.

Women were never permitted into the council hall, nor anywhere near men when discussing town business, or any matter of import. As I sat alone on the meagre stool, ignored by the great men of the region, I felt like an insect. Yes, I thought, I'm a flea or a cockroach, unwelcome and silent. How I wished I could scutter away and hide in the cracks of those cold walls. But I couldn't move even a finger. Only my lips trembled, and my teeth clattered in my mouth. What terrible wrong had I done to be summoned and made to sit behind those men when all I wanted was my home?

The sound of a heavy object hitting a solid surface suddenly rang around the hall. I almost jumped to my feet in fear, my heart banging in my chest. Instead, still frozen to my seat, I looked up as, once again, the place fell silent. Until the shuffling of many leather soles signalled the arrival of a higher power.

The crowd parted like the wood of a cloven pine.

A man dressed in the finest robes I'd ever seen, all gold with scarlet braids and tunics swirling about him, walked briskly toward me. He had a thick beard of red whiskers growing in unruly patches over his face. Although I'd never seen the Governor, I knew the man before me was Barbarossa.

Shaking with fear, I thought I'd fall to the cold stone floor.

Moving ghostlike in the firelight, Afalkay the Beautiful appeared from the crowd to stand by my side. The shaking subsided a little. The good councillor gestured for me to stand but gave me no aid. Using my staff for purchase and support, I struggled to my feet.

So! the Governor suddenly bellowed, his voice so loud I felt myself flinch and shrink. *You're the one telling our captains when to raise their sails.*

I looked hopelessly at Afalkay the Beautiful. He nodded that I should respond.

I'm apt to give my opinion, sire. If it is asked for.

My own voice squeaked like a mouse.

You are?! He laughed with his voice of thunder, as if some great joke had been told.

The sound echoed around the hall and rippled through the company of men. My eyes darted beneath their cover, hoping to find a way of escape. There was none.

What would your opinion be, he continued, *if I asked you, for example . . .* Barbarossa paused, stroked the long straggly ends of his beard, and several men laughed again. He hushed them, bawling once, before continuing. *If I should send out a fighting fleet over the course of the next few days? What would you say? Would the winds be a friend?*

I looked about the chamber.

Faces loomed and stared through the gloom, each one a grotesque mask, flickering like ghouls under the flames of the many torches. Afalkay the Beautiful stepped closer. Snapping my attention to him, his sleeve briefly brushed against my arm. The crow, clacking its claws on the stone floor, lifted its head and gave an almighty caw. As the shriek echoed through the great chamber, purls of unhappy voices grew in volume to a resounding thrum.

Barbarossa waved his hand and silence fell again.

With some difficulty, I lifted the crow to my shoulder. It flapped but didn't protest. If the men in the hall were given leave to show violence, I'd defend the crow with my staff, even if it meant being dashed to pieces myself. I'd not let them hurt my friend. I steadied myself before speaking. My voice would be louder and clearer the next time I used it, I was no scuttling insect nor snuffling rodent.

I would say, sire, that to do so would be to murder your soldiers.

There was an audible intake of breath, but the Governor raised his hand again for the company to be quiet and waved me to continue.

A tempest is coming, mightier than any seen in my lifetime. To put to sea in such a storm would mean nothing but death. No one would be spared.

The murmurs started up in earnest now. This time, when the Governor shushed them, it rang around the hall like a summoning bell.

Did you see this . . . in a vision? Tell me the source of this supposed knowledge.

It's what I feel. I have no visions, sire.

You're a seer? A storm witch?

I shook my head, unable to say any more. How I hated him using the word *witch*. It meant nothing to those men but an imaginary devil's whore. They had no understanding of gifts or glamours, no belief in the power of natural forces. They had no right to it.

What are you, then? Speak!

I'm a beekeeper and a healer, I managed, my voice cracking as tears pricked my covered eyes.

Yet you freely give prophecies, that I'm told have been borne out many times over. So here you are, standing before me. Do you know what you're saying, young woman? Do you understand the import of your words?

My feet were ice-cold on the white stone beneath them. I was shivering, and again had no voice to answer with, so nodded as vigorously as I could.

Good. Then if I were to say a fleet of invaders was on its way here, to sack the town, to kill the men and perform unnatural acts upon the women, would your feelings on the matter I have put to you remain unchanged?

My trembling stopped and I looked at Afalkay the Beautiful, the purpose of my visit suddenly clear. The invaders were on their way. War might be imminent, or worse. If what I said proved true and things went our way, I'd be rewarded with the prettiest silks and the finest oils. If I was wrong, it could only mean death.

I took a shallow breath.

Nothing I said would garner the respect of the men before me. No promise of the good I could do as a healer. No mention of what I'd already done for the merchants, ensuring their safety at sea. I was a wretch with unnatural gifts. A grubby young woman, twisted of hand, bent of back, with a crow on my shoulder. I was a witch and to be suspected of all manner of evils. Closing my eyes, I tried to concentrate on what to say. But my thoughts slid like worms around my mind. Was it Afalkay the Beautiful's wish that I die for the sake of wind and rain? Had this been an elaborate plan to rid the town of me? Gifted women were never safe, I'd known that. I'd been stupid to think people weren't talking behind my back. I'd seen them pointing at me. Every day at the market, rolling their eyes and whispering. Perhaps they'd been plotting and planning. Was the beautiful man sent to lure me to this place, to this nest of shadowy vipers? For that's what they seemed now: serpents from hell, writhing, hissing, waiting for me to say the thing that would give them reason to murder me. I looked at the good councillor. His eyes were full of urgency.

Then it hit: a revelation to knock the air from my lungs.

It wasn't about me at all; I was of no importance.

The life of every man, woman and child was resting on my words. If my prediction proved wrong, who knew what hell might be visited upon the town by the invading army?

I was the weakest, most wretched fool ever to have lived. I should never have told anyone of my gifts, I should have lived quietly, away from the crowds, like my mother had always wanted. As much as I'd been hurt by their sideways looks and spiteful talk, the townsfolk had buried my father. I'd watched them buy my Dreamstones to help quench their most secret desires. They laboured, fed their babes and wished only for full bellies at the end of each day. I wanted no harm to come to them. Taking a breath, I lifted my head and looked at Barbarossa.

If any invader ships appear on the horizon before morning, I would advise not to send our fleet out to meet and fight them, if that is what you're thinking, sire.

Consternation echoed around the hall.

Barbarossa again called for silence, allowing me to continue.

The invading soldiers will be dead before they reach our shore. The wind will gather the sea in its hand and dash their ships to splinters. There will be no mercy. A tempest cares not for men. The sea has no morals or allegiances and would just as easily kill our soldiers if put in its way.

Silence.

The Governor, who'd been smiling and stroking his matted red beard throughout, continued to do so. Every creak or spit from a torch had me jumping like a fox in a trap. If I was about to be seized and thrown into some deep dungeon, then I wished it to be done quickly. All I knew for certain was my hope of a simple life as a healer was in pieces.

Go!

Barbarossa's voice was so loud it felt like a blow to the head.

Panicking, I scrambled for my blanket and things, suddenly unable to pick anything up, dropping my unravelling bundle as men's voices started up behind me, some laughing, others exclaiming loudly that I was an abomination and repeating what I'd said.

Once again, Afalkay the Beautiful appeared at my side. He helped tie up my blanket and fix it to my staff. Then, gently putting his hand to the small of my back, he guided me from the hall.

It was dark outside.

Go home, Sycorax, said Afalkay the Beautiful.

I took in a lungful of night breeze and thanked Setebos for it. The good councillor's soft touch was still resting, warm and heavy, on my back. I did not know if it was a treachery or a comfort. He had brought me to that place with smiles and sweet words, knowing exactly what it would mean.

Are you able to find your way alone? he asked.

I answered yes, but before I could step away, Afalkay the Beautiful took my injured hand in his and stroked it with his long fingers. The intimacy of the act made me flinch. I tried to pull away. He felt my resistance, but his grip was strong. It tightened. Staring at my terrified eyes under their muslin, he held on. And smiled.

Thank you, he said, before releasing me. Then, turning quickly, he disappeared back into the mouth of the great white hall.

I remember little of my journey home, only that it was painful. My sore feet unable to carry me as quickly as I wanted. When at last I felt the sea spray on my face and could smell the wild sage in my garden, I dropped to the ground and wept.

That night I listened for the mountain lion.

I didn't know why, but I was certain he would come. Only, sleep took me quickly to a silent place, and I was glad of it. But when I woke, still in the depths of night, I was sure I heard his steaming breath, snorting and warm by my bed pallet, the pad of his great paws sounding over the newly laid rushes, and I felt the comfort of his animal heat. Curling my legs under me, I pulled my cover over my head and fell again into the world of dreams.

I pictured us together.

The councillor and me.

Climbing the hill.

Storm clouds swirled above like colours of a Dreamstone. We watched, amazed as the sky raged, sending thunder-claps over our heads. Then everything went black. From the thick, silent darkness, a crack cleaved the sky in two, spilling a sliver of golden light onto our faces. There was a roar somewhere in the distance, either a ship's cannon or an animal cry, we couldn't tell. We looked out, over the town.

Everything was gone.

There was no harbour, no houses, no lanes or market, just the golden sands of a rolling desert. I tried to turn, to go to it, to at last feel the warm desert sands under my feet. But the councillor grabbed my waist, and with his fingers pressing into my flesh and as if bound in iron, I couldn't move.

His clench tightened.

My bones snapped.

I cried out in agony.

There was another roar. Only, now I knew it to be the call of the mountain lion, creeping through the cracks of my dream, reaching for my wakeful mind. And I was back on my pallet, sweating and blinking into the night. I couldn't say if the animal's cry was real, or slumber-made. But half asleep, I whispered thanks to the beast for its message of caution. Warning that grace and beauty can hide a bloody nature.

Alluring but terrible.

Charming but violent.

ACT IV

Scene 1

A clutter of starlings, bickering in the oleander by my door, drew me into the day. Opening my eyes, lying as still as a pebble under my thin cover, I blinked.

The pink light of morning was casting shadows around my walls.

I listened for movement outside.

The bees hummed, happy in their hives.

Rising slowly from my pallet, I padded over to the small, unshuttered window and looked out. Not a breath of breeze blew, and the Sun was a large golden ball. Still, I shivered. Pulling a swathe of sapphire silk from the pile by my altar, I wrapped it over my shift, took my staff, and stepped outside. The crow appeared as if conjured by the spell of daylight, jumped up to sit on my shoulder, and we set off to the dunes.

The air was thick, silent and numb.

Voiceless cedars stood sentinel along the way, needles

unruffled on their branches as I passed. Birds fell quiet in their nests now, too; as if lulled by the calm. I moved like a child afraid of waking a sleeping giant, timid and slow. The only sound was the distant ebb of waves on the sand. There were no mists. The day was as clear as well water.

Reaching the Wishing Tree, I leaned against its solid trunk, listened to the hush as sunshine burned holes in the sky and rills of sweat ran down my back. The heat and stillness made no sense. My bones were heavy with the anticipation of a storm, my skin tingled and fizzed with it. It should have been a raging, ravaging thing, bigger than anything I'd known. I couldn't have been mistaken. And what of the birds, set to be tempest-torn? Now they dozed like milk-fed babes. I'd never known a more placid morning.

Arriving at the shore, the crow perched itself on my staff as we looked out to the horizon. A gentle breeze tickled my unbound eyes. I opened them as wide as I could, took in the brightness: the green of the sea, the blue and white of the sky, the dry, russet tones of the rocks. All the colours of the day, so perfectly in focus. It should have been a joyous sight. No wisps of fog hung over the sea; no storm clouds gathered above. Instead, I felt sick to my stomach.

Then, appearing as if by magic, I saw the ships.

At first, they were but a faint, grey block, shapeless and strange. Then a shimmering of light pierced the silhouette, making lines, creating form. Until, gradually, I could see it wasn't one large object filling the horizon, but many smaller entities. I blinked and there were more. Hundreds, maybe thousands of ships' sails, casting their shadows, taking space where sea should meet sky. Fresh, salty sea odours filled my senses, but my mind swam with the dank stench of a dungeon. Sweating and swooning, I gasped for breath.

Leaning on my staff, I unwrapped the sapphire silk and let it fall at my feet. The crow lifted its beak and screamed as my stomach lurched. I tried to shush the bird, but again and again it let out its angry cry, shouting murder at the distant ships, until I touched its neck, stroked its feathers to calm its fury.

I lifted my chin to the glaring blue of the sky, looking for some sort of answer.

The terrible Sun shone.

A wave lapped, gently, at my foot.

The tide was coming in.

I dared not take my eyes from the invading fleet now, so let the water come. When I felt it rise to my ankles and soak the hem of my shift, I glanced down. Heavy with seawater, the sapphire silk was nothing but a rag in the tidal flow. The crow screamed again and at last I stepped away.

There was nothing to be done.

Back in the dunes, I watched the ships. The enormous fleet had stilled and anchored, and the ships hung steady on the horizon. Like me, the invaders were watching.

Waiting.

Weak with fear, I crumpled to the ground. Feeling the silence, heavy on my bones and skin, I thought it might crush me. My mother once said that there are two types of quiet. The hush which exists before words are spoken, pregnant with possibilities. And the emptiness left when everything is said, and all is broken. Perhaps the weight I could feel was the stifled screams of the soon-to-be-dead. I closed my eyes, and I could see them: the young women at the market, giggling as they chose a Dreamstone, breathless with youth; the high townsmen in their finery, parading up and down with their noses in the air and hands clasped at their backs; and the poor, stinking ships' boys, scratching in their rags. I saw all pounced upon, their bodies sliced from bellies to chops, ripped up by glinting swords and the hands of those on the invading ships. I couldn't stand to see any more. I opened my eyes.

The sea was flat calm. Not a single ripple pocked the surface.

Everything was holding its breath.

Thinking I might faint, I lay down, rested on my back. The crow hopped onto my chest and touched my face with its beak, urging me to get to my feet, and I was up again.

The ships hadn't moved.

But through the silence came a voice.

It was low, calling my name. With a racing heart, I looked over the dunes. There was no one. Supposing it a figment of my fear, I steadied my breathing. But then he was there. A hand on my shoulder.

Turning quickly, I let out a startled yelp.

Afalkay the Beautiful, his head covered in a length of clean muslin the colour of mushrooms, stared at me. All the strength in my limbs failed, but his hands were on my shoulders, holding me up.

Do you have somewhere to go? The mountains? Have you family there?

He spoke quickly but I couldn't get words out to reply. He was looking at me so intently I thought he might see my soul. My mouth went dry as sand. I managed a shake of the head and noticed again how wide and penetrating his eyes were, staring into my own like he had never seen another person before.

Then I remembered I wasn't wearing my muslin.

The Governor should never have asked you. I was against it. You're just a girl. I'm sorry I participated. Forgive me.

Again, I searched a way to answer, but could find none.

It was of no importance.

The sky went dark, as if the Sun had suddenly fallen, like a stone, from its place. There was a sharp crack from above, and a bellowing roll of thunder. A spear of silver fire flew across the sky, splitting the world in two. Almost immediately, the thunder came again. We shrank back, instinctively grabbing each other as the heavens blackened to pitch, and just for a moment, the silence returned. Then in a heartbeat the wind came, and a mighty gale began to blow.

As the waves thrashed, the sea transformed into a foaming monster. Gnashing its teeth against rocks and shore, it reared, shaking and splashing its furious head.

The crow flapped and screeched, then flew towards home. Afalkay the Beautiful shaded me from the wind with his cloak and started to guide me away, but I shrugged him off. I knew the coastline better than anyone and could make it home, lame as I was, even in the wildest tempest. I couldn't help but wonder why he wasn't with his wife and babes when the threat to all our lives was so severe. Where did he think to go in my company? To my dwelling, to shelter with me? He was believed a good man. The impropriety alone would be appalling, and to think of the panic for his family up on the hill, alone in the squall. I cared little for virtue, but it would have been foolishness itself to let a man so close to Barbarossa into my intimate space. At last, I found my voice.

You must get home. Quickly. Go! I shouted over the howling, smashing wind and crashing waves.

He hesitated, and hesitated again, until I pushed him in the direction of the town and started over the dunes. For most of the journey I didn't look back, praying he would not follow me.

As the tempest took hold in earnest, I saw how wrong things had been. The times I'd caught him staring at me in the harbour; the way he'd touched my hand the night before; how close he'd be when speaking. Now coming to find me when I should have been the last thing on his mind. It was more than kindness or guilt. And the hesitation, right there as the winds blew, how he stared before turning home to his wife and babes.

Suddenly I remembered my uncovered eyes.

Cursing Atlas and Sunny for ever binding their child in

muslin, I tried to stay my panic. Surely if Afalkay the Beautiful spoke to anyone about the colour of my eyes, there'd be questions. He wouldn't want that.

Finally, I turned to look behind me.

He was gone.

When I reached home the crow was there, waiting for me.

Scene 2

As I pushed the door open, the crow flew about, crashing, cawing and flapping its wet feathers, until at last it settled. But I couldn't rest. Praying to Setebos the bees wouldn't swarm, I knew I'd have to bring the hives inside. Quickly, I worked the fire, already lit with embers. The place filled with smoke. I hoped it would be enough to keep the bees calm. The crow would be no help, squawking, and flapping as the wind screamed around the walls. But I was glad of its fear. It would keep it inside, away from the storm. The last thing I needed was an injured crow, or worse.

The heavy sound of something falling outside shook me back into action and I shouldered my way through the door. The gale was savage now. It whipped my hair up with fearsome strength, wrapped it around my face like a winding sheet. It flattened the high grass, bent the cedars in two, as it screamed around my dwelling like a tortured thing.

With my shift twisting about my legs, I made my way to the bees. Fighting the fabric of my dress with every step, somehow I found the strength and achieved the task. But when the last of the hives were inside, I fell exhausted onto my pallet. It was a comfort to hear the bees, vibrating with furious life. Exhilarated by their noise, I lifted myself from the bed and spun around on my feet, laughing in the firelight. A few insects came out to buzz, angrily joining my strange dance, but they soon settled and most, seeming to understand danger was in the air, remained within the safety of their hives.

The crow grew calm, too.

It stayed on its perch in the corner by my altar, preening its feathers, unbothered now by the battering at our walls and roof. It looked cosy in its small alcove away from the fire, which lapped healthily, giving us plenty of heat and light. My eyes watered, stung by the smoke, and I coughed a little, but I was glad to be home and safe. Only when I could lie back on my pallet to find my rest did I think about the ships again.

Listening to the storm's destruction, I pictured the people on board those many gloomy vessels. The galley slaves so cruelly used; their lives already obliterated. The soldiers, boys not long taken from their mothers' skirts. And I cried out for pity's sake. But the fleet had come to kill us, and those unknown boys I now mourned were our murderers-in-waiting. As for the slaves, we might easily take their place if the ships were allowed to anchor. Better them than us,

I thought, and prayed to Setebos to blow the wind harder.
Yes, pray, I told myself. For something had to be done.
Unable to rest now, I walked about the place, grabbed a
bundle of dried sage and other herbs from a large pot and
threw them on the fire.

Blow the wind harder, I cried.

Repeating the words over and over, I was no longer
praying to my deity, but to the tempest itself. My voice grew
louder, chanting in time with the thunderclaps as they too
came ever stronger, ever booming.

Blow till thou burst thy wind, I cried again.

The smell of burning herbs stirred the stagnant air of
my dwelling, fragrant and woody. My life depended on
the storm. I could not leave my fate to the recklessness of
weather. Sitting before my altar with a pounding heart and
trembling fingers, I took several plain pebbles from the
basket, set them in a pile, and anointed them with sweet oil.
Lifting my arm up in the firelight, I watched the oil drip
over the scars of my injured hand and run down the wrist
to my elbow. It was calming, but it wasn't enough. For the
divine to feel the strength of my plea, there had to be blood.

I pulled my mother's curved knife from its pouch at my
hip and, with the very tip of the blade, made a small nick
in my bent thumb. A bead of shining blood immediately
appeared. In the firelight it was a jewel, a chip from a ruby.
I blew gently on it. The little glob of blood shivered before
mixing with the unctuous liquid and slipping down my arm
in a stream of red, running like a ribbon. Taking more oil,

I spilled the stuff. It fell over my arms and over the pebbles, making thick pools over my altar, speckled with spots and streaks from my still bleeding thumb.

The crow tilted its head, looking at me first with one eye, then the other.

Although my belly flipped and fluttered like a fish in a net, I smiled at my friend as I took the feather from my hair and brushed oil over the stones. It seeped into the dry rock, filling every pit and crevice, until the pebbles began to change. Colours started to swirl on the surface of each one. Deep scarlets, and the ruby red of my own blood, mixed with murky greys and blacks of the angriest skies. I sent my prayer to Setebos. The crow shook its wings and cawed, but I put my finger to my lips and let out a gentle *shhhh*. It settled. For the bird knew I wasn't really praying, not to my god nor any other, not even to the storm.

I was setting a spell.

Wash them away, I whispered. *Wash them all away.*

Scene 3

The tempest took several days to pass. Sometimes I feared it would never stop. It seemed impossible my house could survive its wrath. All about me boomed and clattered. But my father's work was sound and strong. The roof did not yield to the lashing weather. The shutters over my window and door kept the worst of the elements out, although I was sure, as every minute passed, they'd be turned to splinters and all would be lost. The noise was a fiend, resounding and vehement. There was little to do but fret and listen to the destruction of the world beyond my walls as I tried to keep warm. I paced about, prayed to Setebos, begged for the bees to be kept from swarming. His reply saw them docile in their nests. Sometimes I sat on my bed pallet humming as I rocked myself for comfort. There was none to be found. The crow was quiet throughout. It preened and didn't spook. Only its head flicked about, seeming to wonder at the calamity. I fed the bird seeds from my stores. For myself, I ate what I could find; making thin broths with un-fresh water, herbs and honey set aside in my many pots and baskets, and chewing on old pieces of comb, in the hope of staving off the hunger. It didn't.

When, finally, the storm abated, it was quick.

All was calm in an instant.

Once again, rods of light burst through cracks and seams in the wood over my door and window. There was silence. My ears rang with it. And an impossible stillness reigned over everything.

After being inside so long, unable to stretch and move my already aching limbs, I was painfully stiff and horribly sore. Yet I jumped up, tore at the wood over my door until all was open in an explosion of light. Stumbling back, I fell, wincing as I hit the ground.

It was warm.

The golden Sun was firmly lodged in a cerulean sky.

Pulling myself up, I leaned into the doorway.

A light breeze touched my face.

Lifting my chin, I took in a lungful of air, so clean and fresh it made my head spin. But all around was dirt. A crust of sand, mixed with the muddy slop of red earth, covered everything in a thick carapace. Trees lay leafless and broken. The flora was flattened as if trampled into the mire by the feet of a giant. Yet the elements themselves seemed cleansed, made new by the tempest. Struggling, I reached for my staff and stepped out into the day.

The crow was ahead of me, already hopping around the wasted garden. Cawing and shouting its liberty, making me laugh at its noise even as my belly turned like an angry ocean. I swayed, this way and that, an uncertain vessel looking to anchor. Having set off in haste, my face burned as I remembered the stink of my confinement left behind. I'd given no thought to scrubbing out my soil and slops or seeing to the bees.

I pushed on.

Holding my staff between both hands, stabbing at the ground in front, I relied on it more than ever to pull me along. The crow flapped and raised its beak as it hopped beside me, continuing its cries of joy. Catching my friend's mood, shame at my own filth diminished and my heart thrummed as I laughed again. The bird jumped along like an excited child until it could resist no more and lifted into the air, flying circles above my head, climbing higher with each rotation. I watched the fringes of its wings flutter silently as it proudly showed me the way, gliding towards the sea. The reassurance of its soaring shadow was palpable, like a hand to hold in the night. Again, I laughed, so hard now I stopped to bend, to calm my stitching belly. But my pulse raced with something akin to fear. I was all contradiction and couldn't rest on one emotion, torn minute by minute from elation to terror and back again. As we crested the dunes, I saw the Wishing Tree was still standing, unharmed by the storm. My relief was too much to bear, and being so tormented by opposing feelings, by my whirling thoughts, courage failed, and I fell to my knees.

My mind turned to the events at the council building.

My skin bristled.

I couldn't know if the Governor had believed anything I'd told him.

If the storm had merely hindered an invasion rather than halted it, then my predictions had been wrong. Our tormentors would only be angry, brutal and determined on success. My life would be like a nut held in the fist of a pirate, waiting to be crushed, or as meat, to be thrown to the dogs of the enemy.

If, however, things had gone exactly as I'd warned, but Barbarossa hadn't heeded me, I'd still be in danger. After all, he'd have witnessed a most terrible storm, watched as the tragedy of my words was borne out before him. What would it mean for a woman who could foresee storms and predict their consequences? Every which way I turned I was stuck between evil doings. The crow swooped and landed by my side, and I stumbled to my feet, determined to get to the shore. But before taking a step, we stopped in our tracks.

Before us, dark water pressed against the bright sky. It was the blackest sea I'd ever known. There were no ships on the horizon; not a single sail was anywhere to be seen. Thoughts that the storm had indeed defeated the invaders brewed in my gut, but any feelings of celebration soon disappeared when I saw the slaughter cast before me.

The sea wasn't black at all, but the deepest, thickest,

bloodiest red. Slick, and glinting now under the great Sun, as if bejewelled with rubies. I thought my eyes played false, for all I saw was blood. I looked again, harder, for perhaps it was a monstrous dream. But I was awake, and more alert than ever. That we tiny creatures might give out so much of the stuff seemed incredible. Yet before me was carnage I could never have imagined. Nor should anyone ever have to.

The shoreline was thick with the bodies of men and horses. They rolled together in gently moving waves, making the sea-edge more flesh than water. I flinched as the salty air made the nick in my thumb from Atlas's knife sting. Looking up, the sand too, all along the shore, was stained red and scattered with human and equine meat. Terror held me so tight I could neither run nor look away. And so, I looked and looked and took it all in, letting the scene burn into my memory, scar my mind the way fire had once scarred my skin, so I might never forget what I'd done. I would bear witness to the devastation. Feeling the air rush through my throat, I swore I'd never again be afraid of men who would use me for their own gain. Nor would I let anyone force me to speak or act through fear, without first consulting my own reason.

Voices below made me start.

The dead were not alone.

Townsmen and soldiers scattered among them, moving slowly along the beach. The stronger ones were ridding the sand of bodies, flinging them, whole or otherwise, into carts pulled by small boys and old men. Soldiers pointed, shouted orders. Others retched and let go their stomachs as they went about their work; while more busied themselves, moving so swiftly they might have been casting nets for fish, but for such a gruesome catch.

Scared to be seen, I ducked down into the sand dunes and lay on my belly. The crow nestled under my arm for safety. Its beak touched my face, which was wet and salty, not with sea breeze, but with my pathetic, useless tears. When I could look no more, I crawled through the dunes like a snake with the crow on my back until I was sure I couldn't be seen from the beach, then shuffled towards home.

Back at my dwelling I stood, exhausted and useless, before my own mess. My living space was a filthy, stinking hole. The hives had to be returned outside, the bees tended to. But all I'd seen had been too much to comprehend. I was dumb, unable to move in the ever-growing, now breezeless, heat. And I hadn't forgotten Yemma; was desperate to know if she was safe.

Yes, Yemma.

Everything else could wait.

I'd get to town as soon as possible.

For whoever the bodies on the beach were, and however they came to be strewn across the sand, I'd foretold the butchery. And Yemma was known to be my friend.

Scene 4

Setting off, the Sun was high and impossibly strong, turning mud miraculously back into dust. My eyes, free from their binds, squinted out fat tears under the Sun's glare. Long sunbeams, as hot as fire but somehow tender, fell across my skin, stroking like fingers, and I thought about Sunny.

My father was of the Sun, I whispered to myself. *It will do me no harm.*

And then how comforting those warm rays were on my sore bones and my frightened mind. I turned around, almost expecting to see him. But only my shadow followed me, and that of the crow, long-beaked and marching beside me through the storm-devastated landscape.

It wasn't an easy journey. With each step came a new torture. There'd been no time to take remedies or to bind the bits of me that flared, swollen and angry. Raw pain cut through my feet. The bones seemed fused, knitted at each joint. I remembered how I'd danced around the hives as a child, pointing my toes, bending and twisting on them, and snorted at the implausibility that these useless barks were the same appendages. Staring down at them, I willed them on. Pushing forwards, sometimes I cried out in agony. Still, I moved ever on until, after what seemed like hours of struggle, I was anchored by pain and could budge no more. Marooned in the heat, sweating and panting like a beast, I held on to my staff, leaned against it, letting my cheek rest against the smooth surface of the wood.

It's only pain, I told myself.

Then I thought to maybe lie down in the dust, wait for someone to pass and beg for assistance. There'd be no respite from the agony, but at least I'd get some rest. Either that or in the now blasting heat of the Sun, I'd dry out like an old oyster shell and that would be the end of me. Not even my father's spirit could protect me under such conditions. But there was no question of abandoning my journey. I had to see Yemma.

It was yet a long stretch to the town.

I slid down the length of my staff, letting myself fall to the ground, and began dragging my arse through the dust. My thighs, the backs of my legs and the secret place in between grazed as they scraped over dried litter and the brittle needles of many fallen branches. I grunted and moaned as I strained. My shift lifted beneath me, showing the world what I had to give.

All the trees along the way had been blasted away by the storm.

There was no shade.

The Sun beat down.

Now it was a burning eye that never blinked, bending the air in waves with its gaze. Alive and pulsing. It watched me struggle. Its rays had changed into something furious and cruel. Again, I told myself that my father was the Sun, as my mother was the Moon. And he'd loved me. Belief was everything, and anyone could believe in anything with a bit of imagination.

I looked up.

I believed.

I shuffled on.

When, at last, damp with sweat and filthy, I could see the outline of the town, I closed my eyes. Sitting in the dusty scrub, feeling the rise and fall of my chest, I somehow found the strength to pull myself to my feet again.

My stomach was tight.

I took a step.

My mouth opened, and a scream was pulled from my body. Leaning against my staff, feeling the tears roll, hot and many, down my face, I was sorely tempted to fall back onto my rump. But I'd not be seen crawling through the dirt like an insect. Not by the townspeople, not by soldiers or invaders or governors, and not by Afalkay the Beautiful. Because I believed in who I was.

I was the daughter of Atlas.

The ancestor of a great desert queen.

I was the maker of Dreamstones and powerful charms.

A woman with jewels for eyes and a crow at her side.

My father was of the Sun, and my mother of the Moon, I said, gulping at the air.

Dripping in sweat, I wiped my face and wrapped the muslin over my eyes, as I'd done so many times before. Then, taking a deep breath, letting agony run through me in a silent cry, I concentrated on the sound of my mother's bells, tinkling around my ankle, and stumbled on. Forwards again. Step by step. Forwards. Breathing. Living. Moving.

The crow, patient with my slow advance, flew in circles, soaring above the path it knew so well, now lost within the storm's debris. As we reached the lane to the market, it alighted on the branch of an upturned tree, before settling gently on my shoulder. It was a powerful act of solidarity, a message I couldn't help but understand.

We'd enter the town together.

I wasn't alone.

Scene 5

The town was spectral-quiet. Small groups of huddled townswomen were dotted about the place solemnly shaking their heads, voices barely more than blurted whispers. Young girls with startled faces had arms around each other. Every now and then one looked up, her eyes darting, unable to rest on any single subject. Clutches of women busied themselves, lugging the storm's detritus – fallen branches, uprooted flora, and rocks – from the lanes, sweeping dust that rose in clouds around their skirts before it settled again. There were men too, standing around stroking their beards, overlooking the situation. The sounds of the market, the frantic colours of everyday life, were gone. Nothing shone under the hot glow of the now terrible and torturous Sun. A blanket of grey lay over the town and its people.

The tension in my spine gave a little. Straightening, I pushed my shoulders back. There was no sign of violent death, only remnants of the tempest's fury. Walking slowly, I tried not to wince as I pulled myself along, both hands grasping my staff. The crow jumped down and hopped beside me. A few heads turned. Two women I knew from the market stopped their work and leaned upon their brushing sticks, watching as we passed. Their chops were smudged with dirt, their clothes not quite clean enough to be decent, and they looked deathly tired. I nodded, but they'd turned away. Anxious to get to my friend's house, I gave my attention to moving on. But a sudden commotion of women's voices split the air, keening, screaming and wailing. Shaken, I stopped and cast around, hoping for some kind of assurance. No one looked up or even appeared to notice the din, and for a moment I feared some strange magic had touched my ears.

I saw them then, a circle of townswomen whirling down the lane.

The eddy of skirts jostled forwards, hastening something along at the centre of their clutch. I stepped back to let them pass. The women had hands clapped to their cheeks or held before them as though begging for a scrap to eat. No one looked where she was going, faces all turned to the heavens in some desperate prayer. At the centre of their huddle, not some bloody terror as I'd feared, but Yemma. I almost laughed when I saw her, elbowing for space and cursing the women as she was rushed along, pipe still hanging from her lips. My heart leapt and I called her name, rasping at the top of my lungs. The congregation of women halted but did not stop their noise, which only rose in volume and urgency. Yemma pushed the women aside, growling at them to move, holding her arms out for me to go to her. Before I knew it, I was consumed by the shouting, cajoling gaggle, ever more insistently pressing forwards.

When, finally, the knot of women stopped, we were outside a small dwelling. It was one of several at the bottom of the hill, built from clay and straw. Yemma, ordering the throng back to their homes, shooing them off like a skein of geese, suddenly grabbed my arm, shoved us into the house and slammed the door. Stunned, we took a moment to take a breath – me, the crow, Yemma, and a young girl I'd not seen before. The women outside pulled at their hair, wailed and knocked. But they didn't attempt to enter, and soon their voices faded into the distance and their noise disappeared.

Looking around, I saw a homely place, simple and well-tended. There was a chimney with its fire lit under a pot, stifling for such a hot day. The fire-pit was flanked by baskets piled to the top with sweet-smelling, freshly gathered wood, and a small bed pallet sat neatly in an alcove in the corner. A large table was at the centre of the living space, with stools about it and several prettily painted pots upon it. On the far side of the room was a closed door leading to a separate chamber, from which I could hear strange howling and panting. I stared at the door, wondering if they harboured a wounded animal in there. The crow didn't seem to mind the noise, or the heat. It jumped about the table, claws skittering, as the young girl watched with her large, startled eyes. I went over, stroked the bird's head and gave an encouraging look to the child, who nervously stepped forward and did the same, smiling as she felt the soft feathers. A scream broke from behind the door, so guttural it sounded like murder. The girl jumped back, flinching, covering her ears with her hands and I couldn't help but gather the child into my arms. She leaned her weight into me, allowing me to take her burden as she nuzzled into my shoulder. The embrace was but a moment. Still, I felt it linger, long after she pulled away and looked at me with cold, suspicious eyes.

Yemma was a whirl of movement, pulling pots from the fire and grabbing calico strips from a disorderly heap on a stool. She ordered the girl to keep the flames high, even though it was hot and the air was thick with heat; then, dashing to the chamber door, she snapped at me to follow her, *Quickly!*

I whispered to the child that the crow would be good company for her, and the old woman closed the door softly behind us.

Inside, the chamber was small, seemingly unilluminated and dank.

There was a stench, both familiar and strange. Most of the room was taken up by a heavy wooden bed. A marriage gift, I guessed. With my eyes bound and with so little light, it was hard to make out the figure of a small, young woman in the middle of the bed, writhing and moaning as if tormented by devils. She was twisted in sheets, soiled and wet. As Yemma pushed me forwards, I realised they were soaked with blood.

Remembering the carnage on the beach, I yelped and turned away, not wishing to see any more of the stuff, but Yemma pushed me back, tutting and shaking her head.

Go to her. Calm her, the old woman insisted as she pulled the filthy sheets away. Slapping them to the ground, the widow put her hands on the young woman's naked thighs. That's when I saw her belly and understood.

As I approached the woman, she shrieked and lashed from side to side. Yemma ordered me to keep her still. I let my staff fall, bent over the woman and took her head in my hands. I wondered if she minded being touched by a twisted limb. I'd become accustomed to women and girls at the market shrinking away when they caught a glimpse of my injured hand. But this young woman's eyes were clamped shut, screwed up against her suffering. Still, she had strength and I struggled to keep her from flailing, my own pain threatening to buckle the legs from under me. I wished I had my pouch of herbs, or time to scout for weeds and snails' shells outside by the walls. For I could surely make her something, a tincture to ease the agony, to pacify. I leaned in closer, so even as she wrenched away, my mouth brushed her small ear as I started to sing.

There were no real words to my song. I could think of no tale that might take her mind from her labour. I simply made sounds, moving my mouth in a pretence at phrasing, a pale imitation of my mother's voice, like the song she'd sung to the mountain lion. That was the melody that came to me, too. It was a song from an ancient place. I could feel the weight of age upon it. The woman stopped thrashing, opened her eyes and looked at me. She fell still. So much so I was afraid, and wondered what sort of spell the song might have cast. But she blinked and started to breathe, heavy, grinding but slow, regular breaths.

That's it, said Yemma. *Get her to breathe. Good and heavy. Like a thirsty dog.*

I knew how to use pain.

Taking on the rhythm of the young woman's breathing, I continued my song. Her agony melded with my own as it guided both her work and my simple tune. As she looked at me, she lifted a small trembling hand and touched my muslin with the tips of her fingers. I didn't take my eyes off hers, nor did I stop my melody, but I pulled my muslin away. A lone candle flickered by her bed, so I could see her own eyes were large and wet, blinking up at me through the murk, full of fear and torment, but calmed now.

Yemma was all movement and endeavour, telling the woman when to hold off from breathing, when to push and rest. But I didn't look at what was happening down between the woman's legs, afraid of what might be there. The labouring woman obediently followed Yemma's instructions. Yet we were the two united. Yemma was so far from our melody she may as well have been in the next room. It was just the young woman and me, locked together in the communion of my mother's song.

The woman's body suddenly tensed and convulsed.

A scream ripped from her throat.

Panicking, I pulled out the only thing I had in the pocket of my shift and placed it in her hand. It was a Dreamstone. Immediately her fingers wrapped tightly around the pebble. She brought the stone up to her face, placed its cool surface against her cheek and I watched her accept the succour. After a moment of calm there were more convulsions, more screams. I sang louder and she stared at me, panting, breathing, sweating, but all her concentration was on my face, even as she jolted, and the very life was seemingly pulled from her body. I sang louder still, touched her cheek with my own, and she sang with me, only a few notes, until we heard the baby's high shriek. We stopped and I whipped my face around to see Yemma. She was holding the tiny wet thing up, one hand supporting its head, the other under its kicking ankles, as it yelled its life into the world.

As the baby was cleaned and settled, I replaced my muslin. The world went back to being a hazy place. I stroked the woman's burning face, listened to her shallow breath and moved a strand of hair from her eyes, then I turned to Yemma. She shook her head sadly and I wanted to scream the injustice back into hell where it belonged. The young woman looked up, exhausted, weak and bloodless. Yet she was calm, astonished by the swaddled babe Yemma had placed on her breast. I promised myself, as I gazed at them, I'd find a way to save this new mother, as weak and spent as she was. If I could predict tempests, then surely I could heal this girl. Giving her my silent pledge that I'd see her well so she might play with her child in the dunes, collect shells on the seashore, she smiled at me. I asked her name. She said it was Zari. Her voice was cracked and small. Looking around the room, she beckoned me closer, and with my cheek touching hers, I felt our breaths mingle.

Are you an angel? she whispered.

No, I said, brushing rills of sweat from her forehead and placing the Dreamstone under her pillow. *They call me Sycorax.*

Scene 6

Days went by. Barbarossa made no attempt to contact me, no councillors came to advise. The promised rewards for my services appeared nothing but a lie. Uncertain if the townsfolk knew anything of my meeting with the Governor and high council, I was as jumpy as a cat. The slightest noise sent me spinning. Walking the wind-broken lanes, I kept my head tucked to my chest, my muslin-covered eyes, bound so tight it hurt my head, fixed to the ground before me.

I'd imagined, at first, since the storm had saved the town from the terrors of invasion, there might have been a sense of celebration. Instead, the townsfolk wanted the impossible, to forget. To speak its name was to invoke, or to infect. The gruesome death of the invading soldiers, every last man of them, was like a secret weeping wound, a poisoned fog rising from the sea, sweeping through streets and houses, orchards and ornamental gardens. It seeped into the sandy ground and into the hearts of the people. Almost everyone now believed evil forces were at work in the town. Yes, they mumbled, they'd escaped with their lives, but the tide could turn again. To keep the bad at bay, they pretended all was well. Only, it's hard to live a lie. Especially when fear is your bedfellow.

Distrust became a disease.

Acquaintances ignored each other where once smiles and nods had been exchanged. People kept to their own small circles more than ever. Muttering together, they covered their mouths as they spoke, eyes flitting this way and that, searching the shadows for signs of evil doings. Death had never been a stranger, but the violence and magnitude of the storm's bloodlust was beyond understanding. Some of the more meagre dwellings had been lost, torn apart and destroyed. Others were so damaged, any attempt at repair seemed fruitless. Those townspeople unfortunate enough to have been caught in the weather were dealt with quietly. Grieving families abandoned the usual show of rites to lament in their own private ways. No one gathered at the burial place or gave mourning gifts. There was no keening, no singing of souls to their rest.

The bodies of the invaders also had to be seen to.

Beaches were cleared of the grisly remains surprisingly quickly. After the first day the soldiers abandoned the task, leaving orders for the townsmen to do it themselves, or face penalties. It was the fishermen and their wives who did most of the work. The councillors considered it the best way, as their stomachs would hold better than most. After all, they were used to the rot and gore of gutting their catches. But the horrors showed in their vacant stares as the men, women and children wandered like ghosts around the town, loose-jawed or jabbering to themselves.

The Governor, a foreigner who lacked understanding of local rituals, gave orders for the invader remains to be burned on pyres along the beach. For the townsfolk, such a thing was an unclean act. Bodies should never be given to the monstrous fire, only to the good earth. The dead may have been on a mission to kill them, but they were men, not a washed-up whale. The burning of human remains was unholy. Funeral fires would be a gateway for any passing evil to enter the town. In normal times there'd have been protests. People would have come together, shouted in the lanes, pulled at their hair, and begged the man on the hill to change his mind. When he didn't, they'd have refused to carry out the order. Not so now. The desperate townsfolk kept silent, turned their faces away as arrangements were made. A few young fishermen lit the fires and supervised the burning. They wore thick black hoods over their faces, so they alone knew their identity. But everyone felt the weight of the act. All over the town, the air was thick with ash and funeral smoke. Anyone who walked the lanes carried the smell of the dead on their clothes.

Then there was the blood.

The fisherfolk had seen to things as much as they were able, but nothing could be done about the colour of the sea, or the waves, spewing pink along the shore. So much blood had spilled it would take months to roll away with the ebb and flow. Fishing fleets were forced further out to sea for their daily catch. But no one would eat their haul, preferring to live on goat's milk, olives, cherries and dates, anything they had available, rather than risk sinking their teeth into fish flesh fed on human blood. Piles of rotting sea life built up around the shorelines, stinking in the heat and bringing swarms of flies to the town, adding the very real threat of disease to the general dismay, horror and thoughts of demonic interference.

Despair gathered like roosting starlings on every roof. The tempest had saved the town from the slashing swords and violations of invading soldiers, but to the poorest inhabitants this seemed a slower torture. Yemma said she'd heard it whispered, more than once, that a quick death by the blade of an enemy would have at least saved them from the encroaching living hell of panic, need and starvation.

As always, things were easier for the more genteel parts of society. They kept away from the smoke-darkened hubbub of the town, finding comfort in their houses high up the hill. But they too needed to eat. Orders were given. There came an insistence from above that townsfolk shouldn't hide in their homes, no matter how much death or possible disease hung in the air. Life had to go on, said the men from the safety of their high-up places. So the streets were deemed clear enough and traders began to set their blankets out in the market again. Servants were sent down from the hill to get provisions, to walk through the wreckage, and to report back to their masters. They alone saw the storm-weary faces, now sweating under the fierce heat of a Sun so hot, many thought it a divine punishment, or a demonic victory.

The townspeople covered themselves for protection from the heat, and ignored the continuing stink, the flies, the vermin, and went about their days, going through the motions of the life they'd had before. Productivity became a disguise. I was no different. I tended the bees and looked to my garden, which had all but been destroyed. Saving what I could, I made abundant pots of potions and remedies, stacking them along my walls like an apothecary. But mostly, I worked on cures for Zari. For I'd made a promise, and no matter what Yemma said to the contrary, I would save her.

Having plenty of the leaves my mother called *thickening wort*, I knew what to do. There were many different varieties, some bitter and dry, others sharp and juicy, but together, a green stew would strengthen the young woman and replace the blood she'd lost. I administered to her every day and often worked late into the night. Even when there seemed little improvement and she lay limp and weak, her breathing so shallow it was barely there, I consoled myself with one thought: she lives yet, and will be better in time. And at each visit Yemma proclaimed her amazement.

I was sure she'd not see the morn, the old woman would say; then, raising her brows, *You've got the knowledge. It's a gift, all right* – she'd nod knowingly – *but this girl is too sick, even for you. Don't waste your energy on things that can't be fixed. Even magic has its limits.*

I'd not listen to such negative talk. As I worked on my potions, my back bent like a galley slave chained to a sinking vessel. My body and fingers ached from toil and illness, and my mind faltered with fatigue. But I could not be idle. I'd save Zari, I'd show Yemma it was knowledge, not magic — which I had no real sense of how to capture and use. The more I worked, the better she'd be. I believed.

Work also stopped me thinking about Afalkay the Beautiful.

If I rested, I'd wonder why he'd not come to inform me how things were with the Governor. Had my eyes given him such a fright? Were they truly so terrible? And my thoughts would wander back to the day the storm came. Did he care what might become of me, truly? As much as I believed it impossible, the idea rang like bells through my mind. Whatever his feelings, I'd seen nothing of the man that might make me trust him. In truth, even with his pretty mouth and slender fingers, his actions did not sit well with me, and there was something in his eyes that spoke only of deceit. I'd noticed it the first time he'd looked at me, the sensation of being appraised, like an animal or piece of meat. Oh, but how I could not stop my mind from picturing him, from playing scenes where he might happen upon me and beg me to forgive him for ever taking me to Barbarossa.

At the market too, Yemma noticed my distraction. One day I thought I'd caught a glimpse of the fair councillor. I began to sweat and was suddenly laughing with Yemma at the smallest, silliest things, excited that he might see me. But when the man strolled by our blanket with a haughty air, I could plainly see it was just some merchant in gaudy clothes whose beard was far from fine and was a full head shorter than Afalkay the Beautiful. My mood plummeted. I accused Yemma of putting the pots of honey in an untidy fashion so they'd spill. Though the day had barely begun, I packed up my blanket, and with the crow hopping and cawing its disagreement beside me, we left the market. Once home I threw myself onto my bed pallet, hid my face in the rough fabric of the cover and, without understanding why, I wept.

Scene 7

Yemma took me every day to see Zari and her child. We'd go in the afternoon when her husband, a surly fisherman much older than his wife, was away fixing nets, or smoking fragrant pipes with the other landbound fishermen. If ever he was home, he'd grunt and grimace as soon as he lay eyes on us and, scowling, he'd shoo away the crow. The poor thing would be locked outside the house, kicking up dust and screaming its beak off for hell and all its devils to hear; no doubt heralding every kind of look from passing townsmen and women.

The young girl who'd befriended the crow the day Zari gave birth was Zari's husband's daughter from another, older and now dead wife. How she'd howl when the crow was rudely treated. Her seemingly innocent mouth spat such ugly words at her father, it would leave Yemma snorting with laughter. The old woman's amusement only angered the man more. But with her eyes all sparks in their creases, she'd throw her head back and hoot at the top of her voice. Try as I might, I couldn't help but join in as I felt my heart jump with affection. For Yemma loved life and was a powerful balm through bad times.

Before each visit, I'd carefully select what remedies to take for Zari, not wanting to be without important cures, spending time biting my lip, going through all the properties of each powdered shell and dried leaf, saying them out loud, before taking handfuls of this and pinches of that from my stacks of pots, giving each one a sniff first, in case the mould had got in. I'd even speak to the ingredients as I went about choosing, as if they were children, wagging my finger and asking them to be good and do their work well, and then I'd carry them with me in my father's pouch. And over Zari's own fire, using my mother's curved knife for cutting and stirring, I'd make the stew, the brews and infusions, imbuing them all the while with the brightness of the Sun and the paleness of the Moon. Bitter herbs to help heal her womb, and a warm paste of tubers and rich green leaves, so tart it made her eyes water, to aid the strengthening of blood and bones.

Zari was still very weak and abed. Although she never complained of any ailments, I boiled roots to calm the fevers I knew she had from the dull, rheumy look on her chops and the glisten of moisture on her skin.

I have been blessed with angels, she'd rasp, as I lifted the cup to her mouth.

I also took sweet honied water. The elixir was for Zari's husband's daughter. Her own mother had died abed with child. She fretted so for her young stepmother, I thought it a treat worthy of her worry. And it was to pacify Zari's tiny, long-lashed babe. I loved dropping it into his toothless, rose-like mouth, watching him dribble and smack his lips.

He was a beautiful child.

As his large eyes blinked out from his swaddling, I imagined all the things I might show him as he grew. Yemma said it wasn't possible for one so newly born to smile at me when I took him in my arms. But he did. Like he knew me. If he'd been mine, what glamours I might have taught the boy. And I thought I might yet. Like a benevolent aunt. It wasn't just that he'd recognise my face. We were connected, two old spirits, found after centuries of separation. It didn't matter what pain I might be in that day, or how vexed, sad or otherwise my mood was, such joy jumped in my belly the moment I was close to the child. He'd squirm and moan when held to his mother, herself far too weak to grip him. But he never grizzled when he was with me and was as calm as any lambkin. Yemma said I'd enchanted the boy, and she'd shake her head, smiling to see him quiet and happy as I'd rock him. Yet the minute I'd place him in his crib, his throat would open, and he'd scream as if being murdered. The babe had a hunger on him, though. Like a fattening calf, forever wanting to feed. Such were the way of things after the storm, no one could be found to suckle the child. As fond as I was of him, I was no wet nurse. It was up to the young girl, Yemma or me to hold the infant to Zari's breast, take his weight as he hungrily took his fill.

He'll suck her dry and into her grave, Yemma said. *She's not the strength for it.*

But there was no other way.

Zari was as sweet as the honeycomb I brought.

In truth, she was like a child herself, being not much older than her husband's daughter. And so frail. When I helped the babe take her breast, she'd breathlessly call me her angel, her sister. As he suckled, I'd stroke the boy's dear head, full of soft black curls. I saw the pain of every suck, but still, she never asked to stop the babe from feeding.

Do you think he's angry? she asked once as the boy fed. *He's ferocious.*

He's just showing you his own strength, I said. *To make you proud. I'll bring more honey next time, that will soothe him when I'm not here if he gets worrisome.*

He loves you. He sees it in you, like I do.

What does he see?

Your nature.

I said nothing, only shook my head and smiled at her in reply.

I know what you are, she whispered, her eyes closed, her skin damp.

Do you now? I said, a hint of jest in my voice. *Then please enlighten me as, honestly, I haven't a clue.* I laughed.

A divine creature. Here to save us.

I stopped smiling and, a little unsteady, unable to stop

myself, let out a sorrowful sigh. Zari shifted; her babe was done, and was asleep in my hands, his little mouth still on her breast.

I'm not frightened of you, she said. *Not like some.*

People are afraid of me? I asked, raising my voice without thinking.

Yemma would have been angry if she thought I was encouraging Zari to speak. The new mother needed any strength she had for her little one. Quietly, I took the sleeping boy to the crib, then returned to her side for a moment, to check her fever. Zari glanced at my injured hand, then stared into my eyes hidden behind their muslin. I stepped away. The sound of my staff hitting the bare ground and the bells jingling at my ankle seemed to ring hard and loud around the small chamber, reminding me how strange I must seem to a young fisherman's wife.

If they're scared, it's of my illness, of how it sometimes bends and misshapes me, I whispered, *and of my injury. It's not me they're afraid of, only what I might represent.*

Exhausted, she closed her eyes.

Her breathing was shallow, and I could see her heart trembling in her birdlike chest.

Dear Zari, everyone stands a chance of misfortune, of being afflicted by illness, at any time, I said. *Like you, right now. Only you will heal and I'm sure you'll thrive again. But I shuffle along with this stick. It reminds people of their own fragility. So it's better to see me as something different to them. But sleep now. The babe will be hungry again soon enough.*

As I went to leave, I couldn't help but dote on the child for a moment, watching his face so peaceful in slumber, listening to the gentle snuffle of his breath – when I heard a deep painful rasp. I looked up to find Zari staring at me from her pillow; although sleep and sickness were heavy on her lids, there was something startling about the way she looked at me through the darkness.

But I know the truth, she said softly. *I've seen your eyes.*

With that she closed her own, and with strained but steady breathing, fell into the world of the Dreamstone I'd placed beneath her head.

Scene 8

The next day we went to see Zari as usual. It was early afternoon, yet she slept without waking, gently snoring, and safe in her marriage bed. I listened for signs of weakness in her breathing. She seemed stronger. Her babe lay awake in his crib but made no noise. His eyes blinked through the murkiness, little spheres of light twinkling like midnight stars as he blew spittle into bubbles, making them pop on his pretty, happy mouth. We believed her stepdaughter must have already helped to feed him, for there was never a more contented child. A wave of pride washed through me to see Zari, as tremulous and vulnerable as she was, faring so well under our care. I closed the door, leaving her to rest with her son.

In the main room, Yemma was showing the young girl how to weave braids into a headdress. It was to be a gift for her stepmother. The crow picked at strands of the woolly goat's hair, freshly shorn from the family's heavily pregnant nanny, who bleated its relief outside the door. Throwing the stuff about the table, the crow made the girl giggle as she struggled to pay attention to Yemma's instruction.

It was so hot outside, the streets were almost cleared of people. Inside, the Sun streamed through the small window. A wedge of thick yellow dust danced and swirled through the light, reminding me of honey dripping from its comb and making me wonder if I was neglecting the hives. The room was stifling. As the fire blazed under the cooking pot, I was rendered red-faced and damp under my mother's wedding garb. For that morning I'd decided I would no longer wear my thin girl's shift. Atlas had kept her bridal clothes in a basket by the door of our dwelling. Sometimes she'd taken them out to shake away the dust, and tie new cedar branches into the fabric to keep it fresh. I'd always supposed she'd kept them for me to use when it was time. As I'd decided, even if one could be found, I'd never have a husband, I was sure that time had come. Now wet patches grew under my arms and around the waist of the thick skirts and tunic as I sweated in the heavy fabric.

Yemma hadn't contained her laughter when I'd arrived in Atlas's marriage clothes, all glimmering coins and fringes hanging from every hem. I didn't mind. I loved how the garments made me feel. Sensing the hefty swish of the skirts, the fabric prickling my bare ankles as it moved, and how my hips took on a sway all their own when I walked, even if that walk was a painful shuffle. The layers of deep green calico skirts and red tunic, sewn through with patterns and ornately beaded, made it a weighty costume. My shift was as light as air in comparison. Being slighter than Atlas and unused to carrying such a load, there was a drag and pull to the cloth that forced my shoulders forwards. But I loved how the Sun shone through the glass beads, giving the impression I was made entirely of light, and I wanted to show the town how I'd grown.

I wasn't a girl any more.

It was a costume fitting for a town healer, a woman of consequence, someone determined to be seen, to have their voice heard. That's what I was thinking as I stirred the steaming brew over the fire-pit, panting as angry flames lapped at the stagnant air. For all that I loved my new appearance, at that moment I sorely missed my thin old dress.

Scratching where the rough fabric bit into my skin, I reached for a pot of honey to sweeten my infusion when a sudden noise had me spinning around. The door of the little house was flung open and, stooping to fit through the entrance, was the shadow of a large figure, silhouette shimmering in the heat. I squinted, eyes straining under their tightly knotted cover as the man stepped forward. He emerged as if conjured by a spell, the green muslin of his head covering falling over one shoulder. Taking another step, I saw him in the light. He was carrying a fine copper bowl, glinting yellow from the brightness of the Sun. I yelped, and the pot of honey fell from my already weak grip. It hit the ground and smashed. As I watched the golden liquid spill through the dirty rushes, my thoughts scattered like pieces of my broken honey pot. Helpless, I looked up. Without asking permission, the councillor marched in and placed his burden onto the table. The bowl was filled with rich red cherries and dates, oozing and sticky.

Forgive me, he said, addressing no one in particular, smiling as he spoke. *I didn't mean to startle anyone. My wife suggested a gift for her cousin. We have more than we need at home.*

Afalkay the Beautiful's eyes flicked to the chamber door, then to me, then to the honey on the floor and back to my face. There I stood, under his gaze, red and sweating with my mouth open, my bare feet swollen, splashed with spilled honey and glistening like moonlit galleys. I was as still as stone and just as mute.

The fair councillor turned to the young girl and smiled again, showing small gold teeth twinkling in his perfect moon-mouth. But she couldn't stop staring at the luscious fruit in the bowl. Without word or warning, he took the girl in his arms and whirled her around like a babe. She laughed as she threw herself about his neck, then quickly, playfully, pushed him away before falling hungrily onto the bowl of delights. How easy they were together. How unlike them I was. An unmoveable object, lumpen and lost in the lives of these other people. Yemma leaned back on her stool and sucked at her pipe, tilting her head as she watched the unexpected friends. She had one curious eye wide open, the other clamped shut in a twisted wink.

Forgive me, he said again. *I wasn't expecting to see guests, nor did I intend to intrude.*

The crow, who was also paying attention to the bowl of delicious-looking fruit, screamed for its share. Remembering myself, I brushed my skirts, proud as I felt the thick fabric, and stepped over broken bits of unbaked clay pot and spoiled honey, hushing the crow – now bouncing from foot to foot – with a cherry snatched from the copper bowl. I busied myself with the bird, dusting its feathers and fussing at its wings, determined not to look at the councillor lest I gave away the slight tremor that seemed to have taken over my movements.

There's no intrusion, sire, I said, still without looking at him, my voice as steady as iron. *I hadn't realised Zari had such esteemed relations. It's we who should be forgiven for being so undone. Please sit; I will bring mint tea, we've plenty.*

Yes. Stay, said the girl.

Her mouth was filled with dates. When she fed another to the crow, I flicked it away, suddenly worried I'd have to tend to a sick bird. The crow lifted its beak and cawed its displeasure so violently, I stepped back, telling it I wasn't its mistress, and it was free to gorge if it so wished. Yemma howled with laughter, as she often did when I spoke with the bird, and the girl followed suit. None of this did anything to lift my mood, which became more dismal with each heartbeat. The thought of being mocked in front of the councillor sent more heat to my cheeks and I felt them burn. Defiantly, I lifted my face to him, determined not to be cowed.

He wasn't laughing.

His face was bathed in golden beams of sunshine.

There was a slight frown across his forehead, which glistened under the heat. He hesitated before speaking, as if searching for the right thing to say.

I wonder, he asked, *if you've seen or heard anything of the mountain lion everyone's so excited about?*

I didn't understand.

I looked at Yemma but she only shrugged. The confusion must have shown on my face, as the councillor seemed happy to continue with an explanation, his voice taking on a jollity that made no sense to me.

These days I hear of nothing other than the terrible cries of 'The Mighty Beast!' being heard across the town at night. Oh, and what I might be planning to prevent some new catastrophe emanating from the ferocious moans of such a creature, of course. I've proclaimed that phantom roaring through the night is beyond even my strengths. He laughed as I pretended to give my attention to the crow, and Yemma looked at him blankly. *Perhaps I shouldn't be too harsh. It's a distraction, after all, considering everything we've been through with the storm.*

As he spoke that last word his voice slowed and quieted, and he frowned, aware of the clumsy mishap. I wanted only to run from that place. Instead, I flushed and gripped the table with my uninjured hand, afraid I wasn't steady enough to keep upright, and cast about for my staff. In the blink of an eye, Afalkay the Beautiful was at my side, passing it to me.

I'm glad to see you. With you being far from town and alone at this difficult time, I've been worried.

His voice was almost a whisper on my neck, too kindly and intimate for the confines of a small room. Having no reply, I stared at the man from behind my muslin as, once again, I got a whiff of sweet almonds from his clothes and skin. He looked back at me, not once tearing his eyes away from mine, not even to blink. It was a brazen act, I thought, to behave in such a manner when we were far from alone and in no way related. Yemma and the girl saw it and, after exchanging glances, they fell quiet. The crow, too, stopped its noise. Its head twitched from side to side as if trying to fathom a puzzle. The girl even managed to cease chomping on her treats, leaving a pit of silence into which I was certain I would fall. Until the fire spat, breaking the hush, and I grabbed the moment to take my leave.

Scene 9

Grateful for my staff, I hobbled as quickly as I could to the open door, rushing to get out of Zari's house. Brushing past the councillor as I went, my arm knocked into his shoulder and I felt the solid mass of him. I didn't bother to see if the crow was following. Once outside, I walked a little before stopping to get my breath. I had no real thoughts of leaving Zari, only a need of air. But there was no breeze to bathe in as I lifted my chin and leaned against my staff, just the thick, hot, immoveable ether. A heavy tread made me turn, and Afalkay the Beautiful was there.

Forgive me, again. I should be more gracious. Truly, I would not have come had I known you were here.

Of course. I'm no company for fine people, I replied.

The fair councillor shook his head, releasing a single curl from his makeshift turban. It sat against his neck. I couldn't help but wonder what that hair would feel like resting upon my cheek. Surely it would be soft; it looked it, not like the goat hair Yemma and the girl had been using to make their braids, which reminded me of my father's beard. As a child, I'd loved the prickle of it, even though I'd squeal and protest when Sunny picked me up and nuzzled my face. I looked at Afalkay the Beautiful's full beard, oiled and brushed, and a longing to reach out, to tug at his whiskers and pull myself into him the way my mother had done with my father, almost overwhelmed me. I flinched as he spoke.

I meant only that you deserve more attention, a private audience, after all that's come to pass. You've no doubt had a heavy burden to carry these past weeks.

I snorted before I thought not to, mainly through nervousness, but also because I couldn't fathom his response. He owed me nothing, certainly not pretty words.

I'm not child enough to think we get what we deserve. I bear no ill will, but I'd be grateful to know if my appearance at the council and the events thereafter have put me in danger. Or indeed, if anything else you may have seen of me – I took a breath, almost too afraid to think of him looking into my eyes on the day of the storm – *might be held against me.*

Afalkay the Beautiful was so close, even under that raging Sun I thought I felt the blood heat emanating through his skin. Again I wondered at his ease with such intimacy. Floundering slightly, I felt beads of moisture form across my top lip. I wiped them away and leaned a little heavier on my staff. The man reached out to touch my arm and, feeling my imbalance, held me up as he spoke, rapidly, almost breathlessly, his passion confusing and so wrongly spent.

I was going to come to you, soon. To bring word from the Governor and to reassure you that all is well. But my wife . . . her family . . . you can't imagine the strain. They believe I have the power to make things right. They've no idea. I don't sleep for thinking of you, alone and away from the town.

His soft words fell upon me like rocks, and again I asked myself who he thought I was, that he might speak to me of such things and in such a way. Seeing my bemusement, he recovered himself, continuing in a steadier voice.

The Governor is grateful. He knows he owes you a great debt. He will pay; of that I'm sure. For now, he's away.

Away? How can that be? I demanded, shaking my head in disbelief, aware of his grip still on my arm.

Barbarossa has important errands. The world does not stop at the harbour.

But people need him here, I insisted.

They need the idea of him. No one in the town knows of his absence.

I took a breath to speak. But he would not be interrupted.

Rest assured, he'll not let suspicion be directed at you. He's not superstitious of nature. The man believes in science over magic if he believes in anything. You're in no danger.

Air rushed through my mouth like the tail of the tempest. I'd been holding my breath from the moment Atlas first ran to the sea in anger.

I am the storm, I whispered, and the release was like the breaking of a spell.

He heard it, saw my unguarded moment.

As Afalkay the Beautiful put his hand to my face, his long fingers brushed across my muslin, down my cheek to my jaw and slipped under my chin, where he flicked my head back with his fingertips. I jumped away, almost shrieking, but swallowed the scream, not wanting to attract attention, for the lane, although sparse of townsfolk, was not deserted. Feeling a pulse of confusion, I waited so he might apologise for shaming me in such a way, at least to explain what right he thought he had to touch me like that. But he simply looked at me and smiled. It was the same smile I'd seen in my days at the harbour when he'd watch me. Then he rubbed his elegant fingers together as if feeling the quality of goods on sale at the market and adjusted the fabric of his turban.

Go, he ordered. *Rejoin your company, and finish brewing whatever bitter thing it was I could smell in that pot for our new mother.* His voice bubbled with amusement. *I'm sure it will fortify her; I've heard much of your cunning. My wife will be grateful for the care you're showing her cousin and the child. As am I.*

With that, the fair councillor turned on his heel and walked briskly away, leaving me reeling in the dust under the ever-punishing Sun, sweating in the heavy layers of my mother's wedding garb.

Scene 10

Hot and bothered by the councillor's attentions and his subsequent dismissal of me, I returned to Zari's house to finish my infusions. Pouring them into pots, directing her stepdaughter on which potion must be administered the moment Zari woke (from her now deep slumber), and which was for later, I tried to calm my busy mind and restless body. Fighting to keep the girl's attention as she giggled at the crow and fingered the bowl of fruits, my wits unknotted and frayed. Meaning no injury, I lightly slapped the girl's arm away as she reached for yet another cherry. She snapped around to look at me and snarled like a feral cur. Apologising for my bad humour, I tried a smile, but she only sneered and pulled back, pushing me away in the process. Ignoring the slight (I was used to sneers; one more wouldn't kill me), I continued showing the irritated girl exactly how to take a pinch of bark and weed and wort.

Never more than a pinch, for they're mighty strong, I said, in what I believed was a strict and instructive voice. *It helps with any mild delirium induced by the cures. And most important of all – do you mark me? – you must keep your father away from the marriage bed.*

The young girl, surly but attentive now, seemed confused, screwing her face up and curling her lip.

Your stepmother might indeed improve and look stronger, I continued, as stern-faced as I could muster. *It's possible she may sit or start to hold her babe without your aid, but she will be far too weak to . . . for him . . . for a good while yet. Do you understand?*

The girl giggled and shook her head, so I insisted again, saying that even if his urges were strong, as a woman herself she must rally to guard Zari from his passions. I did not cloak my words and thought to have embarrassed her, but there was no bloom to her cheeks, only puzzlement and a creased brow.

He does not go near Zari's bed. The thought wouldn't cross his mind.

She shrugged.

And where does he sleep at night? I asked.

Under the table, she jeered.

I scowled suspiciously.

Father sleeps there, where Zari used to sleep.

She pointed to the spot, the giggle in her voice highlighting my evidently foolish lack of understanding. Being obviously baffled, she made a great show of sighing, letting me know what an effort it was to explain anything to one as witless as me.

Zari came when Mother fell ill with her full belly. The babe ate up all her strength and she couldn't cope, so we took on help. The girl picked at a piece of thread on her shift. *It was better back when Zari slept in here with me. She was quiet and never smelled bad. Father stinks of fish and farts and makes a mighty racket in his sleep, it's like living in the yard with the goat.* She laughed before looking at my still puzzled face with another sigh of exasperation. *When Mother's baby got stuck and she died, it wasn't decent for Zari to live here any more, to help with me and mind the house as she'd been doing, not with Father being without a wife, so he married her. He said it would cost less that way as he wouldn't have to pay her any more . . . but they're not close, not like that.*

The girl looked up from worrying the now loosened thread and pulled a face, but still I shook my head and repeated he must not bother his wife. When she shrugged her whole body and sighed loudly at me again as if I were the stupid child, Yemma snorted and cackled like a jackdaw. I was too tired to keep on at her, and my heart still raged from my encounter with Afalkay the Beautiful, so I left Yemma with the girl, who was now prancing around the room and chattering like a bubbling pot. Neither seemed to notice my distress, and I was grateful for it. The old woman flicked a look at me, but she remained seated at the table, braiding goat's hair for the headdress and sucking on her empty pipe as I made my exit.

★

Slow and steady in the blistering heat, with the crow ever at my side, and struggling to keep a grip on my staff, I made my way home. Walking through the lanes, I crossed a small group of women, fanning themselves with their skirts. They fell silent and stared as I passed. I refused their gaze, looked away, and held my chin high until I was out of the town.

When a fair distance was travelled, I pulled the muslin from my eyes as I kicked a shuffling path through dust and debris. The earth was parched, brittle and mean. Too hard for my soft, swollen feet. I could hear the waves lapping on the other side of the dunes, bringing no relief or bracing salty sting, only the stink of death. There was no breeze to be had, no respite from the storm's damage. Starlings filled every bone branch of the Sun-blasted, tempest-broken trees, packing the stagnant air with their noise. Finally, exhausted, my mind reeling like gulls above a fishing boat, I reached my dwelling.

As soon as I walked through the door, I threw off my mother's heavy wedding garb, replacing it with my old shift. Then I made my way outside to stay with the hives while it was still light. Lying on the ground next to them, I imagined the bees all huddled within, their trembling bodies rubbing against each other, so blessed by togetherness, and I wasn't alone. Listening to their gentle hum, it was easy to picture myself as one of them. They were as much my family as anything else on the great earth. With the bees, I became we.

Night fell quickly and the pain of Aamon was with me. He held on to me with his powerful grip, stuck me with his claws, and breathed fiery breath into every joint and ligament. When I moved there was a crack across my chest. A thousand knives seemed to burst and scatter through my shoulders, neck and jaw, and I screamed out. But I was glad to be home, back in my own universe, filled with the stuff of my life. Every object was a beloved thing.

Inside now, lying on my bed pallet, looking at the Moon through the small window as she shone, pearl bright in the velvet blackness, I thought of every creature who might be seeing her at that precise moment. In lands far away, over the briny sea, animals such as I couldn't imagine, humans and spirits, all looked upon her as I did. And back in the storm-beaten town, through the lanes, the many different folk, some whose faces I knew and strangers, were all living and breathing under the same tent of night.

The mountain lion, too.

I thought of his large paws and yellow eyes, out there some-where. My mother said the Moon had the power to connect. I felt it then. As that silent Moon shone upon my home, I was connected to everything, a small part in a large tapestry. No, I wasn't alone, even if my empty heart ached with want. Just as with the bees, I was one part of a mighty many.

Moving slowly, I rose and went to my altar. It would have been amiss of me not to honour Setebos, even with Aamon so heavy upon me. With a gasp, I knelt and, under my flickering candle, whispered a hasty prayer of thanks for having seen another day. The smell of beeswax was rich and soothing as it crackled under its flame. Giving my libation, lines of sweat ran down my back, and the thin fabric of my shift clung to me. My words quickened. They ran like water from a stream, becoming a furious lament until they fell from my mouth in a desperate passion as I begged Setebos to release us from the heat. My fervour grew until I swayed and swooned. I sang a charm of release then, eyes heavy, parched lips sucking in the humid air. That's when I heard it.

There was a wheeze.

I tried again, pulling the air into my body, and listened to the rattle inside. It sounded like a bee was trapped within my breast. Hot, wet air was not good for people. Tomorrow I would brew a strong-smelling potion, inhale its vapours and rid myself quickly of the rasp. I'd take the remedy to town and give it freely to anyone who might be in need, for a thing like that could not be allowed to take hold.

Just then, the crow screeched.

I knew I'd been neglecting the bird. I looked to it now, as it scuffled about. But it would not settle. Feeling the burden of heat and bad air, the poor thing flapped and cawed its agitation, snapped its beak at tiny flies, invisible in the dark but our constant companions. I tried to go to it, to stroke it or give it water, but the bird would not be still. Finally, with a shake of its great feathery head, it hopped out the window and, with a flash of wing in the candlelight, was gone. I rushed to the door and called out, but it was dark and starless. The Moon was hidden now, too. Not a prick of light pierced the fierce, black firmament. I grabbed the candle and, panicking, wondered how things could change so quickly, just like when Atlas had run into the sea. The light from my tiny flame was insubstantial. I could see nothing. The thought of losing the crow was too much. I let go a howl into that malignant night, offered all the fear and sorrow I had to the darkness, but the air was so dense with heat my voice fell flat. I called out again and again for the crow, shouted and bawled. Until at last, there was an answer.

From above came the unmistakeable scuffle of claws on the roof, the tap-tapping of a beak and a single almighty caw, followed by another, and a third. My howls turned to a raucous, lunatic laugh. It split from my lips, hurting my ribs and almost knocking me to the ground, and I couldn't stop until the wheeze in my chest turned into a cough and I choked and spluttered myself into silence.

Wiping my mouth, I replaced the candle, and went back to my pallet.

My limbs were as heavy as trees. Lying down, shutting my eyes tight, I thought I heard the deep and desperate moans of the invading dead on the distant waves. It was only the cry of gulls, I told myself, though I knew gulls almost always kept their silence at night. But the self-deception gave me comfort, and perhaps the heat had changed their habits. I concentrated on the crow's shuffling on the roof. My thoughts swam towards sleep, but as I ebbed in the slumbering tides, that distant wail came again. It was not the cry of any gull. It sounded like an unholy thing. I raised myself to sit in the dinge, my arms resting on my knees, my head cocked to one side, listening. When it came again, I recognised it. As the stub of my candle flicked and flashed in the corner of my altar, I whispered comforting words to the mountain lion, for his cry was a lament, full of tragedy and loss. Hoping to hear him again, I waited. But his sorrowful song was done.

The crow shuffled and tapped above.

The waves blistered the shore.

And a soft tread stopped outside my door.

I jumped up, desperate to hear the snort of hot animal breath behind my door, and the musky stink of the mountain lion's coat. But the cry had been far away, the beast couldn't be that close. There was a gentle scratching, a fidgeting of bony fingers on splintering wood and the sound of my door being pushed slowly open. It was no lion, but a man.

This time, even in the dark, I recognised his shape.

ACT V

Scene 1

As surprised as I was by the appearance of Afalkay the Beautiful in my dwelling in the depths of night, I did not cry out, nor did I speak. It was unbearably hot, but instinctively I sat up and covered myself as he stepped toward my pallet. My back was against the rough wall, my shift pulled over my knees and my thin cover up around my neck. He reached down and gently took the cover away, pushing it to the ground as he bent to me and took my head in his hands.

The candle hissed.

I flicked a look to the ebbing flame and when I looked back, I was staring into the eyes of Afalkay the Beautiful. His fingers stroked my face as he pulled me to him, as he laid me down and I felt the weight of him on me. My senses were filled with the odour of almond oil and sweet jasmine as his mouth searched my skin. Everything was spinning around me. The spoils of the storm swirled through my mind.

The waves. The blood. The night was full of fever, and I thought myself in a dream. But reality buzzed in the hives outside, scuffled on the roof and wheezed in my chest. I was not afraid of the man looming above me, pressing against me. He looked into my eyes as he lifted my shift, sliding the fabric up and pushing my legs apart. When I closed my eyes, he told me to open them, said he wanted to watch me watch him as he gave me what I needed, for I might have thought myself cunning, but he alone could cure my pain.

I want to help you, he said.

Hadn't I felt his benevolence? Didn't I feel his kindness now? Had it been daylight I might have laughed. I might have pushed him away and ordered him out, called him appalling and many other angry things. But it was night-time. The air was heavy with secrets wanting to be kept, and I was glad he had come. In truth, it was more than that. I was ringing with desire. I wanted to be closer, closer still, to feel the thrumming of his heart under his naked skin, as if it were beating within my own breast. As his fingers touched and moved and rubbed, I pulled him closer still as I cried out. There was a release and I laughed at the terrible and sudden need, the joy of wanting more. I moved my body, tried to coax him on, before he tugged at what was left of his robe and came down hard onto and into me. There was pain and this time when I cried out, it was with dismay. But he put his hand over my mouth, told me not to be afraid, then when he was sure my noise was done, he stroked my head. It was all part of the remedy. I closed my eyes then, for he seemed no longer to care about my state of being, so I was silent as he pushed and heaved until at last, he fell, exhausted and spent, beside me.

He was still and silent for a while.

There was just the swell of his breathing body, the air blowing out of him, into him. I lay like stone in the dark, suddenly afraid even to twitch or try to make myself comfortable, lest I draw his attention. Blinking, I tried to listen to the crow on the roof, to all the usual noises of the things around me, but another reverberation seemed to bellow above all else, invading the sounds of my world: that slow, heavy breathing of the councillor. Suddenly, I found nothing exciting about him. His skin was sweaty, sour and dank in the heat. He was a man like any other, exhausted by the madness since the storm, and so strangely out of place in my dwelling, like an eagle in a lark's nest. How I wished I could cast a spell to make him disappear. He shifted then, moaned, and brought his mouth to my breasts, his tongue wet and warm as he licked, but I moved away. He laughed and his hand brushed up against my thigh, and he pushed his fingers between my legs. But I kicked and pushed him from my pallet. He was still for a moment, then he stood.

Don't say you wish me to leave? he said, almost in jest.

I do, I replied as honestly as I could. *There's no place for you here.*

There was no light to see, but I knew he was staring at me and that this was not the answer he'd expected. For a while he made no reply, and all I could do was wait and hope he'd heed my wishes, until at last he spoke again as he fixed himself.

Do not fret, he said, but his voice was cold now. *There'll be blood, but it's normal for a maid. Next time will be cleaner.* And he was gone.

It was late in the morning when the crow woke me with its bleating and flapping as it flew in through the unshuttered window. The Sun was painting lines through the air, making shapes across the bird's glossy back. I called out a greeting, telling it how beautiful it looked. One tiny pebble eye shone back at me as it cocked its head and clacked its beak, making me laugh so hard I had to hold my belly. The door was wide open, and a fresh and wonderful breeze lifted rushes and dust from the ground.

Sliding from my pallet, an unfamiliar soreness bloomed across my backside, my thighs and the places between, and I remembered the night. For that one waking moment, if I'd thought of it at all, I'd imagined it but a dream. I inhaled, rose quickly and cleaned the mess from between my legs. There was an uncommon aroma on my skin and in my hair. Traces of almond and jasmine, muddied by my usual woody scent of sweet oil. I pushed my hair, woven through with seashells and feathers, away from my face, tied it up with a rag, and dragged a cloth over each part of me, trying to ignore any residual foreign odours.

My body felt like a stranger.

I looked at my arms and legs, followed the familiar

patterns of hair and flesh, but couldn't find myself wholly there. The councillor had somehow erased bits of me, or maybe I'd done it myself for I apportioned no blame. The man had not been gentle, though, that was sure. Several bruises blossomed under the curve of my belly and across my thighs, fingermarks from elegant hands, like budding flowers. When I touched them, they were tender. But there was no sadness in my heart, no shame in my gut. In truth, I was in good spirits. Yet there was a flipping sensation in my stomach. It made me light-headed, and although I hadn't eaten for many hours, the thought of food left a sting of sickness.

Again I noticed a rattle when I took a breath, so prepared a strong tincture, rubbed it over my chest and shoulders and inhaled its potent vapours. It made my eyes water, but I could feel its goodness rushing into me like fresh sea air blowing about my ribcage and masking any unwanted aromas. Seeing no reason to miss my visit to Yemma and Zari, I bottled the tincture, knowing it would likely be needed in town, put it in my pouch and left.

Scene 2

The bottles of tincture in my pouch were heavy as they bounced at my hip. I smiled to myself, so wide my cheeks ached. How good it was to do good, how light and airy it made me feel. The heat of the past few weeks had finally broken, too. The relief was palpable, even the dusty earth beneath my feet seemed to sigh with it.

A melody came to me, so I stopped for a moment to listen to the chirruping grasshoppers. How lucky we are, I thought, to be surrounded by music, and hummed along as I continued on my way.

I am the daughter of night, I sang to the breeze. *The holder of gifts, the healer and granter of wishes. My father was of the Sun, but my mother was of the Moon.*

It was warm and pleasant.

There was a gentle movement of air.

As the crow hopped at my side, I believed it was doing a

merry dance. With an uplifted heart, I sang again, louder. Each note was heavy with gratitude, yet weightless. For in that moment, I had all I needed in the world. Thoughts of Afalkay the Beautiful were pushed from my mind, replaced by the landscape of my home, the life I was making as a healer. Unfathomably, if I did picture the councillor's face, I couldn't help but smile more, until my jawbone begged for release. Even so, I hoped never to be in his company again, and certainly not alone. He'd surely feel the same, so I had no reason to fret. No one need ever know of his one nocturnal visit to my dwelling. All was done with. Nevertheless, it was hard to ignore the new ache between my legs and across my hips. And that slight feeling of erasure lingered and nagged at me still. I told myself, again, not to worry. Every bird needs to shed a few old, heavy feathers now and then. To enable them not only to fly, but to soar.

And I was more than ready to lift into the air.

As we approached the lane to the market, there was a small crowd of townsmen and -women looking up toward the dunes. Surprised, I fumbled for my muslin and covered my eyes, tying it a little too tight. The gathered folk seemed excitable, speaking softly but with agitation, creating a low murmur on the breeze. It was almost beautiful, like Aeolian music. This time, I thought it best not to add my own song to the melody, so simply smiled as I approached. Several men were pointing in the direction of the dunes. When they saw me, hobbling towards them, grinning and waving, the tone of the crowd gradually changed into a quiver of hisses. It made me think of the snakes I'd teased with sticks as a child, and then as I neared them, there was a hush.

Suddenly nervous, my heartbeat quickened and pulsed at my throat. How could they know what had taken place in the depths of night in my own dwelling? It was impossible to think Afalkay the Beautiful had told anyone. He'd never risk such a thing.

With the crow marching at my side, I held my head high and made my way through the now silent throng. People stepped back, opening a path for us to pass through, which dissolved again behind us. A woman I vaguely recognised caught my eye and gave a weak smile. Taking it as a sign of kindness, an invitation, I stopped and told her I was looking for Yemma. But the man beside the woman yanked her arm and pulled her away. After a few steps he turned back, stopped briefly, and kicked dirt at the crow, causing it to scream defiance at him. The man rasped and spat on the ground before scuttling off, pulling the woman with him. My heart lifted toward that good wife, tripping over her skirts as she looked back. There was compassion on her face. I smiled at her, hoping it might be charm enough to alleviate some of the force with which her husband grasped her arm, and to let her know I could see her goodness and was thankful.

The crow jumped up to perch on my staff.

It pecked my hair and nuzzled my ear, and I stroked its feathery head, wondering if the woman, whose husband was so keen on kicking birds, had ever bought a Dreamstone.

Did she hide it under her bed to sate the desires of her sleeping hours? I hoped so, and whispered a glamour to keep her dreams vivid and joyous. Feeling emboldened, I considered following her, but Yemma's hand landed on my shoulder, and she ushered me briskly away, pushing me down toward the harbour lanes.

It was stifling inside Yemma's tiny dwelling. I swooned, and my empty belly growled. The old woman caught my elbow and helped me to sit on a low stool. It pained me to bend so low but I recognised her kindness and willingly took my place. Thankful for the care, I smiled as my friend gave me a bowl of cold broth.

Be nourished, she said, *for you must pay heed to my every word.*

I blinked compliance, took the smallest sip and tried not to wince as the bitter liquid slid down my throat.

In the deepest hours of the night, she told me, *there was much commotion at Zari's house.*

Fearful of what that might mean, I gasped. Yemma raised her hand for peace, instructing me not interject, that she might finish her tale. I respectfully complied.

Earlier in the evening, a sound was heard rolling through the town, she began. *Terrible it was, that's what folk were saying, and full of murderous anger. Everyone knew it to be the mountain lion, come back to do the mischief Atlas had once prevented.* The old woman shook her head and chewed on her bone pipe, clicking it between her few remaining teeth. *After all we've been through with the storm and the invaders, another threat was too much for most to take. For terror now runs through every home and heart. Did you not feel it, walking through the lanes?*

But what of Zari and the commotion you spoke of? I snapped, too anxious to be courteous. *Give me news, as I won't listen to fireside stories.*

Heed me, and you'll know all.

I sighed, nodded apologetically, and she went on.

You remember the old pregnant goat, the one we'd shorn the previous day to have hair for the girl's headdress?

I do, I said.

An old nanny like that, little wonder she was easily spooked, poor beast. As the Moon shone, she broke free of her ties, kicking and bleating, rolling her eyes and lolling her tongue like a thing possessed of a demon. It caused such a din men ran from their beds to see what the matter was and if aid was needed. But it was too late. The goat was rendered a lunatic. Demented by her own fear, they said, no matter how much I insisted it was old, too weak and sickly to be bearing kids and any number of influences might have caused her lunacy. But folks blamed the sound and scent of the lion, or spoke in terrified whispers of other unknown, demonic and evil forces.

Yemma sniffed and shook her head again.

And Zari? I asked, impatient now.

Be comforted, child. Mother and son rested well throughout the drama. Neither made a peep nor woke at all. Now let me continue, you must listen.

Again I nodded, and the old woman took a breath before going on with her tale.

Those who hadn't rushed into the night to witness the nanny in her distress, too scared themselves of the lion's roar to venture out, had at least heard the noise. But they ran from their homes this morning all right, with wails and cries for action, calling for blood as menfolk put themselves forwards for a hunting party.

Hunting? No! The lion has no interest in the town and its people. It's merely afraid of them, I protested. *No doubt it was lost, in need of help or looking for its cub.*

Aye, but fear is a powerful force, a mighty weapon, she replied. *I've gone too far, let me go back, as you must know all.*

Lowering my eyes in a promise to listen, I held on to the pot of broth in my lap.

I stayed the night at the house, she went on. *Not for the babe and mother, who as I said were sleeping like nesting birds, but for the girl. How she fretted for that old goat and bit at her fingers. I dared not leave her. And with Zari's husband having sent word he'd not be back at night-times while his wife was weak, it was all I could do. We found the nanny and brought her home, me and the girl. We did our best to give her comfort, but she frothed at the mouth like a mad thing and raged against us. Then she gave birth. Only the kid, having been thrust into the world in a moment of terror and before its time, was a twisted thing and never took a breath.*

I'm sorry to hear it. The girl must have been in some distress.

She was, but there was nought to be done but await the fisherman's return from the harbour, for he'd surely had word of the night-time calamity at his dwelling. And so it was. On seeing the dead kid and his faithful old nanny only half alive, rolling around in the bloodied straw, he fell into a fury, making his daughter sob and carry on in a terrible agitation. The goat was slaughtered, then, to save its pain.

When all was done – for his anger would not be contained – I took it upon myself to ban the man from his own home, sending him from whence he came until he could be calm, fitting and right.

I couldn't help but laugh, imagining this tiny woman, bone pipe clenched between her almost toothless gums, ordering the man away. Yemma did not smile. She grew quiet, only urging me to drink my broth. But it was too cold and pallid to swallow. I put the bowl on the floor and the crow happily plashed its beak around in the liquid, shaking its head and flashing its beady eyes. Again I laughed, for there was always joy in watching that bird.

How can you grin so? demanded Yemma. *There's no time for merriment. You must try to comprehend the damage this has done.*

The death of an animal for people as poor as Zari's husband and with a family and new babe was a terrible loss, I knew that, of course, but such upset seemed indulgent.

I'll bring the family a bolt of fine cloth with which they can procure two new and healthy young goats, I said, trying to keep my words light, kind and understanding.

Your gifts will never be accepted by that man. Have you no mind to what this means?

I looked to the crow, still making a mess of the broth, and shrugged. Yemma crouched by my side and placed a calloused hand on my knee.

They say you took goat hair from yesterday's shearing, she said, her voice soft now.

We did, and plenty of it. For the girl's headdress, I replied.

Folks are saying it was for you to put in a potion, to make a spell.

Again I shrugged, shook my head and carried on watching the crow.

Some believe you cursed the nanny. I had all hell on my hands through the night, men barging into the house, terrifying the girl, picking up pots of anything lying about as proof of devilry and shouting all manner of accusations.

I tried to stand, but being too tired and sore, raised my voice instead.

Are you sure Zari is well? Did anyone hurt her? And the child?

I've said twice already. She never woke. Nor did her babe. But do you heed me?

Yes. Some stupid people believe I cursed a goat with leafy broth and tea.

This is serious. Your mother would never have let this happen.

There was a choke in my throat. I grew hot and itchy under Atlas's wedding garb, which I'd seen fit to wear again. The crow caught my discomfort, stopped sploshing around in the bowl, cocked its head from side to side and moved closer, hopping onto my lap.

I'm not Atlas, I said, quietly. *She's gone, so I do my best without her guidance. Surely my cures prove I'm doing well, as well as my mother ever did and better. For my gifts are stronger.*

Yemma sighed and there was care in that breath, but I picked up my staff, coaxed the crow to rest upon it and, struggling to stand from the low stool, shuffled out into the stinking harbour lane. Yemma followed, speaking quick and low, buzzing about me like one of my bees, asking where I thought I was going and that I must hold my tongue and be careful who I looked at or what I did. When she saw I was making my way to Zari's house, she tried to grab my arms. But I wouldn't be stopped, and she wouldn't let me go alone.

Scene 3

We passed through the centre of the town, where the market should have been a long line of noise and colour, but all was sand and dust. None sat out on their blanket to wait for trade. Several small groups of townswomen stood around, and some of the older townsmen also gathered in huddles. I tried not to look at anyone but couldn't help glancing at the people there. With the heat now subdued and a gentle breeze lifting the ends of their tunics, I was glad, at least, to see that relief on all their faces. Some of the women stood back as I walked by, something like fear in their eyes, others gave me a half-smile and a nod. I felt those small acts of solidarity stronger than I'd ever perceived the distaste of those who turned their noses up at me, as if I stank of the cesspit.

At Zari's house, although Yemma begged me not to, without knocking I opened the door, and with the old woman still at my heels, slipped inside. The girl was alone

by the cooking pot. When we entered, she turned and
ran quickly to Yemma, throwing her arms around the old
woman, who stroked her, told her to be calm and that all was
well. But the girl looked at me suspiciously and frowned.
At least the fisherman wasn't there, I thought, when a noise
from Zari's chamber made us turn and gasp. Panicking,
before the young girl could open her snarling mouth to
protest, I threw the chamber door open.

Zari was awake, her wet eyes blinking through the gloom.
I could see she was soaked in sweat and shaking with fever.
Her breathing was nothing more than a heavy, painful
wheeze.

She wasn't alone.

My empty stomach lurched and if it hadn't been for my
steadying staff, I might have lost all balance. Standing beside
the marriage bed, holding Zari's sleeping babe in his arms,
was the unmistakeable figure of Afalkay the Beautiful. He
flinched when he saw me, but only briefly, then he raised an
eyebrow and smiled. Again I thought my legs, still aching
and bruised from his carelessness, might fall from under
me. Instead, I moved, as swiftly as I could, to be by Zari's
side. There she lay, helpless between me and the councillor,
floating on her large bed. Weak, struggling for breath, her
mouth opened and closed. Slowly then, as if made of something heavier than stone, she lifted her arms as if to heaven.

Both my angels are here, she rasped, painfully.

Even in sickness and distress, Zari had a look of serenity
about her. You are the angel, I thought, but there was no

time to reply. Trembling and stiff-fingered, I fumbled in the dark to take the potion from my pouch. When the bottle was in my grasp, I leaned over her shaking frame and held her head gently up so she could smell the contents. I whispered for her to breathe as deeply as she could, to take in the vapours as if they were air. My sweet young friend tried to inhale. I felt the deep rattle in her birdlike frame until she began to splutter, wrenching forth a coughing fit that seemed to shake the world. Suddenly aware of a commotion and shouting behind me, I spun around.

Witch!

With a voice as loud as thunderclaps, Zari's husband stood in the gloom of the chamber door, arm outstretched, staring, and pointing at me.

Move away from her, and take your devil with you.

I turned back to my patient, quickly applying the tincture to her temples. But before I'd finished, a great force fell upon me, and I was thrown to the ground.

I dropped the bottle.

It rolled and spilled, letting go its potent stink. Paying no attention to the violence or to the two men in the chamber, I crawled on my belly and reached to rescue the potion. The vessel was kicked away. A leather-shod foot shoved me onto my back and fell against my chest, pinning me down.

I'll have no more of your devilry here. Leave before I crush you like a beetle.

A heavy shadow flew across the chamber.

Afalkay the Beautiful was fleeing without a word, Zari's

babe still cradled in his arms. Extracting myself from the fisherman's foothold, whose threats were hollow enough to allow my freedom, I grabbed my staff and followed the councillor. Yemma held on to the girl as I pushed past, and with the crow flapping on my skirt tails, we rushed out into the day.

Where are you going with that child? I bellowed across the lane.

He did not stop nor look around.

The townspeople still standing about in small groups, awaiting a spectacle, gasped.

It's the babe she wants, someone cried.

Several voices began calling out; others joined them. Until disjointed words and accusations buzzed and swarmed.

Storm witch. Like her mother. Desert hag. Deformed lump. Murdered her father. Killed her dam. The crow's a devil. Feeds it her own blood. Suckles it on her dugs. Devilry. Crow queen. Witch. Witch.

Sycorax the witch.

Afalkay the Beautiful swiftly made his way down the lane towards the old stone steps. Exhausted, confused by all the shouting, I knew I'd never catch him. I watched with the crow as a length of soft green muslin waved gently behind him. The smell of sweet almonds lingered on the breeze, and the high squeal of the babe in his arms broke the air.

Something hard suddenly struck me in the back.

Winded, I yelped, and the crow screeched as I snapped around. Three young boys, just children, stood before me.

Two of them had stones nestled in their small hands; the other, a look of thrilled terror on his face, had his fists shoved into his mouth. I bawled at them, threw my arms up to shoo them away like ravens around a cherry basket. They shrieked and ran to the skirts of their waiting mothers, who'd watched in silence but now howled with the fires of hell at me until they moved away, cooing at their poor mites.

Left standing with the crow in the dust, I looked around at the now silent, staring faces of the townsfolk. Not knowing which way to turn to hide from so many pairs of eyes, I opened my mouth and let go a scream.

The pageant was done.

Townsmen snaked their arms gently around women and children, who craned their necks to look back as they slowly walked away, shaking their heads, disappearing into dwellings or up along the harbour lanes.

In a matter of moments, I was alone with the crow.

All was quiet.

Only the sound of distant waves remained.

Then the chatter of starlings began.

The birds appeared in soot-coloured clouds of beaks and feathers. They blackened the skies and hung on to the swaying, clattering bone branches of devastated trees.

I looked up.

It wasn't time for the birds to roost.

Their noise grew until I could stand no more and, resting my staff against my chest, I covered my ears. Such a darkening could only be a sign. Death lay in their message, that much I understood. I cried out to thank them, and as quickly as they'd appeared, the birds took off. I watched as they created shadow patterns, inky wheels whirling and dancing in the great blue of the sky. Until, at last, they flew to the horizon and were gone. Cold air crawled along my spine. I shuddered.

Yemma floated towards me. I turned and saw the young girl behind her, watching from her doorway. The old woman touched me lightly on my arm. I winced. The crow jumped up to rest on my shoulder, and on the ground I saw the thing that had struck me. It was a beautiful pebble, shiny and colourful, just big enough to fit comfortably into a child's hand. Even through my muslin its patterns were gem-bright. They swirled, as if in recognition of its maker. I wanted to pick it up, rescue it from the brutality we'd been subjected to. But I was exhausted and almost bent double with pain. All I could do was stare at the magnificent little stone and remember the child who made it.

How I missed her.

I dropped my staff. Yemma grabbed it. She put her arms around me, and somehow, with the crow screaming as it flew around our heads, we made our way back to my dwelling.

At the door, Yemma hesitated as she looked inside. Only then did I see how I'd been living, with little care to myself, as I'd worked to save Zari. The general filth of life had left its stink. Along with it, a crust of bird shit splattered the floor and walls, and it had been some time since I'd swilled out my own slops. I looked at the bloody mess on my bed, hung my head and sobbed.

I'll stay with you now, she said. *We'll make it right.*

Scene 4

Yemma replaced the soiled covers on my pallet with clean muslins. I hadn't used them since Atlas washed them with her olive soap and folded them into a basket. The fresh smell caught at my throat, and a thousand pictures of my mother flew through my mind. The old woman shook and beat my goatskins, so I'd have a more comfortable bed to sleep upon, and there I lay, watching my friend.

Dragging everything outside to air in the wind-battered garden, Yemma even pulled my altar out into the Sun, complete with its beeswax candles that melted in the heat. When the place was empty, she scrubbed the walls and ground around me. I stayed immoveable in my bed, my heart beating its gratitude in heavy thuds. Using salt and olive soap, she then carefully washed all my precious things – sea-smoothed pebbles, fishbones found on the beach, feathers, mother-of-pearl, seed pods, and my pots and bottles – and shook out the bolts of cloth I'd abandoned in a corner, where they'd been left to the mercy of rot and damage. When all was cleaned and dried by the Sun, she neatly replaced everything, lay new grasses and lit bowls of mountain thyme. The place was as lovely and fragrant as it had ever been when I was a child.

Even with so pleasant a home, my mind was confused as my body raged. Agony left me helpless, breathless and sleepless. At least the wheeze had gone from my chest. My tincture had worked. It gave me hope for a good future, something to believe in.

Belief is everything, I heard my mother's voice whisper through the walls.

I watched the Moon come and go through the open door.

I saw sunrises and sunsets.

Nothing much happened.

Life was calm, and Yemma's presence, rustling about the cooking pot or sitting on the low stool, sucking at her pipe, was a blessing. Though she would not allow the crow inside at night, and only for short spells during daylight, so I wouldn't fret, there was a quiet complicity between us. The bird perched in the window anyway, watched our goings-on, and when dusk fell, I heard it on the roof pecking out messages of comfort and love.

Yemma nurtured and fed me.

There were figs from the garden, tubers and mushrooms from the earth, and leaves from the wild bushes on the path to the dunes. Every day there was cool, fresh water she'd pulled from the well at the back of the dwelling. So much more refreshing than the stagnant jugs I'd kept around the place, speckled with the floating bodies of spiders and flies.

In the evenings I'd ask Yemma about her life. Bit by bit she told me her history, so that, finally, I knew my friend. Like my mother, she'd come from the desert. But Yemma arrived at the town when still a girl. Her own mother had died, leaving her father with a thirst for adventures new. Moving away from everything he'd known seemed a fair way to forget his loss. Not even a year had passed since they'd made a home in the harbour town when he too caught a fever and died. To save herself, as young as she was, she married a sailor whom she saw little of (*Praise the heavens*, she cackled). Nevertheless, the couple had two boy babes who lived to be children but never to be men, and when her husband was lost at sea, Yemma became a wise woman. It's what her mother had done in the desert, and even as a child she knew the way to a good birth, the consequences of a bad one. Not being from a family of gifted desert women meant she had no powers of charm or glamour. But she'd learned to make a few herbal remedies at her mother's knee, and could use them well with the women she tended. Eventually she'd married again. This time it was a love match. He was much older than her, with white whiskers and a rounded belly, but it had been a passionate marriage. They had three children: one girl who died when still a babe, and two strong sons who'd lived to see manhood. Somehow, for reasons she never cared to uncover, there was bad blood between her boys. Eventually they killed each other in a brawl. Both were run through with blades; neither survived for more than a few hours after the skirmish. Her husband, an old man by then, was broken-hearted, and the loss was too much for him. Once again, Yemma was on her own.

Her work had always been more than just a way to earn coins, so she married herself to it and carved her way into town life. That's how it was until, one day, when out gathering herbs, she met another desert woman, freshly landed and desperate with love. Realising at once that this was a gifted woman, Yemma felt sure their meeting was more than mere chance. When she asked the young woman her name, she told her it was Atlas, *like the mountains*.

I loved to listen to Yemma, and would ask again and again for her to tell me about the day she met my mother. In the mornings we craved the feel of flatbread in our mouths and the sharp sting of salty cheese on our tongues. So along with Yemma's life story, we'd spend hours describing the taste of this or that dish to each other until our bellies growled and we'd lie on our backs like upturned beetles, moaning for food. Even so, we did not go without nourishment. Each morning and evening as she chewed on her dry pipe, Yemma administered the warm broth she'd cooked up, full of spices from my pots.

Yemma never once shrank from the gems in my head, even as she'd untied my muslin when she first put me to bed. She'd only looked for a moment, flinching almost imperceptibly, before going about the business of making me comfortable. It was a relief, as finally I didn't have to hide from my friend. I believed those were happy days.

But this is not the complete truth.

Love and nostalgia make an easy mist, lying thick upon the things we'd rather not see. During that time, the weight of fear and dread lay upon us, always. It was not a thing we could see or taste, nor was it a subject of conversation. But it pulled us down with each breath we drew. It pushed at us as we tried to live out the days in our tiny space in the world. And it struck us with a silent terror that showed in the strain of our mouths as we laughed, and in the creases forever on our brows. Each rustle of a leaf from behind the door, each movement of air or cormorant cry, made our hearts leap, our hands reach for our throats in anticipation of treachery. We listened for footsteps, for surely it was only a matter of time before the townsmen would come with ropes and ever more accusations of witchcraft and evil deeds. There wasn't a moment I did not expect to be accosted in my bed. But there was nowhere safe to go, and at least I was home.

For a while, at night we heard the distant roar of the mountain lion. When its cry suddenly stopped, I looked to Yemma for a sign of hope. She shook her head in the firelight. I knew then, even though it had done them no wrong, the townsfolk had finally hunted and killed the beast. I knew it was wrong to wish it, but I hoped, in its fight, that the beautiful creature of grace and majesty, had at least found some revenge.

When I was able to sit, I attempted to stand.

Although Yemma waved her hands and fussed, I told her not to hold me back. I could bear my pain. Still, I needed her help to dress. Not in my mother's heavy wedding garb, which Yemma had shaken out and hung on the trees in the garden to air, but back in my young girl's shift, washed in olive soap, then dried and bleached in the Sun. My friend tied my hair away from my face, brushing it through her fingers to catch any crawling thing that might have snuck in, just as Atlas had once done.

With my staff in my uninjured hand, my other arm around Yemma's small but solid frame, at last the day came when we made our way down to the dunes. The crow circled above us, showing the majesty of itself in flight, and we spoke about the bees. They desperately needed tending. I promised to show Yemma how to smoke the hives and collect the honey. It was a fine treat to see her excitement. Her wrinkled face had the look of the girl she'd once been as she smiled and bounced on her toes, for she loved the sweetness of honeycomb. As we reached the Wishing Tree and looked out over the dunes to the sea, back to cerulean blue as if the violence of the storm had never happened, all seemed calm. Any thoughts of the dead still lying in the depths, pearls for eyes, their bones nibbled by fishes, were gone.

My heart leapt to see the brine again, to taste sea salt in my mouth and feel its crust on my skin, and then it was I who was like a child. I'd had an idea to go down to the sea and bathe my feet, but Yemma wouldn't hear of it, which left me sighing as, jealous of the sand and pebbles, I watched each lapping wave.

Thoughts of Afalkay the Beautiful had gone from my mind. But my sex still felt bruised, and I would sorely have loved to wash any lingering trace of him from my body in the salty sea. Even then, I felt sure he'd left something indelible there. I couldn't tell Yemma any of it. I felt no shame, yet something rotten burned in my breast. When I pictured Zari's babe, screaming in his arms, there was a tug in my heart. I pushed the thoughts away. There was no use in fretting about Zari, not until I was in a better state. Instead, I enjoyed the sea sounds and looked to the horizon with the warm breeze on my face.

The sky was bright, the sand as golden as the Sun. We stood for a long while, each in contemplation, until Yemma's belly moaned so loudly it seemed to echo through the dunes. Laughter burst from our mouths until our eyes blinked away tears. There's no joy in hunger, though. Thin broth was all well and good, but we couldn't sustain ourselves on figs and flavoured water for much longer. For myself, I'd lost any appetite. The mere thought of solid food sent a swell of sickness through me. Now I suddenly reeled when she mentioned olives and goat's cheese. Seeing my pallor, Yemma insisted we turn back home. We could always go to the sea again tomorrow, she said, maybe to venture further out and along the shore, look for pebbles and shells and other precious things.

Before we left, I embraced the Wishing Tree. Yemma

laughed, saying, *You are so very like Atlas.* I loved her for it, and for the first time I sensed it, too. My mother living within me. Under my skin. In every beat of my heart and trickle of blood. Sunny was also there, shining above and all around me. I closed my eyes to catch my thoughts, then said them aloud so I wouldn't forget:

My father was of the Sun, which is the giver, not of glamours but of sweetness and light. When I feel its heat on my skin, he is all without. My mother was of the Moon, full of enchantment and secret magic, the seer in the dark, the healer. She is all within.

At last I understood a great and wonderful truth. I turned to Yemma, my voice faded to no more than a whisper.

I'm more than a receiver of gifts, I said. *I'm the perfect balance of dark and light.*

She smiled.

We returned as we'd come, with me leaning on my friend, but now the crow marched alongside us. In our communion we'd almost forgotten our worries, the cruelties of the townspeople, the ache between my legs and the fingermarks on my skin. I thought, then, that maybe Yemma might leave her rotting dwelling on the harbour lane to stay with me always, so we might live as Atlas had wanted, away from society, making remedies and candles, collecting honey, doing good when and where we could, keeping our own business, free from torment.

A smell of smoke drifted on the warm breeze. Yemma and I looked at each other and craned to see back toward the beach.

Perhaps a warning fire at the harbour, though I see no ships on the horizon, Yemma said. *Probably some foolish ceremony to ward off danger. It's strange, not knowing what's happening back there.*

I shrugged, so used to being out of kilter with the life of the town. I didn't even know that people lit fires for protection. But then, I knew so little of the customs, fears and superstitions of the townsfolk.

We walked on in silence.

The odour grew deeper, the air thicker. My eyes began to sting and water as I blinked. Curls of soft grey smoke drifted around us. Motes of ash floated past and landed on our faces. We started to lose sight of the path. When Yemma began to cough, the crow lifted its beak, squawked and took to the air. After a moment, my old friend got her breath back, and we started to hurry on home. A panic was rising in my gut. That's when I noticed the strips of cloth. Torn, cut to pieces and tattered, caught on the dry branches of trees and fluttering in bushes all around me. More and bigger remnants sat in small heaps on the ground. I picked up a piece of rag and recognised it.

Rubbing the thick green fabric of what had been my mother's wedding costume between the fingers of my uninjured hand, I felt a fury so intense I believed I might burst into flames. I cursed and wished a thousand plagues on the town and its hateful people, a scourge so terrible, so full of agony that none would survive.

I heard the fire before I saw it or felt its heat.

I'd lost sight of Yemma, but her voice came rushing

through the now dense smoke, shouting over the sound of roaring, blazing flames. I lifted my staff, the wind changed, and my path cleared for a moment. Struggling, shuffling, dragging myself along as quickly as I could, suddenly there it was: my house, engulfed.

The fire was infernal and wild.

Flames seemed to dance in every direction as they rose into the air, celebrating, like prisoners suddenly released from a dungeon. Although I couldn't see her, I could hear Yemma shouting. Her voice wasn't alone. Someone was answering her calls in deep, urgent tones.

I thought of the bees.

Dropping my staff, I fell to the ground, thinking it quicker to crawl than to shuffle. The hives were gone. Not taken by fire but smashed by heavy hands and unjust rage. A gulp of hot, smoke-fetid air caught and lodged in my chest. I was sure I'd die for lack of breath. The thought was almost a blessing. For how could I live when such violence had been set against the creatures my father had taught me to nurture? As I opened my mouth, air rushed down my gullet and I screamed my fury. But pain in my lungs from breathing in the acrid murk wrenched me down further. I landed on my belly, wormed myself towards the door of my burning home, but could not enter. The fire was too fierce, the flames too hot, barring my way like an angry beast.

My injured hand sang with the memory of flame and heat. I didn't care. I wanted to be with my things. Those precious objects, which had become friends and family, had given me a sense of belonging, and a channel for my desperate affections. I thought of my altar, created for me by Atlas; of all my remedies sitting neatly in their pots; of my bed pallet made by my father for my mother when her belly was big and full of me – and I couldn't bear to be without them. I would have been happy in that moment to have thrown myself into the fire, to have been made ash and cinders alongside all my useless treasures. I already knew the pain of flames. I was prepared to take it. I tried again to approach, but the heat scorched my hair, my eyelashes and skin, and try as I might, I could go no further. I screamed at the flames then, begged them to come to me, to take my flesh and bones, begged them to consume me, not to leave me in a world so full of cruelty it would see me homeless and alone, but their only reply was to beat me back. How I hated myself for being too weak to throw myself to the fire.

Suddenly I was pulled away.

A deep voice shouted over the blazing racket of flames.

Cinders flew all around, setting light to our clothes before long fingers patted them out and they sizzled on our skin.

When at last I turned around, I saw who had hold of me.

Afalkay the Beautiful was on his knees, dragging me, still shouting, sobbing and kicking in protest, from the conflagration to where Yemma sat on the ground, swaying back and forth, whispering some private prayer under her breath.

What have you done? I screamed at the councillor, hitting out, pummelling his chest and face. *How have I ever injured you?*

He caught my arms and held me, tight, at each wrist. I thought of how he'd rubbed his elegant fingers between my legs, the rough feel of his chin and the wet slither of his tongue, of how he'd moved above me and into me, and of the thatch of hair around his sex, warm and soft on my belly. Now all I wanted was to spit in his face, but my mouth was as dry as the desert.

I had no hand in this, woman, he said.

Reeling and sobbing, my throat already raw, I screamed again and again until I was too exhausted to continue, and dropped into Afalkay the Beautiful's lap. We stayed like that for a while, watching the fire and the smoke.

There was nothing left to fight for.

Why did you come here? I croaked at last without moving to look at him.

I came to bring news, and to help you, if possible.

Help? Yes, you are so very good at helping me, councillor, I managed to say. Then, looking up, *Who did this?* I asked.

I don't know. They were gone when I got here.

Barbarossa? Did he order my destruction?

Never — though he has returned, and I'll inform him of this. He'll find the culprits.

I'll destroy them first, I growled, through heavy breaths, choking and coughing. *Crush them like they've done to my hives. Don't think I can't.*

He began to stroke my scorched hair and, horrified, I jerked away.

I'm sorry, he said.

I didn't know which of his wrongs he was sorry for. It was at his suggestion, young and ignorant as I was, that I had given auguries and predictions to the barbaric Barbarossa, knowing full well if I was wrong or inept it would mean my punishment or death. Such a thing was nothing less than cruel. For the rest, I'd never felt shame at wanting him; after all, why shouldn't I have the same desires as anyone else? But there was nothing right and correct in him coming to me the way he did. Was it for his own amusement, then, that he'd watched me and used me? I could see no other reason. No, there was no magic in that word *sorry*, no poetry or power. It could undo nothing of what had come to pass since he'd come for me in the rain at the market, smiling and smelling of sweet almond oil. Every bad thing that had happened to me stemmed from that moment, and I felt my own foolish complicity in it.

Yemma stopped her murmuring and slid forwards.

She pulled me, like a rag, toward her, and took all my weight onto her breast. She held me as she began to sway again, backwards and forwards. Then she started singing. Her voice was gruff, but the words, although strange, were familiar to me. They were in the language of my mother. I wanted to look at her, to show my gratitude, but I was too tired and broken. I let her rock me, and tried to lose myself in her growling song, charmless, but from the place of my foremothers. Then she stopped abruptly and turned to Afalkay the Beautiful.

Go away, councillor, she said.

I have news. There are things you must know, especially now. I can help.

Go, she said again.

This time, he nodded and stood.

The fire was still burning behind him. It cast his shadow, long and narrow over the singed ground. Yemma sucked at the few teeth in her mouth. She was missing her pipe. The old woman squinted up to the large man looming over us, shabby now his good clothes were charred and blackened.

Understand, she said to him. *I know what you are.*

He snorted as he turned, and we watched him walk away, disappearing like a ghost into the smoke-filled air.

Scene 5

Gone the walls, built by my father's gentle hands.

Gone the matted ground my mother fussed over with broom and fresh grasses.

Gone my altar.

Gone my pallet.

Gone the echo of each life lived under the protection of the roof.

Gone the roof.

Gone the smell of wax and honey, sweet and deep.

Gone the sleepy buzz of bees.

Gone, hummed the wind.

Gone, sang the sea.

Gone.

Flames reflected in our eyes as we sat quietly, watching the fire spit and lap like a starved dog hungry for every scrap of air, turning the last pieces of my life to ashes. Each plume of smoke diminished me. Soon, I thought, there'd be nothing left of my bodily self but a trace of bones under my filthy shift. Wanting to escape but with no will or muster to move, I closed my eyes in the hope I could lose myself in the darkness there. A sickness was growing in my belly, making my head sway. It moved up to my throat. I swallowed and wished myself away again.

There was no magic to be had.

I had nowhere to go.

The day ebbed as we lay there.

Eventually the flames grew less intense. When we heard the familiar *caw-caw* of the crow, felt the shadow of its wings cross our faces, I was so filled with relief to see it, I sobbed. It swooped down by my side, shook its head and lifted its beak to baulk at the final sparks of flickering fire, sending spears of love through my heart.

The breeze changed.

The fire was almost out.

Seeing a clearer picture of the destruction now, everything was cinders. Still, I looked hard at the scene, searched with my tired eyes for something to be saved. And there in the embers, in the smoking ashes, was a pile of grey pebbles. I slid, then crawled toward the smoking ashes. Yemma opened an eye and went to call out but stopped before the words could come. With great effort, I pushed myself up. Crawling at first, I managed to stand, unsupported, where the door of my dwelling had been.

Look, I called to Yemma. *The ground is glowing.*

Scorching heat rose up as if from hell itself. Lifting my chin to the dying Sun, I pulled down its paternal strength.

Fire must be met with fire, I whispered to the remnants of the furnace, before placing first one foot, then the other, onto the red-hot embers.

I heard Yemma yelp behind me, saw the sparks rise beneath my feet from the orange underbelly of the grey ash as I took another step. But I didn't fret, nor did I scream out. I sang, softly. For, now I believed in the strength of my Gift, the beauty of my magic. My song would render the ground of clinker and cinders as cold as stone. The soles of my feet would neither scorch nor blister. I walked with purpose over to my pile of pebbles, enjoying the strange, cool sensation underfoot, drawing strength from each shaky step. Bending with some difficulty then, I gathered the stones, still hot from the fire, into the skirt of my shift and made my way back to Yemma.

The old woman frowned.

They were just rocks: smooth, collected from the beach, and left in a basket for a time when I might brush them with my feather.

I smiled for a moment, remembering the delight I would have had watching their colours appear. Then a sigh pushed its way through my body and twisted my mouth. Now the pebbles would be forever grey, their hearts closed, locked into the stone by fire. But they were mine and I wanted them with me. I tied and knotted the pebbles into the skirt of my shift and held the heavy bundle under my arm, leaving my legs bared to the world. I didn't care. What did acts of social immorality matter now? What did they ever matter?

I found my staff on the ground nearby and Yemma stood, readying herself for whatever journey we would endeavour to take next. But I told her she must go home, back to her own dwelling. She argued, and refused to leave me. Even the crow lent its voice to her cause, but I was stern, and insisted. If she went back to town without me, I explained, the townsfolk would not molest her. Their suspicion and anger were toward me, not an old woman who'd lived among them for longer than most could remember. A wise woman who had brought them and their children into the world. The good wife who'd slapped a first breath into them and buried their babes when there was nothing else to be done. No matter that she'd come to them from the desert, as Atlas had done; she, at least, was one of them. A townswoman.

Exhausted, she eventually agreed, and I watched with the crow as she started down the track towards the town. Hobbling, she was stooped and slow in her movements. My friend had never looked so small and huddled, so old and alone. Wanting more than anything to protect her, and without knowing what to do or how to do it, I whispered a charm of safe keeping. How I hoped, as the words left my lips, that the Gift would serve me.

Believe, I told myself. *Believe.*

Then I saw my spell appear before me; gasped as I watched it spin and twist around Yemma like leaves on a breeze, each whispered word a small piece of armour as she plodded on.

I felt it, too. A force, a magic, a spark of joy through the misery; a power. How beautiful it was. How good. Perhaps, just for a moment, I even smiled. When at last Yemma disappeared into the dying light, with the crow at my side, we made our way through the dunes and down to the beach.

My spirit was strangely calm, as if there were no space left in me for anger (I'd learned from my father that fury was a beast I couldn't fight and win. To let it in for too long would only see me rip apart). Still, my eyes were as heavy as my heart was sad, my legs so weak I tripped as I shuffled along. More than anything I needed to rest, so turned my thoughts to practical things.

The mighty red-whiskered Governor was the only person who could protect me from the fear and violence of the townsfolk. Somehow, I needed to get to Barbarossa.

Scene 6

When I reached the shore, I stood for a while looking out to the familiar horizon. The wind swept over me, gave voice to the whispering waves. They spoke of my childhood, told tales of happy days. I was still holding the bundle of stones under my arm, warm within the fabric of my shift (I thought of them as Firestones now). They were a comfort, but heavy, and my back ached more than ever. I wondered, then, if my past had been but a dream, easily bought for coins at the market, nothing more than a few secret utterances murmured through ancient sorcery into a hard pebble and hidden under a child's bedtime covers.

I opened my eyes as wide as I could, remembering how they were the colour of noontide skies over a sparkling sea, felt the salt sting hit them. There was a keening of seabirds and something else crying from beneath the waves. I thought I heard my mother's voice calling from the water.

She howled her need for me, wailed her loneliness. The desire to be pulled in until I was nothing but another drowned thing, weighed down by the stones in my dress, almost overpowered me. It was all I could do not to fall into the spume. How cunning old Neptune was, to wrap me in Atlas's song, siren-like and gentle.

But I knew she did not rest beneath the waves. I'd not let him have me.

I stepped back.

I felt with my feet for drier sand, until there it was, slipping between my toes, and I was safe from any sea glamour, or the vagaries of my own exhausted mind. There was no point to self-destruction. I'd not follow my mother down such a path. In truth, more than anything at that moment, I wanted to live. More than that. Even with all that had come to pass, as alone as I was, I wanted to thrive.

As the Moon rose, a swell of cold crept from sea to land. It slid over me like a silken coat, but how barbed it was, how sharp its teeth. The shivering took me by surprise, shaking me so violently I thought I'd been taken by a sickness. The crow flapped about, pushed me with its big beak in the direction of the only shelter on the beach. As much as I was filled with a dread of the place, and retched at the memories of Sunny's drenched corpse laid out on the covered rocks, I needed sanctuary, so started toward the sea caves.

The wind had picked up, making it harder than ever to walk, and still I wouldn't discard my heavy bundle of pebbles. I clung to it like a child with her poppet, something so beloved it must never be abandoned, no matter how it hampered me. With my hand hooked around my staff, I managed to drag myself across the beach. The crow had flown on ahead, and I could hear its cries, hurrying me on through the moaning sea-wind.

The Moon was high, the prick of a pin in a black vastness, making the night bitter, and dense. I saw no stars, only a thin sliver of pale light emanating from the void. It seemed to point my way. I pulled myself forwards, but my back was bent, and before long I was on my knees. Still I pushed on, dragging my legs through the sand.

It was useless.

I lay down and closed my eyes, feeling sure death would not be far off.

I cursed it.

But then hands were upon me.

They lifted me as easily as a heap of rags, and before I could fathom what was happening, I was carried to the rocks.

Once in the cave, Afalkay the Beautiful undid the knot in my shift. I felt the bundle loosen as my pebbles tumbled to the ground, making pleasant crick-cracking sounds as they landed on the damp rock, and a sudden lightness took me. As he went to lay me down in the very place my father's corpse had waited for its shroud, I cried out. The councillor hummed words I didn't hear as he continued to put me to my rest, like a babe in its crib. Shocked to find it was not the cold smack of rock that greeted me, but the smooth feel of close-woven blankets, I softened. In moments I was wrapped in delicate threads. My cheek wanted to bury itself into the weave, feel the comfort and warmth. But recovering myself, I baulked, and demanded to be helped to sit. I'd not lie before that man again. He complied.

A familiar smell pulled at my heart, causing such confusion I almost cried out again. The cave was flickering with the orange light of many candles, scattered around, hissing in the dampness. The melting wax sang of my lost bees and hives. Of the many hours spent rolling the cire into sticks for market. Of the grease I'd work into my sore fingers. Of the sleepy hum of the insects as I worked my father's smoker. Of all that was lost. I looked down to my pebbles, afraid to lose sight of the only things left in the world that truly belonged to me. Beside them were two baskets. One was heaped with fabric, clothes and covers. The other had a feast of flatbreads, olives, skins of water, and cheese. My stomach lurched and I reached for the food, but the councillor flew to my side before I could grasp a morsel. He passed me chunks of flatbread, tearing them into manageable pieces that I grabbed and shoved too quickly into my mouth. He held my head as he gave me water and told me to sip. It was cool, sweet and freshly pulled. I guzzled, choked and spat out a mouthful of slop. He helped me to sit higher, with a straighter back, and wiped away the mess from my chin. After I'd caught my breath, I nodded thanks.

I thought this was where you'd come, he said. *I brought clothes.*

I looked at him, unable to find my voice and unsure how to respond.

You must be frozen, he went on, pulling out a garment, feeling a piece of it between his fingers. *See? They're fine.*

I almost laughed.

What good was fine clothing to me?

But I was shivering and grateful, so nodded again.

Struggling under the blanket I'd been swaddled in, I pulled my shift – now no more than a filthy, stinking rag – over my head and dropped it by the baskets. The finely woven covers slipped like water to my waist. I didn't care about my nakedness, but the man's eyes flicked over my breasts in the dancing light before he helped to lift the fine tunic over my head, and to settle it into place on my shoulders. It was even softer than the blankets, with deep sleeves and a skirt that rested around my ankles. I stroked the cloth.

Your wife's? I croaked, finding to my surprise that I could speak.

She has more than she needs, he said.

We sat for a moment. Only then did I recognise the baskets he'd brought.

It was you who left the food at my door, after the sandstorm took my father and mother, I gasped. *Why?*

It's strange, even to me, how I noticed you when you were little more than a girl, tripping at your mother's heels, small breasts blooming on your chest. I believe you enchanted me. He laughed. *I remember imagining my fingers untying the muslin from around your eyes. I couldn't have you starve to death just as I was reaching for you.*

I was about to lash out, to slap and kick the arrogance

from the man, when I saw the crow, marching around the rocks, pecking between the guttering candles, and a tightness released from my chest.

I have news, he offered, his eyes sparking in the candlelight.

From Barbarossa?

Yes. But there are things you must know first. They won't be easy to hear.

He still held the sleeve of the tunic between his fingers as it rested at my wrist. His arm brushed the scars of my injured hand as he again rubbed the cloth, as if he were a merchant testing wares at the market. I moved gently away, almost expecting him not to let go. But he allowed the garment to fall from his grasp.

No news can hurt me now. I've nothing left to lose.

He looked at the crow and lifted his brow. *There's always something*, he said quietly, and panic rose like bile to my throat.

Yemma? I gasped, and tried to stand, but my strength failed me.

The old woman is in no danger. She's home and well.

He leaned toward me, pushed my shoulders down and started to stroke my leg through the fine weft of his wife's borrowed garb. I flinched and pulled away, quickly this time, pulling the fabric tightly around my thighs, and pressing my back into the cave wall.

And Zari? I asked.

Afalkay the Beautiful briefly turned away.

The strange light in the cave caught the hairs on his chin,

making them gleam a vibrant rich red. The side of his face shone like a crescent Moon in summer, before he looked back, wetted his lips with his tongue and shifted closer to me.

I couldn't escape him.

The rocky walls of the cave were all about me.

I pushed further into them, felt keen edges snag the soft cloth of the fine tunic. I would have pushed my flesh into those rocks at that moment if only I could have done so. I'd have locked myself into the very fabric of the cave walls with a glamour, had I the wits to conjure one. Anything to avoid his closeness. There was a terrible silence between us, though he was so near I could feel his breath blowing in warm, rhythmic gusts across my nose and mouth. I thought he would not answer me, and my ears filled with the void, as thick and acrid as the smoke from my burning home. When at last he spoke, his voice was almost kind, but there was an edge, like the sharpened blade of a dagger, that might sing as it slit to cleave a body in two.

She was weak and ill after the birth of—

No! I screamed in his face.

He did not flinch, nor did he move away. But his eyes moved over my face as he spoke. Checking. Inspecting.

There's an illness in the town, a fever. After the storm, many have been taken with it. People can't breathe, they wheeze and seem to drown in the very air about them. Some call it sorcery. And Zari . . . she was never going to survive much longer after the birth anyway.

He looked into my eyes and blinked once before continuing.

She was too weak to fight, he said again. *There was no hope.*

At last he moved back. He shook his head as if he were regretting no more than the loss of his best honey pot.

I could have saved her, I spat. *She thought you an angel, but you're the very devil.*

He snarled at me, but in it was the satisfied look I'd first seen at the harbour.

Stay your anger, it does you no good. Only know, you do not grieve alone. Never have I known such sweetness as that dear girl. How she loved me.

Instinctively, I felt for my mother's knife at my hip, but it was another thing lost to me. Afalkay the Beautiful saw the gesture. I couldn't be sure, but I thought a trace of a smile curled across his mouth. He snorted.

She was mad with her womb before I saved her from its torture, he explained. *I concede, I had desires; I am but a man, after all.* And as he said it, the smile grew into a smirk. *I helped her, and she showed her gratitude in many wonderful ways, not least by giving me another son.*

Where is he? I growled, the image of the babe's face suddenly pulling at my guts.

Cared for.

The councillor shifted along the rock, allowing me room to pull away from the cave wall. A quiet moan guttered from my throat. My voice was weak with exhaustion, rasping from the inhaled smoke, but I'd not be silenced.

You stole him and left her to die.

She had no milk. None would nurse the child after what happened with the old goat, lest they be cursed themselves. For since the storm, they see curses everywhere.

A look of triumph crossed his face.

I swayed, my eyes heavy with fatigue, but I forced them open, determined to look him in the eye.

Are you attempting to put blame my way, sire?

But he did not, or would not, answer, only continued to tell me how heroic and selfless he was.

The boy was dangerously undernourished; had my wife not taken on the task, he would have died. You should be thankful for that. As plain and witless as she is, my wife's a good woman.

You put your seed in an innocent young woman and it destroyed her, I spat.

Unlike you, Zari was full of joy and gratitude. Now, enough!

No! You took what you wanted and discarded her like a piece of fish skin.

What would you have me do? Women are such a torment. Even a twisted wretch such as you. Look how you made me follow and seek you out. You were so desperate for my attention, so in need of me to give sustenance to your dried-out womb. The fair sex is a scourge on the lives of men, he said.

You did not care for Zari. Not for her life, nor her death.

You know nothing of what you speak.

I know everything.

Enough, I said! What's done is done.

He stood; so suddenly, I jumped and winced.

As he paced around the cave, the flickering orange light danced in time with his movements. I thought maybe a flame might catch the cloth of his coat; there was a charm on my tongue, but I'd had enough of fire, enough of burning and destruction.

When he stopped and turned to me again, his face glistened as he pushed a hand through his uncovered hair. There was a pleading look on his face, a heavy furrow to his brow, and I couldn't fathom what emotions now took him.

I've brought all this to you, he said, looking around the cave at the baskets and candles, *and still you are as hard as the ancient stone you sit upon.*

He threw himself before me, kneeling upon the rocks.

What must I do to soften you? he begged.

Leave me to my peace, I answered in a whisper.

Springing to his feet again, he wheeled around and laughed as if moonstruck.

That I should be shunned by such as you!

His voice echoed around the cave, the words melting into one another as he continued to rave and laugh.

Oh, that I'd meet my match in one so bent of body! I should mould you like clay, you should whimper at my every word, yet you snarl and bark like some rabid dog and turn away. The heavens have played a fine trick on me.

I never asked for your attentions.

You're an ungrateful, foul slut, he shouted, and his voice echoed around the cave.

No. I'm grateful for the food and clothes, but I've nothing to give in return. All I have left in this world are grief and sadness. You brought them upon me when you came to find me at the market, you forced them upon me when I sat trembling before Barbarossa. Now they're mine to keep.

Afalkay the Beautiful whirled around, and his coats flew about him in a display of absurd finery in that damp, rocky place, as he growled with impatience.

These things! These cast-offs! he raged, pulling a piece of fabric from the basket. *You're grateful for* them? He laughed again, throwing his head back.

The crow had stayed silent and still in the shadows until then, but now it flapped and swooped around the cave, taking its lead from the councillor, who stomped after it, threatening to break its wings, before it flew out into the night. There'd been too much misery to enjoy the ludicrousness of the moment; all I could do was watch and despair at the vile comedy playing out before me. When the crow was gone, the councillor calmed himself, breathing heavily and pushing his damp hair away from his face.

For weeks, months, years I've watched you, such a weird creature, your eyes bound, and then with that bird at your side. I saw how you'd look for me. Of course, you did, your virgin breast trembling at the thought of a mere glance from me. When I heard you were going to the harbour, selling prophecies, like a whore sells her cunt, I admit the intrigue was too much.

His eyes flashed.

I did no harm, I said. *I was of help there.*

But he wasn't listening.

With news of the invasion, he continued, *I thought providence had intervened and I could finally get to you. What a romantic fool I was.*

You used me badly. You killed Zari, and your wife is much abused. I see no romance.

Afalkay the Beautiful stared at me, his rage so acute his body trembled in the candlelight.

Moments passed.

He neither spoke nor moved.

When he did, I gave a start.

Barbarossa will see you. Tomorrow night, only when the Moon is high. Do not try to go to the town in daylight. It would not be safe. I'll help you no more.

And with that, the good councillor marched from the cave and, without torch or guide, melted into the darkness beyond.

Scene 7

I didn't move for a while, but sat, as still as the rocks around me, eyes pinned to the mouth of the cave. All the sounds of the world – waves, wind and gulls – seemed louder, more pronounced, as if everything were moving in on me, getting closer, and there I was, waiting to be swallowed up, washed away.

Once I was sure Afalkay the Beautiful was not coming back, I grabbed the blankets he'd left, holding their softness close to my chest, hooked the basket of food with my foot, and pulled everything to a dry crevice between the jutting rocks. I couldn't bear to stay any longer in the same spot Sunny's body had lain. And I desperately needed to feel safe, to curl up in a hidey-hole, like a lost thing, unknown to anyone, anywhere.

Then I ate.

Chewing carefully and slowly, I filled my belly with

far more than it needed. The food tasted so good I almost wept. To enjoy such a feast in that place seemed strange and perverse. Not for the first time, I felt like an animal, a small, nibbling, filthy thing, like the rats in the harbour. But I let myself savour each morsel, then licked my fingers clean of salt and oil, and rummaged again in the food basket. There was something at the bottom I hadn't noticed before. A small pot wrapped in muslin. I unwound the layers to find exactly what I knew I would. Honey, crushed from the comb by my own hands, worked on my father's table that was now ashes, and poured into one of my unbaked pots.

The thick liquid glinted under the sputtering candles, golden and flecked with light. I didn't dip my finger in to feel the viscous drip, though I ached to do so. Instead, I held the pot of honey close to my face and thanked the lost bees that made it, hoping their tiny souls might somehow be blessed. And with a low, broken voice, I asked any that yet lived to forgive me for not protecting their colonies as I'd promised I would. Then I thought of the hand that placed the pot in the basket for me to find, and of the mind that would be cruel enough to do such a thing. It was only then I decided, without any doubt in my heart, that I would not be killed by all that had come to pass. Somehow, even after everything I'd been through and living with the pain of Aamon, I would have a free and full life, just as my mother had always wanted.

The candles guttered.

Some hissed and burned out.

Another reminder of home, but I was glad of them, not just the light, but the smell, so pregnant with the knowledge of who I was, of where and what I'd come from. It lulled me as I pulled the almost unbearably soft covers over my body. I was so broken and numbed by pain I thought myself incorporeal, a spirit or entity that might dwell eternally in the rocks of that cave, forever unknown and unseen, just living, feeling and thriving in the darkness, until I closed my eyes and fell into the deep well of sleep.

Seagulls screamed.

I woke with a start, and winced at the bright sunlight blasting through the mouth of the cave like a violent assault. My head swam and my guts churned as nausea took me. I moved as quickly as I could to the light and salt air, took a deep breath and promptly retched, spilling the contents of my stomach over the shingle in front of the caves. Just when I felt mistress of myself once more, I suddenly reeled, and was sick again. And again, until I spat nothing but bile. When I was sure all was done, I moved away from the mess, and lying on my back with my arms and legs open to the world like a marooned starfish, splayed myself against the wet rocks.

The Sun was warm, the sea breeze pleasant and a little reviving. I forced myself to sit and looked about for the crow, listened for its familiar bleat, but heard only the twittering of starlings, the distant *tchack* of bickering jackdaws and the cries of gulls. The sea was choppier than I thought normal considering the weather, and wondered what it might mean. I checked for signs, but my head was heavy, and I could read nothing. There was a strange bloating in my belly too, and my breasts felt tender, bruised and swollen. I took little notice, other than to mark the change, blaming the effects of sleeping in a damp cave with all the ravages of Aamon pressing upon me.

It felt good to be outside.

The fabric of my new tunic, so smooth against my skin, gave unexpected frissons of delight as the breeze swept over it. As always, there was something soothing about the smell of the sea, the ebb of the waves.

Ebb and flow, I called out to the mighty brine.

But today their constant movement also made me swoon.

All my instincts were heightened, as if I'd been peeled down to my essential, animal self. I felt raw and exposed, snapping my head this way and that at the smallest sound or change in the wind. The fear of being found by the fire-setters was all-encompassing. Reluctantly, I dragged myself back into the murk of the cave and hid under the rocks to wait out the day.

Feeling the crow's absence so keenly, I worried my bottom lip, biting down until the metal taste of blood scorched my tongue. Alone in that cavern, I thought my mind might break. With no other distractions, I ate more bread and olives, not through hunger, but to take my thoughts away from feathers and wings, the feel of a beak nuzzling and nipping at my chin. Eating also helped to pass the time, which seemed to have slowed almost to a stop as rays of bright sunlight insistently reached into my dark sanctuary, and the day stubbornly refused to fall away.

I chanted.

I shouted and hummed, listened to my voice ring around the cave and come back to me. Sometimes, swaying, I counted the whorls in the rocks all about, and traced them with my sore, gnarled fingers. Finding patterns and faces hidden in the stone, I wondered what would happen if I brushed my feather over the cave walls. Would it show me its heart colours, lighting up the entire cave in spiralling hues? And what dreams might I whisper to them? Might I make a world there, in that dank place, with nothing but magic and any spirits who might be hidden, deep within the minerals and sediment? I was sure I could, for I was the holder of a Gift, a most powerful magic, I knew that now.

I believed it.

I looked up. Still the daylight persisted, making me sigh and rail and quiet myself again, scattering my thoughts across the cave floor.

I pictured Zari with her child.

I rocked myself back and forth.

I sobbed and pulled at my hair.

I pissed and shat and cleaned myself with salt water.

I stared unblinking at the pool of light at the cave mouth.

I listened to the waves and the seabirds, encroaching, closer, ever closer, but never reaching me, there in my dank hole. And to the wind as it picked up or slowed until, at last, night began to fall.

Then, I readied myself.

As the last orange band of sunlight deepened to blood-red and disappeared behind the sea, there was a throbbing in my belly, as if my heart had slipped down and landed in my guts. The candles had sputtered their last some hours before, and I'd no way of making a torch. It was a blessing. I needed the darkness more than ever. The night was a disguise. It would guard me from the mistrustful eyes of the town; like the blanket I was to use as a cloak, it would cover me. I pulled the soft fabric around my shoulders, tucked my hair under it, reached for my staff and stepped out of the cave onto the cool, wet sand.

Absence filled me.

I sighed to my very soul.

How I missed the crow.

But I dared not call out.

All around was as thick as pitch. Although the heavens were alive with stars, they sent no light. A thin crescent Moon gave a crooked smile, but it seemed a dulled thing, sending not even a sliver of a ray down to earth. My eyes were useless, so I closed them. Only then did I remember they weren't covered. I flinched at the thought, but there was nothing to be done and I had more pressing concerns.

Though I knew the tracks and unmade roads as much as I knew my own mind, I needed all my wits in the blackness of that night. But try as I might, I couldn't banish my whirling thoughts. What if I'd been tricked and Barbarossa wasn't back? Getting me to sneak into town might have been a trap, and I'd find a horde of angry townsfolk waiting for me, councillors, fishermen, merchants and ships' boys, all gathered together. The men would hold flaming torches, while the women and children would stand just behind, each with a Dreamstone sitting neatly in the palm of their hands, ready to hurl them at me, to pummel me until I was nothing but a heap of lifeless flesh. Afalkay the Beautiful had used me before, and with suspicion so high in the town it would be easy to get rid of me, now I'd become a nuisance to him.

When at last I saw the harbour, with its perpetual fires all aflame, and the tiny flashes of candlelight from the windows of anchored ships, my heart banged furiously in my chest. Still, I moved on.

Scene 8

The town was silent and seemed deserted. The torch in the main square was blazing, so I could at least see where I was going, be attentive of anyone who might want to sneak up behind to murder me. But there was no one. Windows were shuttered tight and dark. Not a voice spilled from the dwellings nor from the lanes down to the harbour. I wondered where the thieves, the desperate women and malingerers that folk so often spoke of, could be. With my heart in my mouth, I shuffled, hunched under my blanket, and moved through the town like a spirit. When at last I reached the stone steps leading up the hill to the council building, as tired as I was, I didn't stop for breath.

Further away from the town's beacon, the higher I climbed the deeper the night became. But the Moon, at least, was a little brighter now. My breathing was quick and shallow, and sweat ran rivulets under my blanket and new clothes.

When I thought it safe, I finally stopped to rest a moment, and almost screamed as a large hand grasped under my arms, and fat fingers pressed hard against my mouth.

My first thought was to bite, but my lips were fastened by a strength far greater than my own. I was spun around, the blanket pulled away from my head. The face of my assailant was so close I could smell his sour stink, feel the bristle of long, untidy whiskers brushing my cheek. It was too dark to see much more than the shadow of his face, but even before he spoke, I knew it to be Barbarossa. With a gentle *shhhh*, he slowly loosened his grip and freed my mouth.

Did anyone see you? he asked.

Not daring to speak, I shook my head vigorously, hoping he'd see through the gloom.

Are you sure of it?

As certain as I can be, I gasped.

Forgive my brutality. I cannot risk having you too near the council hall. Not now.

With that, he grabbed my shoulders and pushed me along before him. I suddenly had no idea where I might be or where we were going. On we walked, on and on, his quick, long steps too much for my pained limbs. I fell. Over and again, I tripped under his stride. When I began to whimper, he pulled me off my feet and I was hauled up, cradled in his arms like a babe, grasping at my staff, afraid to lose it to the night. At least I could rest a little. Gently, I leaned my head against his enormous chest, felt its rise and fall with each step. As the streets fell away, we were plunged into blackness again. With only the starry canopy to show the way, I blinked up at the sky, until even that disappeared. I opened my eyes as wide as I could, tried to make out shapes in the darkness, but all was black. I could see nothing. Then the air changed.

Suddenly it was damp and chill.

There was an echo, but not clear like in the cave.

It was a thin, sorrowful sound.

And the smell was of musty, cut stone, like the walls of a building, or an old well, barely used and left to rot. We seemed to be spiralling around, and ever downwards. When we turned a final round, before us was a door with strips of dim light escaping through cracks in the shrunken wood. At last I could see. It seemed as if we were standing in the bowels of the earth. I shivered. Barbarossa set me gently down in front of the door, took a key from a large ring at his hip, and put it into the heavy-looking lock. It turned slowly with two loud clunks. He looked at me and, with a nod of his enormous head, pushed the creaking door open. There was a soft shove at my back, and with my eyes adjusting to the light, I stepped into a small, enclosed chamber.

The smell hit me before anything else. It didn't seem an unclean place, but the flames of four tallow candles swayed in the draught from the open door, giving out an animal stench along with their pale halos of light. It was an acrid and filthy stink compared to my bees' wax, and I reeled as I tried to understand where I was. For a moment, I longed to be back in the cave and thought to turn and protest, but recovered when, blinking into the dimness, I saw Yemma.

The old woman was sitting on a low stool in the centre of the room, bone pipe hanging from her lips. There was no greeting, she remained where she was, as still as stone, though I sorely wished to run to her, to bury my head in her lap.

The candle flames flattened and dimmed for a moment as Barbarossa took a few steps forward. It was shocking how his mighty presence filled that small space, and his odour of freshly cut wood, leather and old sweat smothered everything, even the rancid tallow. He respectfully bowed his wildly thatched head, then handed Yemma the key to the chamber door. The old woman grunted by way of recognition, slipped it into her pocket, and went on sucking loudly on her pipe.

The chamber floor was made of thick, cold slabs of cut stone, recently covered with new straw. There was a pallet in one corner, covered in blankets that looked far too good to be in such a dank and dismal place. Next to the pallet was a low table with a wooden plate and cup upon it, and baskets filled with fruit, flatbreads and all manner of comestibles. In another corner were two large pots. One was filled with water, while the other, smaller pot had nothing in it, there to receive my dirt and slops. I looked at the large man beside me and frowned my confusion.

You'll stay here now. It's safe, he explained. *I know about the fire. I'm sorry for it.*

I shook my head, unable to grasp the situation or put words to my thoughts.

She will bring your daily provisions, provided by me, Barbarossa said, as he pointed at Yemma. *You won't starve. She can take your soils away, keep the place clean for you,* he went on, stroking his beard.

Yemma is not my servant, I said, again shaking my head.

No, but you'll need help and there's no one else. Trust is not easily bought. She can stay with you during the day, for company. But she'll bring the key to me each evening and fetch it again in the morning.

I'm to be a prisoner?

This is no prison. You're here as my guest. The Governor sighed as he spoke, and there was a heady sense of exhaustion in his voice and manner.

But I'm to be locked up, unable to leave?

For your own protection.

I looked to Yemma. She was as blank as the walls and would not catch my eye. There was a lull. Barbarossa was so big, he looked uncomfortable in such a small chamber. Had things been different, I might have laughed. He felt it and shifted uneasily.

If I refuse?

You cannot.

Yet you say I'm not a prisoner.

Please, don't test my patience. You've nowhere else to go. The superstitious elements of this town would have you killed for devilry. I'm offering you sanctuary. Let's call it a gift.

I flicked a look at him. He saw the anger spark within me.

No, he corrected himself. *You're quite right. It's payment, for the great favour you have done for the town — if they did but know it — and for me.*

Yemma moved on her stool.

I flinched before realising it was a signal. I dropped my head and cast my eyes down.

Thank you, sire, I said.

You should take your rest, Barbarossa replied, before turning on his heels and disappearing through the open door and up into the shadows.

My old friend and I sat alone in the deep hush of that strange place. Neither of us spoke, but it was a companionable silence, peaceful in its way. Until with some audible effort, Yemma stood from her stool.

He's not a bad man, for a murderer and a brute, she said as she walked to the door. *Sent a lackey to find me, saying a friend was in need, if I'd be willing to help. I knew it was you, for I know no other to have dealings with the mighty Barbarossa. And he's right, you need sleep, and much of it.*

Wait, I said. *Where is this?*

The town's old water cistern. It's not been used since I've known the place, and that's longer than most of the townsfolk have been alive. You're safe enough.

Without thinking, I reached up to her, but she didn't move toward me or take my hand, only looked around quizzically.

Where's the crow? she asked.

I shrugged sadly, feeling its absence more than ever. She

came over to me then, laid a soft but firm hand on my shoulder, and squeezed.

I'll be back at sunrise, she said, and plodded to the door in her baggy leather slippers, closing it behind her.

I listened for the clunk-clunk of the heavy key in the lock, but all I heard were slow, shuffling footsteps, echoing, making their way up, ever up. She hadn't locked me in.

Scene 9

It was impossible to sleep in that deep, sunken place. As the candle stubs spat their rancid last, I forced myself not to flail about in the pitch-black. The sounds of worms and beetles and other blind, slithering things behind the cold walls made me think of rotting bodies shifting, as mushrooms pushed through winding sheets. I thought I'd suffocate in there. Or perhaps, at that moment I was drowning, as Sunny had done, and I was in my final throes, starved of air, and this was but a dream of burial.

Then the sickness came again.

Falling from the pallet, I crawled. My stiff, swollen fingers felt about the stone and straw. Agony stole the breath from my lungs as I searched blindly for the empty pot. The temptation to push the heavy door open, to pull myself up and clamber until I was out and could breathe a fresher, freer air, and call for the crow, was strong. But I was too weak.

Oh, how the thought of my feathered friend hurt my heart.

I craved the company of the crow. As the retching finally stopped, I closed my eyes and tried to sing to the cold earth and all its tiny beasts beyond the walls, to reach them. But want stilled my tongue, my voice lost to loneliness.

When at last Yemma pushed the door open with lighted candle in her hand, and announced it to be morning, I was standing in the darkness, in the middle of the now stinking chamber, doing nothing other than waiting. I smiled when I saw her and half expected the crow to be at her side, shaking its beak and flapping in agitation, and I craned my head to see if it was hiding behind her skirts.

She was alone.

The old woman covered her face against the stench of my sickness, but before she could even lay down her light, I'd found my staff and was breathlessly asking her to help me scale the stone steps. She didn't protest, but put her arm around my waist, let me lean my weight against her, and guided me as we ascended.

The way up seemed eternal.

I've been sent to hell, I said, and Yemma snorted.

I've lived in worse places, child. You will know hell when you truly see it. For it exists on this good earth, and that's the truth.

Once out under the Sun's warm rays, and when my eyes had adjusted to the light, I could see we were atop the great hill overlooking the town, high above all the dwellings and buildings. It was nowhere I'd been before. A shadow passed overhead. For a moment I looked up at the clouds and imagined Atlas there, on the back of her great black bird flying to the shore to meet her love. My mother's tales were always the place my mind sought when in need of comfort, and I even thought I heard the beating of heavy wings above, but it was just the wind. I looked about me again. But for the familiar shape of the harbour, small and far below, I might have been in a different land altogether.

It smelled sweet and was a vibrant green up there on the hill. So different from my dank cell or the filth of the harbour and sweat of the town, like a brave new world waiting to be discovered. How I wanted that newness. It almost felt like freedom, and I smiled at the thought. But the call of starlings somewhere in the distance shook me to my senses. I was nowhere new, just higher up.

I need to get back to the beach, to the caves. The crow will be waiting. It might be roosting at the Wishing Tree. It's done it before. Can we get there from here? I asked feverishly.

There's a way around the town, over to the dunes. I've not walked it since I was a young woman, but I've not forgotten. And no one will ever see us up here, even in plain day, Yemma said, smiling. Then, as if she'd heard my thoughts, she said, *We are free as birds, child.*

That notion of feathers was enough to stir us both. Yemma, despite her shooing and nagging, had fond affection for the crow and would have been happy indeed to be reunited. I leaned half my weight upon my staff, the other half taken by my old friend's shoulder, and we set off.

A breeze blew.

I lifted my chin to fill myself with the fresh air, felt my soft tunic flutter around, then cling to me like water. Yemma pressed her warm hand against my hard belly.

You're showing early, my girl, she said.

I looked down at myself, then back at her, and frowned.

When did you last bleed? she asked.

I don't know, I haven't been thinking about it. It's been a good while, I suppose. I shrugged, but my mind was reeling. In truth, I'd done nothing but think about it. I knew the nature and ways of the body more than most. And of course, Yemma of all people would know, would see it. But I'd never imagined myself a mother, only a daughter, someone's child. I pictured him then, Zari's dear boy, and my heart lurched – that I might have a babe of my own, just like him, that no one could ever take away from me.

It's not my place to ask questions. But you'll need to start thinking, and soon. At least it explains the stink down there. She nodded back toward the cistern. *Thank heavens it's not the illness spread through the town; that was my first worry when I opened that door and got a whiff of your guts. You need care, mind. Things can be difficult.*

Stopping, I stared at her so intensely my eyes began to sting. I wanted to laugh, to twirl and sing. There was no confusion now, no hiding from what I knew to be true, only determination. I'd not be killed. I couldn't save Zari, but I'd bring the babe growing in my belly safely into the world and, somehow, the child would live. Yemma lifted an eyebrow, and I smiled in reply. She shook her head, gave a gentle chuckle and we pushed on.

As we staggered over the hill with its cherry trees and tall verdant grasses, I looked again at my stomach, then lightly touched the fabric over the mound with my injured hand. The tightness of my skin underneath the tunic was still a shocking truth, and I pulled away. A memory of fire caught. My body was flame-hot. There was a moment of panic, but I pictured him then, still just a tiny fish, golden, glistering, rippling and eager to grow. He was warm, that was all, spreading his heat as he swam around my belly. I sang to him, though it was a silent song. He alone could hear the voice of his mother coursing through her sore and broken body, carried by her blood and spirit down to his cosy den, where it could soothe him – for I was certain I carried a son. He sang his answer, so I might know his name. I was glad of it. To bring a girl into a world where she would be born to serve, to slave and suffer under the basest orders of men, would have grieved me. My son would be free.

The rest of our journey was silent. Yemma held me at the waist, the ease of being in each other's company flowing like the freshest spring water. We were two beings, moving as one spirit. When we saw the dunes appear below us, the joy of seeing the nearest thing I had to a home pulled at every sinew and I wished I could run. Instead, we staggered down the hill, slipping and sliding in our haste, falling gently on our arses, giggling and hooting like playful children. Yemma held the bulk of my weight against her body until grass turned to sand under our feet, and I stepped into my own shadow. It was warmer in the dunes than up on the hill, and although the sea brought in the whisper of a familiar salty breeze, I missed the cleansing high wind on our faces with the lie of freedom on its breath.

The Wishing Tree was just ahead of us.

Its branches swayed like beckoning fingers. Small flies started to appear and circled our heads. We swiped at them with our hands, spat them out as they landed in our open mouths, sticking like pips on our tongues. Flies also looked to be gathered around the trunk of the tree, hovering there in great clumps. It didn't seem hot enough for them to be congregated like that. We stopped and I looked at Yemma. She put her arm out to bar my way, preventing me moving further on.

Best not get close, she said, waving her hand in front of her face to swat away more flies. *Nothing good is there.*

We both knew what we'd find. Still, nothing would stop me from seeing the cruelty for myself, of bearing witness so that every spirit, every visible and invisible thing of this world, might know of it too, and weep.

I pushed past her, sticking my staff into the sand as hard as I could, determined to get close to the Wishing Tree. When I heard her plodding steps and muttered words following behind, I thanked Setebos for her dear friendship.

But grief had already set in.

I felt it, raging and pulsing from toes to chops, a great ball of panic sticking in my throat. The fish in my belly turned and turned, and I thought it spoke, willing me not to look at the large black shape fastened to the trunk of the Wishing Tree. Flies crawled about the thing. At first glance it looked like it might be moving and there was a moment of hope. But then I saw the maggots, squirming within.

The crow was hanging, wings outstretched, body limp and dead. A sharpened stick was run through the crow's neck and stuck into the trunk of the tree. As I got closer, I saw care had been taken to ensure its wings were propped wide open with twigs. They were held with pins, making its head slump forwards as its beak lolled upon its breast. Twine had been wrapped around the bird and the trunk to secure it, making tracks in its feathers, cutting into its flesh.

Bellowing to Yemma for help, I pulled furiously at the twine until my fingers split and bled. The old woman tried to prise me away, but I screamed at her to aid me or leave. When, finally, it was free, I held the crow to me as I'd held Zari's babe. Close to my breast where it could hear my heartbeat. The flies did not abate but I didn't care. I bawled at them, flicked them away as tears and spittle fell onto the still shining feathers of the crow. Through my wailing and sobbing, I could hear the sea in the distance. The ebb and flow sounded a sorrowful rhythm. How soothing it was, the familiar constancy of waves touching the shore. I listened as their whispering voices seemed to grow and reach out, wrapping the crow and me in a blanket of calm, like the coddling arms of a mother. Quiet now, still holding the body of my dear companion, I began to rock. My mouth opened, and gently I sang the song of the sea so that, somehow, my friend might feel the love pouring from my shuddering frame. When at last I looked up, Yemma was singing with me. She gave a nod. It was time to let go.

We buried it there, under the Wishing Tree. Digging a hole with sticks and our hands, we covered the body with sand and silty earth. Yemma wanted to look for pebbles to pile upon the grave, but I worried the weight would trap the crow's soul, bind it to its bones, forever imprisoning it in the hole.

No, I said. *It needs to be free.*

Louder now, I keened an undulating melody to release its spirit from the pain of a world so full of cruel men. Looking up through the branches of the Wishing Tree, I felt the dappled light play across my face.

This is my wish, I said.

The leaves of that old pine shimmered and sighed. Sweet sap oozed through its ancient wood and ran down the trunk like thick tears. The waves stopped then. The breeze disappeared, and all the flies fell from the air, peppering the sand beneath. I opened my eyes and swayed back and forth by the small burial plot. As I wiped my own tears away, the soft outline of wings rose from the ground. The shape moved and changed as it assembled itself above me. It was the crow, made massive but wispy and of no substance. The huge bird seemed to be drawn in smoke, not like anything I'd seen from fire or candle, but pure, gleaming silver.

Its wings beat.

We watched as sparks of shining silver darted this way and that. They were everywhere, touching me like falling ash from a lustrous fire, engulfing but cold.

The crow is an angel now, I said, turning to Yemma, her hands clasped to her heart as if in prayer.

I sang on.

I sang my sorrow.

I sang my love.

I sang the crow to its rest.

It swooped and, floating above me, lifted its beak in a final silent cry before up it flew, up and up, wheeling and twirling. Then, as it turned over the dunes toward the sea, I saw the outline of a young woman sitting upon its back, but so faint she was barely there at all. Her thighs were clamped around the bird's body as her head fell backwards and her long hair trailed behind. I watched until the angel crow and its passenger disappeared into the clouds over the big brine and melted into the horizon.

When it was gone, I stopped singing and howled my pain again.

After a moment the waves ebbed once more, shushing against the shore, and the breeze moved the branches of the Wishing Tree, which clattered sadly above us.

I lifted my arms up to Yemma like a babe to its mother and my old friend helped me to my feet. As she wrapped her arms around me, she shook her head; guessing my intentions before I could say a word.

No, child. We must go to the cistern. It's safe there, she said.

Begging her, I feverishly described how she must go back the same way we'd come, find Barbarossa and, wringing her hands, tell him she'd been foolish. Tell him, with eyes full of guilt and shame, that before she'd left the previous evening, I'd showered her with desperate appeals. Being unable to calm me and afraid I might commit some ungodly act against myself, she'd conceded to leave the cistern door unlocked, asking only that I'd promise to stay in the safety of that refuge. Of course, when she'd arrived back that morning, I'd betrayed my word and escaped.

I'd not let her suffer on my behalf.

I've done no wrong and will hide no more, I said, my voice straining with the need for my friend to comply. *There's nothing left for me on this earth, but you have a good life, dear Yemma. I have been but a small mark, a little shadow on your path, and I'm forever grateful for that. But I could not bear to bring more ill winds to your door.*

The old woman took a breath, but I could not allow her to speak.

Look what they have done. I pointed to the crow's blood, spilled over the Wishing Tree, my voice cracking, my hand trembling. *You wish only to help me: then be kind now, as you've always been, and do this last thing for me. Live what life you have left in peace. Leave me now.*

There was no more protest.

She nodded and I watched her walk the way back to the hill.

I'd go alone to face the townsfolk.

There'd be no need for charms, potions and glamours. When they saw me, I'd simply be the mirror to their cruelty, forcing them to look upon their own brutality. All I could do was hope their shame would force them to ask my forgiveness. And so that we might all live in harmony, I would give it.

Scene 10

The market was awash with traders on their blankets showing their wares. A smell of meat cooking on an open fire, mixed with odours from baskets of sweated fish, sweet oils, burning herbs and muck from the filthy lanes, hung, as always, in the air. Merchants of every race and fashion marched this way and that, taking a break from the harbour, casting around for deals to be made. Ships' boys jangled the few coins they had in their pockets. Ragged women scrapped about in the dirt, scrounging for a bite of food, as fine-looking men in richly woven fabrics stood in small groups, speaking of important things. All the colours and the noises of everyday life were in full swing as the towns-people went about their business under the great golden Sun.

Shuffling, head down, covered and hidden, I was a stranger in the only place I'd ever known. Alone among the many, I felt huge and monstrous, like a beached whale fit only to be carved to pieces and burned as an unclean thing. Dangerous, like a mountain lion, all teeth and claws, to be treated with the highest caution lest it might pounce. Hated, like a cunning woman come from afar to aid and cure in ways few could understand. I felt afraid, like every woman in that market whose body wasn't allowed to be her own, and with no agency or influence, lived under the orders of men.

I didn't wait to be noticed.

Throwing off my covering, I watched with strange satisfaction as Afalkay the Beautiful's soft blanket was trampled into the dirt. Like that, in my fine, borrowed tunic, I continued through the bustle of the market, showing myself. Not one person looked my way. I began to shout, to scream, insisting I be told who had killed the crow. The towns-women going about their day made way for me, as if I were a poor wanderer, a strange old hag, bloated of belly and bent almost to a hoop, not the young woman they'd known all my life. How changed I must have been to be so invisible. Perhaps with my eyes free from their binds, far from their colour being a thing to distract or even fear, as I'd always been led to believe, I was just another townswoman. No, they'd simply not looked, not seen the jewels embedded in my head. Frustrated, I wailed and shouted louder, beckoned all to walk with me and listen as I demanded them to see me, to know my name; the name the town, not my mother, had given me, and hear the story it carried: of how even as a child, strangers decided who I was to be.

I am Sycorax, I cried. *Look upon me here. My mother called*

*me Raven, but you made me a pig and a crow. Now you've taken
everything, all I have is this name. So hear it, see me. Your own
Sycorax.*

When at last, people recognised me, they stopped to
gawp, and I came to a halt in the middle of a crowd. The
throng huffed and snorted as I insisted the crow killers be
brought forward at once, so I might at least look upon the
faces of those who would cruelly slaughter an innocent bird,
and forgive them.

Young women giggled.

The older ones shook their heads.

I shouted louder, repeated my demands and proclaimed
my rights as someone born of the town, a healer who'd
helped many in their moments of need. Pointing to indi-
viduals I recognised who'd come to me for herbs and
potions, for Dreamstones or soothing words, I asked them to
remember how I'd tended them. Discomfort spread, smiles
disappeared and the crowd about me grew. Faces peeked
around shoulders to get a look at the screaming woman. The
kindly-looking good wife whose husband had so roughly
pulled her away on the day I'd looked for Yemma, shrank
from me now. Zari's husband's daughter, her eyes wide in
her head, drew her bottom lip back behind her teeth in a
look of horror. What a sight I must have been, so undone
and seemingly out of my mind.

Atlas would have wept to see me.

But what did that matter?

I shouted as loud as I could, demanded again to be heard.

Only when a group of men rushed towards me, with their coats flapping and several soldiers at their sides, did I stop.

The crowd fell quiet. But they did not peel away or flee in fear. Catching my breath in the lull, I held my head up as best I could to look at each of the women gathered there, hoping they'd recognise something of themselves in my tired face. Mostly, they turned their gazes to the ground. Only a small girl stared straight at me. Her hair was neatly combed and covered. I returned her gawp, tilted my head to one side and arched my brows, thinking I might garner a smile from the child. Her face crumpled as she started to cry and screech. She stamped her little feet, pointed at me, screaming to all that she'd been cursed by the evil eyes of the sorceress.

There was a low rumble of voices as at last the crowd looked at me.

I grabbed the moment and shouted again, asking for the men who'd set my home aflame and for those who murdered the crow to show themselves. No one was listening. Women gasped as they looked upon me, staring now at the violet-blue of my blinking eyes. The absurdity of it made me snort and laugh loudly, causing several people to flinch and yelp, as many in the crowd nervously stepped back.

Yet, still no one walked away.

Catching the mood like a fever, more children began to cry out. They threw themselves to the ground and sobbed, claiming they too had been looked upon by the Storm Witch and could feel the curse. Some said they choked;

others claimed to burn. A boy with a shaven head, a sack for a tunic and a feeling for dramatics was now the star attraction. He rolled in the dirt frothing at the mouth, screaming of how invisible spikes were stabbing him and he was being cut to pieces from the inside.

Wait! I cried. *Look at me!*

The voices hushed, the boy was suddenly still, and all heads turned toward me again, though many shielded their faces from my eyes with their hands.

What are you afraid of? Do you really imagine the colour of my eyes will cut the flesh from your bodies, or burn you up like you burned my home? These children do not suffer, other than from the fear you give them.

The babes, quiet again, sucked on their fingers and blinked up to their mothers. I laughed once more, but there was no joy in it. I thought the people heard it, my sadness, I even imagined I felt it in their breathing as at last they seemed to listen.

What lunacy is this? Spreading the same fear that made my mother cover and bind my eyes when I was but a babe. Do you understand the injustice? The world you see so clearly, for me, has always been under a veil of shadow. Can you think how afraid and ashamed I was, even as a child. Think of your own little ones enduring such a thing. Have you no humility? No sense of what is decent and good?

The silence grew. People shuffled their feet.

You've stood aside, every one of you, to allow the destruction of all I had. I was but a girl who'd lost my family. Then you permitted the murder of a poor crow. Its only crime was loyalty to the lonely young woman who'd shown it care and attention. Are these the deeds of good people? And am I now to be accused of fabulous acts by excited children? I asked, my voice catching in my throat and growing hoarse. *Was the burning of my home and the killing of a crow brave measures, or were they the cruel actions of cowards and fools?*

People began muttering, until one voice rose above all the others. A man I did not know pushed his way through and stepped forward.

There are no cowards here. Only good people protecting our families against your unnatural ways.

A murmur of agreement made its way through the crowd, growing louder as it went.

I saw your altar, he suddenly spat. *I know what you are.*

There was a gasp from the crowd. Some of the women covered their mouths with their hands, wiped the sweat from their brows with the corners of their tunics.

You are the murderer, shouted the man.

Several voices rose from his audience, giving him even more confidence to speak.

Yes. I was one of the good men who put fire to your pit. But I alone killed your demon, he said, stepping closer to me with his arms in the air, hands open as if in declaration. *I wrung its filthy neck with these fingers, just as you killed your poor father, you and your deviant whore of a mother.*

There were cheers as people began to shout their agreement.

Men proudly claimed they too had a hand in putting fire to my dwelling and destroying my hives. Women accused me of trying to poison them with potions and send them mad with bad, unholy dreams.

A man afraid of his own women is unnatural, my accuser continued, turning to the crowd, now. *I knew Sunny, he could have been a good man had he not been put under their spell. They kept him like an animal, desert witches, both. And this one –* he raised his voice higher as he turned back to face me, one arm outstretched and trembling, finger pointing – *twisted by the very demon she gave suck to.*

Another cheer.

He went on.

Perhaps this buckled and bent creature killed her mother too. Boiled her bones and ate her flesh. Why not? For where is that stinking bitch now? There are no remains, there's been no burial. We know this depraved wench, this Sycorax, brought the storm, then put herself in favour with the Governor, poured lies and charms upon him. The councillor here among us, who we know is a good, honest man and has the ear of Barbarossa, witnessed all. Ask him. For he knows the truth.

The accuser's swooping arm moved so quickly the air sang around it. His finger now pointed to somewhere deep within the crowd, and it parted.

Afalkay the Beautiful made no attempt to move, nor did he cast about as if in confusion. He stood steady and lifted his chin. The thin green muslin of his headpiece fluttered in the breeze as he gave a solemn nod. Then he turned and disappeared, consumed again by the crowd. He did not look at me once.

The crow's killer seemed to grow wider, his breast fuller, his voice louder.

All the death, the destruction we've seen, the blood and disease many of us still face as we watch our loved ones cough up clods and suffer, all due to her evil curses on the town. How many more horrors must our eyes see, how many will die before she's stopped? Is there any doubt? She is a monster. Look upon her foul, lumpen aspect. Gaze into those demon eyes if you dare. They are all the proof of devilry we could need. And see the belly! It holds the spawn of the devil she worshipped when she gave it her cunt and her womb on the altar I destroyed. But it won't be born. It must be ripped from her.

There was a swell as the crowd moved forwards.

A rush from behind made me flick around and I was suddenly seized by unseen hands. As my arms were grabbed, I dropped my staff. Screaming, I was pulled from my feet and swept away. I tried to kick but my legs were held fast. My stomach flipped and I thought only of the life inside. That little golden fish. My head swam in confusion. All I knew was the blue of a clear sky passing above, the crowd, cheering and screeching with delight somewhere behind me as I was hauled away. I twisted around but the ground beneath me seemed to turn and bend. There was a dizzying sensation as I was lifted higher into the air. The colour of the sky filled my eyes. I could see nothing but blue. Blue, like my eyes. Then all around was spinning, deepest blue, and spinning, spinning. Until landing heavily, I was thrown into a cart and held down.

Everything blurred.

Suddenly hot, I imagined I was burning.

Was it, as I'd always feared, that fire was to be my fate?

I screamed over and again, begging for the flames to be put out. There was laughter, men's voices, and all at once I was cold and soaked to the bones, as if plunged into a moonlit sea. A rolling bucket struck my head and the salt water that had been thrown over me seemed mixed with some corrosive thing. I began to shiver, uncontrollably. The person holding my arms down tightened their grip.

As colours swirled through my mind like a Dreamstone, causing me to see nothing but shades and tones, I thought myself a child again. I tried to shout for my mother. Surely, she would come; save me, as she'd always done with her stories and calm ways, with her sweet songs, boiled herbs and thin broths. *Atlas*, I tried to say, but my mouth was filled with bees. Their trembling bodies buzzed behind my teeth. Tiny bee-legs pricked with each step as they picked their way across my parched, cracked lips. I tried again. Opening my mouth as wide as it would go, I attempted to make a noise, any sound so I might be heard. Finally, the bees flew out. But her name stuck to my tongue. So I said it in my mind, quietly, like a tale so sweetly told, like a child at bedtime whispering and sleepy: *Atlas*.

At last she was there, stroking my face, singing her strange words to an ancient melody, inviting me to cleave my voice to hers so we could become one. Then all would be silver. All would shine. My flesh would dissolve into the earth,

I'd be gone, and the pain would finally stop. There were others, too. All the women, the desert ancestors, were with her, standing behind and lifting their voices, calling me to unite with them. I caught the tune, it hovered about my lips, but then I remembered the cormorant cry across the waves, and I wanted to hear it again. It was too soon to join their song, I needed to feed the fish in my belly, bear my son and watch him grow, discover all the magical things I knew I had in me. More than anything, I wanted to live. I told myself again all I knew of me.

My father was of the Sun.

My mother was of the Moon.

My birth was a coming together, a powerful charm, a strength, and an earthly magic. I turned away from my mother, closed my eyes, and the world went black.

Scene 11

When I opened my eyes, it was gloomy.

I blinked into the haze of a gentle light.

Recognising the dense silence of a buried place, the musty smell of mushrooms and damp, I realised with some surprise I was back on the pallet in the ancient cistern. There was another odour there now, too. A strong, sour smell, curiously mixed with something sweet, like oil or incense. The place had been swilled out, new grasses spread around the stone floor and my old slops disposed of. The dim light came from a single dancing flame; a tallow candle, smoking and spitting on the small, otherwise empty, table. Even as its filthy odour added to the general hum, I was grateful for its muted yellow halo and gave thanks for the considerate hand that lit it.

Somehow, Barbarossa had saved me from the mob.

I pushed myself up to sit with my back against the

unforgiving cold, stone wall. A thick, rough blanket woven from some sort of animal hair covered me. It smelled of its original owner but that wasn't so unpleasant, and again I thought only of the care someone had taken to put it there. My own hair and my tunic were dry, but held the memory of a saltwater soaking and felt gritty to the touch. I did not know how long I'd been lying in that place. When I looked at the candle it was about the length of my thumb. Judging by the smell, it had been burning for some time. I wondered how much longer it would be before it fizzled, and I'd be plunged again into the abyss. A wave of panic washed through me, but I grabbed the feeling and pushed it down, felt it fall through my body, pool on the ground around me and evaporate.

Fear could not help me.

But magic might.

Without much bidding, a melody came to me, and I sang a charm of everlasting light to the stick of melting tallow, watching my breath blow the flame gently back and forth as I made the spell. I was still uncertain of my gifts but knew that to tap an ancient stream you must dive to its depths, plunge through its history, and accept what's there. To use the powers of my foremothers, first I had to truly believe in them. I closed my eyes.

For my own sake, I believed.

For the babe in my belly, I believed.

For the kindness of Yemma, I believed.

For a love of life, I believed.

My voice was strong, my song loud.

I took my power.

The flame bloomed like a flower before me, warming my face with its light, then fell back to a gentle, steady and eternal flicker.

Thirsty, I found the pot of clean water. It had been filled to the brim. Putting my lips to it, I sipped. It was fresh and told me for certain I'd not been abandoned. Why would I have been allowed the luxury of a candle, the warmth of a blanket and the chance to quench my thirst if I was to be left to rot?

The relief of knowing someone would come was a blessing. For now, I was safe; away from the townsfolk, away from Afalkay the Unbeautiful, as I'd come to think of him, and away from the sad remnants of my life. Nevertheless, I couldn't help but wonder how long I would be alone in that place. Not that I craved company. By then I felt sure a life of solitude would be the finest thing for myself and my little one. After all, my existence had been a series of different isolations. I knew how to be on my own. Alone, we could live in harmony with the stuff of the world, and we need never do harm to anyone, nor they to us. I looked at my bulging belly, rubbed and cradled it with my uninjured hand.

A sudden and urgent need to piss broke me from my thoughts. I cast around quickly, but the pot for that use had been taken and not replaced. I lifted my tunic and crouched just in time. Before I finished there was a noise from without. An unrushed plod, heavy and echoing down the stone steps. The sound crept under the door and into the chamber. Although welcome, it was a shock. Fumbling, I hurried to fix myself just as the footsteps stopped and the clunk-clunk of the turning key rang like thunderbolts around my cell.

Good, you're awake.

Barbarossa's voice, so loud after the silence, made me jump and I fell back onto the pallet.

Fear not, he said, his tone only a little softer. *I've not come to kill you, but to save you. After a fashion.*

I'm to be saved?

A deep sigh seemed to roar from the enormous man before me. I tried to peep around his huge form, to see if Yemma, or some soldiers, or anyone had followed him down into my pit, but he was alone.

Only if you do exactly as I say.

My confusion showed, for he hardly took a breath before continuing.

The town wants you dead. They'll not rest until they see your broken corpse carted through the lanes, and your body hung on a hook in the harbour to rot. They call you the devil's whore, blame every pestilence, every death of an old man or demise of a goat, upon your living presence. He snorted. *But I'll not have the death of an innocent on my hands.* Nodding at my belly, he stroked his beard thoughtfully. I found no words to form an answer, so he carried on. *Heaven knows I am in your debt, not that I bother much about what lies beyond the great blue. A crook I may be, and many things besides, but I pay what I owe. Can you walk?*

355

I shook my head before finally finding my voice:

It will be difficult without my staff. My limbs are stiff and pained, though not as badly as they might be, all considered. I could try — if you'll allow me to lean against your arm, sire. Though I will be slow.

There's no time for trying, he barked. *Take up the blanket I left, and the candle. You'll need both.*

Standing, blinking up at him, I felt small and weak again. With no idea what was happening and suddenly frozen by fear, I couldn't move. Seeing my distress, Barbarossa sighed again, moved to the bed pallet and sat. I almost laughed to see the great pirate of the seas, that deadly menace to all nations and men alike, sitting so uncomfortably, his knees sticking under his chin. When he spoke next, his voice was gentler, almost kind.

Sit beside me, he said, *for I'll speak with you in the manner I know you'd prefer, that of an equal. It's the least I can do. Pirates might be brutes, but we are men of honour and understand the meaning of respect.*

A little stunned, I nodded, managing to shift my limbs into action, I perched, uncomfortably, on the corner of the pallet. He cleared his throat and pulled at the skin between his thick fingers.

Do you know what time of day it is? he asked, casually, as if this was all he could think to say to pass the time away.

No, sire, I replied. *In truth, my senses are all in confusion. I'd be glad to know.*

It's the dead of night, he said, then waited, as if expecting a response.

Bafflement was my only reply as I frowned.

The townsfolk fear the darkness these days, he explained. *So we shall not be molested on the way.*

Where are we to go? I asked.

There was a pause before he spoke again.

We will cover you in the blanket, see — and my coat, he explained, as he started to remove the massive garment. *I'll keep the flame to light our way, and I'll carry you, for we need to be swift and cannot risk a slow journey.*

I ask again, sire: to where are we journeying?

My voice was high and small, and I was frowning so hard my head began to ache. I'd been my own mistress since the death of Sunny and Atlas. The thought of now simply being taken away, pushed around like an animal and expected to obey at every turn both scared and appalled me. Barbarossa shook his head and looked at me from under his thick brows.

We can take the hills around the back of the town, he said. *Then down through the dunes and to the shore near the caves. There'll be a small boat waiting and a single boatman. We can't risk going anywhere near the harbour. I'll leave you there to be carried hence to a carrack anchored out in the bay. The boatman is a soldier in my pay. When you go aboard the carrack, you'll find a small crew. They're a rough lot and do not speak your tongue, so there'll be no way to ask for anything. I've given orders for you to be left unchained.*

Unchained?!

Aye. The men are used to prisoners and the paraphernalia of

357

capture, and they are not what you might call good men. But I've made it clear you are not to come to harm at their hands, on pain of death. So you'll be free to walk the deck, but I'll warn you to keep to yourself.

I could make no sense of it.

I'm to be taken onto a ship? To sail? I asked, my words drawn out and slow.

He nodded.

You did me a good deed. Your counsel saved our fleet and the town, if they did but know it. This is as near to payment I can give you now. I'll not let you be killed by the townsfolk. Once you're gone, I will accurately reassure them of your banishment.

Banishment?

I'll claim your belly as sufficient good reason. The town will accept your punishment, they'll soon forget you, and everything will fall back to how it's always been.

And me? Where am I to go? Where will I live?

I've not promised that you will live, Sycorax. Only that I won't see you killed.

Somehow I managed to hold my guts, but like a wreck that had slipped its anchor, I was slack, bobbing and utterly adrift. Barbarossa waited a moment, as though he expected a perfectly voiced response. When there was none, he continued to explain my fate.

On a privateer ship, if a member of the crew is disobedient, not necessarily against the captain, but against the other men, he is abandoned, alone, on the first uninhabited island we find. There have been stories, of course, about how such men have fared, escaping to

become *tricksters and players, making a show of their experiences.
But I must warn you that they are fireside tales. For most, if not
all, such solitary abandonment with few, if any, provisions, is a slow
and almost certain death.*

I stared at the man, my eyes trembling in the dim, flickering light.

*You will take three barrels of water and three barrels of food. I'll
not be the cause of your starvation. You've a head on your shoulders, perhaps you'll bring that child into the world, find shelter and
a way to live. If it's true what they say, about your . . . gifts . . .
perhaps you will cast a spell to save yourself.* He snorted again,
and smirked. *At the very least you can read the birds, understand
the elements, so you have more than most in your favour. I almost
look forward to hearing the stories told about you in years to come.
Your abandonment will make you immortal. Your name will be
whispered in halls both great and small for centuries to come. You will
be a subject for scribes, a topic of debate around the tables of learned
men. It might be said that I am your saviour.*

He dragged a hand through his whiskers, stood and offered
me his heavy coat. I took it. The weight hurt my already
sore fingers as I clumsily wrapped it and the blanket around
myself until I was cocooned, like a grotesque swaddled
babe. Then he scooped me easily into his arms. And with
the eternal flame spitting in one hand, and me held tight
against his chest, the mighty Governor, the decider of fates
and the false deliverer, slowly pushed the cistern door open.

Scene 12

When Barbarossa set me down on the shore, my legs buckled slightly, but I kept on my feet. The familiar sound of waves and the taste of salt on my tongue tugged at something deep and visceral. I might have believed I was taking the night air with a new friend before returning to a warm home. But home was a dream now. Shivering, I straightened my shoulders, dug my toes into the cold sand to steady myself and stared out to sea.

The boatman was waiting by the caves.

The gibbous Moon, brighter than I'd ever seen it, glowed on the wane. Turning, I looked toward the dunes. How I wanted to see the branches of the Wishing Tree one final time, glimpse their soft outline silhouetted through the night, that they might calm my thumping heart, stay my trembling hands. I squinted.

A figure was trudging slowly toward us.

It was Yemma.

Bathed in moonbeams, holding my staff before her like a precious thing, she seemed the very picture of an angel. I glanced at Barbarossa. He made no attempt to hurry us on. I held my breath until she stood before me, and I fell into her arms. I tried to be strong, to contain myself and show no weakness, but couldn't stop the fear from spilling over. For as long as I could remember I'd lived with physical pain and knew its cruelty in many intimate ways. But this was a different agony. I thought it more than I could bear.

Yemma held me up.

That small woman took my weight as she stroked my hair and hummed into my ear. It was the melody I'd sung to Zari as she'd laboured, Atlas's song used to calm the mountain lion. The old woman spoke. I didn't know the meaning of her words but recognised them as the language of my mother and knew enough to understand they were sacred. I took them with gratitude and thanked my friend with a kiss as she handed me my staff.

I cannot stand here all night. It's time.

Barbarossa's voice was not harsh, yet it split the air like a thunderbolt. He was right. It was best to go quickly, there was nothing else left. I handed him his heavy coat, but he shook his head and placed it over my already slumping shoulders. He signalled to the boatman then, and carrying me like a child, waded through the waves toward him.

The small moonlit craft bobbed in the water as I was lowered in.

The feeling was strange and startling. The sea swayed the boat so I could not stand, and even sitting brought a terrible panic. At first, I'd clung to the Governor's sleeve, but he'd shrugged me off and turned to shore without looking back. So, clutching the still flickering candle, I held my staff tight to my chest until I was lying flat in the bottom of the boat, looking up at the stars.

Silently, the boatman took up his oars, and we rowed out into the night.

Not daring to move as the boat undulated through the waves, my stomach churned with each small swell and roll. My head spun and there was a falling sensation. If I kept my eyes open, looked at the stars passing overhead, listened to the boatman's oars steadily pushing through the water, I could keep my sickness at bay. In truth, once the first terrors subsided, there was a curious peacefulness in that little boat. I kept it close, knowing it would not be long before it was gone.

And so it was.

Far too soon we came to a stop.

There was shouting. I was manoeuvred around and dragged up by rough hands. Thick ropes, that rubbed and burned my skin, were slung about my shoulders and hips. I was no more than a captured animal. My tunic was pulled up above my waist as unknown men grabbed my bare legs, dug stubby fingers into my thighs and buttocks, and shoved me onto the deck of the waiting carrack. It stank of the harbour, of dead and rotting things, of sweat and filth. Left there alone, like a fisherman's landed catch, I untangled myself from the tethers, and watched the boatman row away. It took all my strength not to cry out, beg him to let me stay in his boat until the world's end. But the night swallowed him, and when I looked again, he was gone.

The crew were six-strong and worse than any I'd seen.

They snarled at me. Laughing and barking at one another in the flat tones of an unmelodious language, they seemed to shout at the tops of their very lungs all their waking moments. After I was thrown atop a stack of rotting rope and discarded oyster shells at the back of the vessel and left a small basket of food, the crew went about the business of sailing the ship, bellowing at each other. There on my heap I clasped my staff. Felt its strength. There was something magical between us. The wood was warm and alive, and held the fresh smell of the Wishing Tree. I also kept my spitting, flickering candle close, watched it with satisfaction, burning yet never melting.

The breeze was mightily cold, and the ship moved faster than I'd imagined possible. I gasped as we smashed into waves at speed and lost my stomach, yet there was a strange liberty in it. My life was now unknowable and unrecognisable, so that along with the fear came an overwhelming sense of freedom and possibility. As my hair lifted into the air and my face was scorched and battered by wind and sea spray, I stroked the bulge of my belly, whispered words of hope to my little fish within.

There was no routine for me on board, it seemed. I ate

little but drank much water, making me constantly need to piss, which I did behind my stack of ropes and oyster shells. Crick-cracking my neck each time, turning this way and that, vigilant lest some gawping crewmen might pounce and grab me in my most vulnerable moment.

We sailed all night and all day, and all the pitch-black night again, but never reached the horizon. I wondered what would happen if we did. Would the ship fall from the earth into a sea hole, and we'd all be drowned, our sunken bodies fated to become dinner for the fishes? With no one to ask, I wore myself out thinking. At least it stayed my shock at the never-ending expanse of sea. I'd known it was mighty but never contemplated its true enormity before. Now I saw the sea was an eternal thing, more than big enough to hold a thousand monsters and a thousand whales, and the bones of ten thousand drowned men.

When the Sun came up, I exhaustedly covered myself with the coat and blanket, tried to ignore the noise of the crew – who became bolder and more raucous in the daylight – and slept. When night came again, I rose, walked the slippery wooden deck with my candle to again stare into the blackness of sky and sea. Many a time I wondered if I might yet be dead and this was hell, with its repetitive and endless nights. But other than the crewmen, I saw no devils. As I leaned onto the side of the ship the wind and spray were a blessing now I wasn't sick, and I hummed its sweetness to my unborn child. He shifted inside me, rolled with the waves, found his own harmony through my chaos. How I wished I could share the feeling with Yemma, get her to touch my belly and feel the life of the boy inside. If it wasn't for the sound of shouting from the men up front, grown loud and excitable and making my nerves twitch, I might have thought myself happy in that sliver of a moment. Then the boatswain cried out and once again all seemed lost and unfathomable. The gruff man's words were incomprehensible to my ears, but it was the same loud message repeated over and again. It sounded like a call to prayer. But then the heavy fall of the anchor juddered and hit. I went back to my pile, tucked in and peeked over my covers. There was a lot of movement. Lanterns swung, beams of light criss-crossed this way and that, allowing me to catch glimpses of the crew, all action and diligence but wretched.

An insubstantial-looking boat was lowered with a great deal of cheer. I pulled my coat and blanket over my head, listened to the noise of the sailors, until the heavy blow of the shipmaster's boot stuck me in the back. There were no concessions or courtesies. I was roughly handled, pushed this way and that, until I too was lowered, to choruses of laughter, into the already leaking craft. The man who rowed me and my barrels (only three, not as Barbarossa had promised) to the island had a filthy face and stank. He grinned, not taking his eyes from me until we abruptly stopped. Gesturing to the pool of slowly rising water in the boat, he hauled my barrels into the sea, making it clear I should follow. I shook my head and pointed to the shore, which was surely close enough to row to. But he growled

and shoved me with such violence I tumbled into the sea as
he turned the boat quickly around and made his way back
to the carrack in the greatest of haste.

The sea was cold.

It took the breath from me.

The laughter of the sailors in their ship was a ghoulish echo
behind me. I cursed them and wished pain upon each one,
but they were not my concern, now. Surprised I was able to
stand with my chin free of the waves, for the water was not
so deep, my thoughts turned to my barrels as they bobbed
around me. With my staff and candle in hand (burning still,
even under the sea), I used my shoulder to push one of the
barrels to the shore. The water took its weight, but wrapped
in my blanket and coat, my limbs were as heavy as stone.

There was no beach to the island that I could see.

All was rocks and caves.

I was too cold, panicked and weighed down by my clothes
to search for a better spot. Pushing the barrel to a ledge of
flat rocks before a dry cave, the thing split, and in an explosion of splinters, burst open, spilling the already spoiled
goods into the salty brine. There was no time for anger or
regret, for what could I do? I hurled myself onto the rocks,
pulled off my clothes, so heavy with seawater they seemed
to want to crush me to death, and looked out. The Sun had
started to come up and there was a haze of rosy light.

It was beautiful.

How could it be so lovely when all seemed lost?

There was the carrack, small now as it finally approached

the horizon, and there the other two barrels, floating out to sea.

I screamed the unfairness of it.

But I screamed once and no more, and never again, for I was tired and cold, and I'd had my fill of despair.

I sat shivering and watched until the carrack disappeared. With nothing else to do, I lay back on the rock and listened to the sounds of my body.

My panting breath.

The movement in my throat as I swallowed.

The thud of my heart.

Taking control, exhaling slowly, I felt something shift. The rock beneath me seemed to give, to move and sigh gently under me, as if my touch, my mere presence, were giving it life, releasing it from a mighty, holding force.

Then the light changed.

Around me was a play of different hues, encompassing me and everything thereabouts. As wretched as I was, I couldn't contain my joy. I laughed, loud and hearty, until my body shook, and I kicked my legs in the air like an upturned beetle. The stuff of the island, its stony, rocky element, was opening its heart to me, just like the pebbles I'd so easily made into Dreamstones. In a moment the colours faded and there was a deep rumble. It was loud but without threat or violence. As I looked around, small cracks and fissures yawned and gaped in the stone, like the loosening skin of some soft fruit.

I felt it then; the power of my magic, fizzing through

me and about me. And I believed it. There was no need to be afraid: my gifts would bring life to that barren place. Settling in, I spoke with tender tones.

Shhhh, dear earth of the island. We are free now.

And closing my eyes, I remembered what Atlas had said, that I'd find her waiting for me in the goodness of the world. My mother was the rocks, she was the sea and the sky, the fading Moon and the rising Sun.

The cold began falling from my bones as the rosy light of dawn changed to gold. And the Sun shone down, warming my nakedness, dispatching the last of any shivers and shakes. Thinking I should try to stand, look around my rock in the middle of the sea, I reached for my staff and saw the candle was next to me. Its flame danced and the tallow spit-spat, causing me again to laugh out loud.

There was no rush.

Everything could wait.

Lying back on the rock – my rock – I sang Atlas's tune.

There was no fear of being heard but I was strangely timid at first, so let the sound flow only in muted tones. Even so, the song was a thing I could see now, a swirling silver mist emanating from my mouth, my breast and my belly. It moved around the caves and danced upon the surface of the sea.

My confidence grew.

I picked up my staff.

It was shining and shimmering with light, patterned with every moving colour. Growing bolder as I wondered at its magnificence, I sang louder, changed the ancient notes for my own. Sharpening some. Flattening others to create different twists in the melody. Like this I watched my song take different journeys, guided it with each strain. It was a powerful coming together of new and old. A melody full of history, of future, and of that very moment, which now I saw was the most precious time in the world. For in truth, it was the only time.

I sang it loud.

The song was within, as it was without.

It resonated in my chest and buzzed over my tongue, it went into my cheeks and around my head, and it moved something deep within my fleshy shell, shifted things, turning like a key in a lock.

Clunk-clunk.

It's unlocking me, I thought, and opened my mouth wider to let the song out, to watch its dance of freedom. It echoed and rang around each stone and rock. As the notes changed the song morphed into new and extraordinary shapes, making the island bloom and blossom as it went. It was a lizard, a beetle, a bat and every crawling thing. It was a mouse and a bear. It was a forest of pine trees. It was a glade with every beautiful flower and leaf. When it flew it was a butterfly and a bird with colourful feathers, its wings beating, its beak clacking and chirruping. It was a raven and a jackdaw. And as the thump of my heart beat out the rhythm of my song, the music swooped and dived, all feathered and iridescent, for it was a crow.

Out of breath, my head light and dizzy with the joy of making, I saw just how my song had truly changed things. A bubbling of bright springy moss had appeared on bare stones and pebbles around me, with a froth of foamy flowers at my feet. The hard rock under me had softened, giving me a bed of lichen, of soft tendrils adorned with nap-covered leaves that had knitted together for me to lay my head upon. At last, I fell silent and nestled in. Did I sleep then? For I thought I heard a voice from within the stone under the lush green plants beneath me, the spirit of the rock, speaking a language I could understand. Its timbre was deep. Its utterance quiet and beautiful.

And the air, too, seemed to join in, so the voice when it spoke was a harmony of many, as if the island itself were answering my song with its own sweet music, and speaking to me.

At last, it said, *you're here. Welcome home.*

Epilogue

The Island Speaks

The waiting was long.

For thousands of years my only real company was the constant battering of waves upon my rocks, slowly eating me away. Nothing grew upon my back, but the crust of salt crystals left by the ever spitting, forever foaming sea. Days and nights were eternally the same – wind, water and brine – and there I was, nought but a boulder and a blighted thing. Through all that time, I kept my silence. No doubt Neptune, his friends and enemies, and the myriad armies of watery divinities thought I slept. So still was I, so inert.

But that was a mistake.

I was only what you might call dozing.

Half awake.

Lest she came.

Don't get me wrong, there were visitors. Cormorants, terns, gulls of every kind, and guillemots, all came to rest

371

and leave their muck on my rocks. Other creatures too, crawling things with or without shells, jellied creatures and fishy types. Perhaps very long ago, in the time of monsters, mermen and harpies stopped to rest a while, it's hard to recall. One thing I do know is their respite wouldn't have been long. I was an inhospitable place and could not have been made a home. If the sea was cruel, then I could do nothing but sit within its angry grasp, my edges reaching dangerously up, jagged and sharp, a mess of hard, vicious spikes. If the Sun was hot, my caves were too dank for shelter, and I was full of noxious, poisoned air. In the human world I was fit only to make wrecks or be a tomb to broken men.

But this was not who I was.

For although made of nothing but rock and gaseous air, I had a heart, and I mourned the sailors whose bodies I could not save as their boats crashed upon me. Such a lonely place for mortal men to die, with nothing around but sea and sky. If you can believe that tears might fall from rocks and stone, then I entreat you to understand that I wept.

Ah, but do not fret for me.

In reality, I was not completely alone.

Many ancient spirits (who thought themselves quite youthful, actually) lived within my mineral breast.

They weren't the best company, to be frank.

Sometimes they were so quiet I thought them gone. But then they would howl and moan, cry out with pain and fury. For they were locked away within my solid, impenetrable depths, and although I felt myself a fantastical place, dreamed it to be true, I was but a stone and had no way of releasing the wailing sprites. So, you see, I was prison and prisoner both, and how I felt it, to my sad and craggy core. Yet I did not despair. There was a nub of hope, the feeling that one day things would change. Truth be told, I'm as old as the earth itself. No, I *am* the earth. It's only natural that I've always believed in magic. Yes, I might have been a lumpen thing in a lost place, but as part of the very fabric of the world, I was connected to everything that ever was or would be and could feel all eventual possibilities.

I had sensed her from her very beginnings.

When she was grown big enough to suck her thumb and kick at the walls of the belly that contained her, that's when my excitement grew. At that first kick, when her mother cried out, it was like a shove from somewhere far away. Of course, I didn't know if she would live to be born, as these things are complicated.

I hoped.

I believed.

The spirits held their breaths, too – although this is only a manner of speaking, as spirits have no lungs, and no breaths to hold, but I'm sure you get my meaning. And on the day of her birth there was such a feeling of joy that although she was far away, and I had no idea if she'd ever be close to me, my belief grew mountains. Literally. Faith is everything, I told myself. So, I continued to wait. But now I did so with the knowledge she was out there, living and preparing, and one day, somehow, she would come.

And she did.

The first day, the day of her arrival, I was at my most
excited and very sensitive to her charms. All it took was the
sound of her voice to send me into a flurry of movement.
Within moments, in all the places her song could reach,
I was covered with a rich loamy soil. Worms and grubs
appeared next, and chomped their way through my newly
made earth, making it even richer and loamier. Carpets
of soft green mosses and meadow grasses sprang forth as
her melody summoned yet more life. Trees and saplings
popped up, waving their woody arms as leaves began to
bud and grow. Thorny bushes appeared, too. They wrapped
their roots about the place and at first this bothered me, as
I didn't wish to cause harm. But what flowers they grew,
what petals. And so perfumed, they filled my very air with
scents divine. My bliss was as great as her power. Without
knowing it, she then invoked the spirits, and in doing so,
freed them from their confines.

Oh, grateful spirits!

Happy spirits!

The first one to speak was the spirit of the stones.

I felt it shake itself as it burrowed up to greet her. It gave
us voice, welcomed her in her own tongue so she'd understand how happy we were to finally have her with us. The
new plant and tree spirits, eager to show their art, made a
blanket of moss and covered her, so her skin would not burn
under the Sun, and she could rest her tired bones. She slept
then, as all the pucks and sprites and fairies of every kind

came together, stretched their corporeal selves, gathered about her slumbering form, and marvelled.

When she awoke, it was the spirit of the air who first befriended her.

He made himself beautiful for her to see and danced with joy at their meeting. How she laughed and reached out to touch his insubstantial form, and how sad she looked when he could not be touched. For he was but an airy thing. After that, he was always at her side, jigging around and learning from her. She had such a wealth of knowledge, there was much we all wished to know, and in return she asked many questions.

The first was about food, as very soon, hunger had begun to worry her.

The airy spirit spoke frankly, saying he could conjure something for her to eat, but it wouldn't sustain her. The food would be as insubstantial as air. Only her enchantments were powerful enough to enable me to grow the food she'd need to live, for I was barren of nature. If she used her gifts, then I would forever bear the fruits she wished to eat. She nodded and sang to me, again. Fig trees took root and gave her what she needed. Later, when she learned better how to use her magic, she gave me cherries and berries of every kind, along with pretty pigs to snuffle the truffle, woolly sheep and goats, who produced milk for her to drink with their gambolling lambs and kids for the petting.

The earthy spirits urged her to explore all my craggy outcrops, to not leave any boulder or rock untouched by her charms, and she seemed pleased with the idea. After all, I was her island and her home, she could mould me as she wished. She navigated well, even when bent of back and aching of limb, and when she touched her staff to my remaining barren ground, humming or singing in high voice, oh the rapture! the ecstasy! Cool clear water pools appeared, so she might drink without fear of contamination. There were streams, too, homes for freshwater sprites and new winged creatures that flashed with colour as they hovered over the water, and gloriously shimmering, shining fish. No matter if her pain flared or if it calmed, her magic was always present and strong.

There were mushrooms then, grains and tubers. All of which she cooked in a pot worked from my own stone, on a fire taken from the flickering flame she carried with her. By then, my pride at being the one to provide her such a home was beyond measure. As more birds and insects came to settle on me, when bees buzzed at my flowers and made nests in the branches of my pine trees, I thought myself the happiest I could be. It was the best and most joyous of times.

But not all was well for my maker and mistress.

Right away it was clear there was physical pain.

I sensed it was caused by a disease that lived in her.

I admit, it took me by surprise at first. That with all the glamours available to us, we could not stop the thing that ravaged her. It didn't take long for me to realise why. She seemed less enlightened. She shouted, called this thing a

demon, but there was no devil. It struck me that the illness
didn't live in her, it was a part of her, like blood and bones
and flesh. We watched as she stumbled, grasping painfully
on to her beauteous staff. It was hard to see, but then again,
she was resourceful. Her charms might not have been able to
cure her but, cleverly, they made my soil and grass springy,
ensuring I was as soft as possible so her tread would always
find a gentle home.

One day she declared a wish to be covered by dresses,
for she could not get used to being naked all the time and
dreamed of wearing elegant robes. My creatures answered
her call. Worms and spiders made silk. The spirits came
together, showed her how to weave a strong but pleasing
garment to keep the Sun's rays from her skin, and the cold of
any zephyr away. It would not be a heavy fabric that might
press or injure, but something airy and light, easy to wear.
In the end her dresses were softer than a whisper of breath.
She wanted them long, so she could feel the precious cloth
move in the slightest breeze. Schooled in the ways of leaves
and herbs, my mistress took the greenest shoots to give the
brightest colour to her clothes. And in them, she looked like
the very soul of the forests – which now covered a large part
of me. Such beauty, as divine as nature itself.

As her belly grew to enormous and delightful propor-
tions, at last I understood why I could feel a second presence.
For indeed, she carried another inside that huge hump. One
that would need even more of our care. The first ever living
being to be born to my land. The excitement for the spirits

and myself at such a prospect was intense. We were quite giddy and couldn't wait to meet our own little person.

All except one.

The airy spirit, who'd always been a flighty thing, grew morose.

You see, he'd come to think of my mistress as his own special play friend, and was unhappy that he'd have to share favour, especially with one so precious. Of course, when the time came, he was the one at her side. He soothed her, found ways to calm and help her through the labour. I have to say, it was an ugly and bloody affair, but she seemed to know what to do, so that at least was a blessing.

He was a big babe!

Brown eyes, not like hers at all. Forever hungry so I thought he'd suck the very life from her. The way he constantly went at her breast! He was certainly a fine and healthy child, but he had no glamours. She knew it almost immediately, as did I. The shame wasn't in his lack of charm, or in his desperate belief that one day he'd find his own magical gifts, rather that it made him vulnerable. Don't get me wrong, he learned well – he was no fool, and soon the boy knew everything about my flora and fauna, could navigate my very topography better even than her. But I was (and am) an enchanted place. As such, magic was in everything, except him.

How fiercely protective she was of her boy.

The envy of the airy spirit grew.

Of course, he was the boy's biggest playmate. He was

his nanny, always available to take care of the lad when the mother was off collecting water or herbs or strolling along the shore, which she loved to do. But he teased the child so. More than once did he get the lad to roll about in a field of nettles, even though the boy knew it to be folly. But the airy spirit told him to use magic, saying he felt sure it was in him, to put a charm on the plants so they could not sting. What a wonderful surprise that would be for his mother, said the spirit. Of course, the boy ended up covered in itching bumps and screaming in pain. That sort of thing went on for years. The lad was loyal and always told his mother it was his own fault, even nodded when the airy spirit was false, saying he'd warned the child and only turned his back for a second.

When a group of water sprites saved the boy from a possible drowning, the truth came out. They told of all the airy spirit's mischief, for they'd become fearful for the child's life. My mistress's anger shook me to my very core. There came storm clouds and thunderclaps. Great forks split the sky and the sea lashed at me again. Then came the sadness. I'd never seen my mistress grieve so, for anything. It was horrible, for she loved that spirit almost like a second child. But almost was not enough for clemency.

How the airy spirit begged her forgiveness, confessing his carelessness but promising he loved the boy and was always in control, would never let anything really harm him. Alas, all his grovelling and whimpering were for nought.

The deeds had been done.

She punished him.

With a wave of her staff, she locked the spirit deep within a cloven pine. There, she said, he could watch with envy as her beautiful boy grew, without ever being able to interfere or cause harm. My mistress was fair, and promised the spirit he'd be released once the child became a man. Only (and I did try to make her realise at the time), in her rage she forgot to put that last part of the enchantment in place.

Forgive me if I sigh, but this is now my greatest sorrow.

For my mistress has gone. Only her staff remains, dropped and abandoned on my sandy shore as she vanished into the strange mist come from the sea, to be eternally with her foremothers. I thrive still, for her magic here remains powerfully strong. The boy is a man. He lives well but misses his mother. As do I and all the other spirits and sprites and fairies. We live in harmony but for the one thing we cannot change. It sits in the cloven pine, locked in, eternally present but forever unseen. We try to ignore the groans that shadow our joys, for the airy spirit is rarely quiet.

There we have it.

My mistress made a magical place of me.

She nurtured the good things found about her, banished the bad. For now, her charmless child lives his solitary life. Of course, if a jealous man ever comes along, one who knows enchantment, and sees all she has done, he might be inclined to claim the work as his own. He might even cast her in an evil, wicked role, make her invisible, and silent. Men do so hate to be outdone by a woman. Now that is an old, old story! I might be an enchanted rock in the middle of a wide sea, but I know the power of stories and of voices. Even silenced ones. So let me end mine with what I have seen of Sycorax, and assure you again that once, she had a voice, and it was loud and melodious and filled with magic. What I know of her grows upon my rocks, lives within deep roots twisting through my earth. She holds my heart, and in the darkness, I see her still.

There she is now.

A woman bent through illness and pain, holding a little flickering flame to light her way, and a wooden staff to keep her steady.

Sycorax, who lived.

Sycorax, who made.

Sycorax, who sang.

Sycorax, who thrived.

CALIBAN:

Be not afeard; the isle is full of noises,
Sounds and sweet airs, that give delight, and hurt not.
Sometimes a thousand twangling instruments
Will hum about mine ears; and sometime voices,
That, if I then had waked after long sleep,
Will make me sleep again; and then, in dreaming,
The clouds methought would open, and show riches
Ready to drop upon me; that, when I waked,
I cried to dream again.

William Shakespeare, *The Tempest*, Act III, Scene II

Acknowledgements

This is a very personal novel, and it means a great deal to me. So it's with a full heart that I extend my thanks to those who've made it possible. To my agent, Samar Hammam, thank you for always being beside me, even through difficult times, and for cheering me on with unflinching belief. Thank you also to my editor, Emma Capron, for your guidance and encouragement, but especially for your kindness and deep understanding of my passion to give Sycorax her own story. To Gaby Puleston-Vaudrey, for your keen eyes and pitch-perfect precision, and to the whole Quercus team: I'm so grateful. Thank you to Ayo Okojie and Alex Haywood for taking care of Sycorax, for your dedication and commitment. Also, to my copyeditor Nick de Somogyi, thank you for your excellence. And to Thembe Mvula, who has treated this book with such care and attention, thank you.

Thanks to the Taner Baybars Award, which was granted to me through the Authors' Foundation of the Society of Authors. The money was a precious gift and a great help in allowing me the time and space to write this novel.

The genesis of this book came from a place of pain. In 2012, after a year of pure agony, I was finally diagnosed with Rheumatoid Arthritis. RA is a systemic auto-immune disease. Living with chronic illness is mostly a lifelong exercise of management. It involves the constant monitoring of pain and fatigue; understanding the outcomes of everyday activities; managing medications and their sometimes appalling side effects; and as someone vulnerable to infection, there's the daily management of risk. Not to mention the many hospital visits and difficulties within clinical care. Since my diagnosis I've experienced everything from excellent caregiving to gaslighting, misogyny, not being listened to, and being left under-medicated, unable even to get myself to the bathroom. It is a frightening and isolating way to live. I am therefore indebted to the community I've found through the ADCI (Authors with Disabilities and Chronic Illnesses) network. I'd like to especially thank Claire Wade, Penny Batchelor, Anna Biggs and Paula Knight for their friendship and solidarity.

I'd also like to acknowledge the work of the NRAS (the National Rheumatoid Arthritis Society). Knowing that NRAS volunteers are only a phone call away has been a lifeline. They've let me cry, listened to me, and given sage advice when there was nowhere else to go. I don't know your names, but thank you from the very bottom of my heart.

Finally, thank you to my oldest friend, my kindred, my dearest Suzy Fairchild. You are a light in my darkness now as you've always been, ever since we sat in the rain at the age of five telling stories about a yellow dog. I'm grateful beyond words for all that you are, and for a lifelong friendship that was recently so deeply manifested in four words: *What can I do?* And to my husband Andy, who lives through it all with me. Your grace is great, and I'm honoured to be beside you. Thank you.

About the Author

Originally from Leeds, **Nydia Hetherington** moved to London in her twenties to embark on an acting career. Later she moved to Paris, where she continued her drama training and set up a theatre company. When she returned to London almost a decade later, her attentions moved from the stage to the page. She gained a first class degree in Creative Writing and began writing novels. Her debut, *A Girl Made of Air*, published in 2020. This is her second novel.